Praise for *In Harm's Way*

"*In Harm's Way*, EJ Kindred's debut novel, is a terrific read you won't want to put down. Nice pacing with funny, nostalgic, tragic scenes, twists and surprises. Very well done. The cast of characters is somewhat large, but I had no trouble keeping track of who was who, and I cared about what happened to them. In particular, I loved the realism of the average, every day people, the settings, and the jobs portrayed. The conflict was well-written between Downton Abbey upper crust nasty and Americana rural life with working people who care about each other. Highly recommended."

~Sue Hardesty, author of the Loni Wagner Mystery Series

"There's nothing I like better than a mystery/thriller where the characters are in a serious situation and still have a funny way of observing the world. EJ Kindred strikes just the right balance. Annie Velasquez is in the middle of a big muddle, but she retains her sense of humor. And I loved her Harley-riding gramma! This was such a good read, and I look forward to more in book two in this sleuth's world."

~Jessie Chandler, author of the Shay O'Hanlon Caper Series

In Harm's Way

Book One
The Annie Velasquez Mystery Series

EJ Kindred

Launch Point Press
Portland, Oregon

ISBN: 978-1-63304-205-6
E-Book: 978-1-63304-217-9

FIRST EDITION
First Printing: 2019

Cover: Jove Belle

Published by:
Launch Point Press
Portland, Oregon
www.LaunchPointPress.com

Author's Note

Like many Oregonians, I value our connection with the Lewis and Clark Expedition. Toussaint Charbonneau was a member of the expedition as a guide and translator, but is perhaps better known as Sacagawea's husband. An unincorporated community south of Portland is named in his honor.

In appreciation for Oregon history and just because I like it, I decided to use his name for the small town in which most of this story takes place; however, I decided to place the town of Charbonneau in this book in the low mountains west of Portland.

I hope sticklers for Oregon geography will permit me this small transgression.

To all aspiring writers, I offer this poem first published in 1917 by Edgar Albert Guest (1881 - 1959):

It Couldn't Be Done

Somebody said that it couldn't be done,
But, he with a chuckle replied,
That "maybe it couldn't," but he would be one
Who wouldn't say so till he'd tried.
So he buckled right in with the trace of a grin
On his face. If he worried he hid it.
He started to sing as he tackled the thing
That couldn't be done, and he did it.

Somebody scoffed: "Oh, you'll never do that;
At least no one has ever done it,"
But he took off his coat and he took off his hat,
And the first thing we knew he'd begun it.
With a lift of his chin and a bit of a grin,
Without any doubting or quiddit,
He started to sing as he tackled the thing
That couldn't be done, and he did it.

There are thousands to tell you it cannot be done,
There are thousands to prophesy failure;
There are thousands to point out to you one by one,
The dangers that wait to assail you.
But just buckle it in with a bit of a grin,
Just take off your coat and go to it;
Just start to sing as you tackle the thing
That "couldn't be done," and you'll do it.

Acknowledgments

This novel would never have seen the light of day without the encouragement, prompting, and occasional application of a cattle prod from many people.

To Lori L. Lake, thank you for the "this shit got real" moment you gave me by offering to publish *In Harm's Way*. You might have put your reputation in harm's way by doing that, but if so, you have only yourself to blame.

To Luca Hart, for her unrelenting support and being willing to let me know when I've wandered off into a ditch somewhere, and then giving me a hand back up.

To Jessie Chandler and MB Panichi, for your invaluable help brainstorming when all I had was the kernel of an idea and a few hundred words. Many of your ideas are here.

To Lee Lynch, for making me finally hand the draft off to Lori instead of picking at it endlessly.

To the Portland Lesbian Writers Group, for constant support and just being there as a sounding board.

And to Terri Valentine, who believed in me long ago. I'm sorry we've lost touch.

EJ Kindred
April 2019

For the most part, the act of writing takes place in solitude, but the art of writing requires a community to give it meaning. A writer might derive a sense of accomplishment from the act of creation, but without readers, writing is a voice in a void.

This book is dedicated to readers. Without you, this book would have no reason to exist.

Chapter One

Annie Velasquez, I distinctly remember kicking you out of here."

Startled, I turned to find myself face to face with my employer, Doctor Carlton Wentworth, who was grinning widely at having surprised me.

"Or am I mistaken?" He tried to give me a stern glare, but the glee in his eyes ruined the effect.

"Of course not. I'm on my way. I came to wish Mo a happy Thanksgiving since I won't be here tomorrow."

Mo was the live-in chef for the doctor and his fourth wife, Elise. She seemed as surprised as I was at the doctor's sudden appearance.

"Are you keeping her from making my midnight snack?" He lifted one eyebrow in mock severity in the direction of the chef.

"No, doc," Mo said. "I've got you covered. There's the small matter of tonight's party and Thanksgiving dinner tomorrow, but you don't have to worry. I have my priorities in order."

"I should hope so," he said with a laugh. "And you, young lady, get your butt out of here. The house is fine. Amscray, vamoose, beat it, hit the road. Go home and enjoy your own holiday. I don't want to see your face until Monday."

"If you need help—"

He held up a hand. "The house will not fall apart if you're not here for a few days. Relax and enjoy your time off. You work hard every day and deserve time for yourself. I hear it's good for your health or some such. I'm a doctor. I know these things." In a low voice, he added, "Don't worry. I'll take care of the missus."

With that, he was gone.

"Young lady?" I said. "Nobody's called me that since my Grandma Natalie caught me sneaking a smoke when I was fourteen."

"From what you've told me about your grandmother, I'll bet you never picked up another cigarette."

"Never even thought about it."

The Wentworths' kitchen was a wonder of stainless steel and maple butcher blocks, almost industrial in feel after the excessive luxury of the rest of the house, and I loved it. I leaned one hip against the counter and watched Mo put the finishing touches on a platter of exquisitely designed hors d'oeuvres or, as she preferred to call them, fussy little bits.

"Midnight snack?" I asked.

"Well, see, he doesn't like to make waves on the home front, so at dinner he eats the microscopic portions Elise demands I serve, because it's elegant, don't you know." She waved a dismissive hand. "By halfway through the evening, the poor man is starving. I fix him a plate, nothing fancy, a sandwich or something he can heat in the microwave, and something sweet, and I stash it in the walk-in."

"And she doesn't find it?"

"Oh, heaven forfend that she'd step foot into the kitchen, much less go poking around where there's actual food. A calorie might stick to her skinny butt, and then there'd be hell to pay." Mo shook her head at our employer's foibles. "Besides, I think the doc gets a kick sneaking around in the dark like a kid raiding the cookie jar."

"Anything I can to do help?"

"No, but thanks for asking." Mo put the hors d'oeuvres into the walk-in refrigerator, closed the big door behind her, and stretched her back. "Everything I can do ahead of time is done. Tonight they invited only six people for dinner, but tomorrow, I think half the population of Oregon will be here. I'll be glad to have the weekend off after tomorrow. It's been nuts lately with all of these holiday parties."

"And to think," I said, feigning innocence, "it's only another four weeks until Christmas." I caught the damp kitchen towel Mo threw at me and tossed it back to her.

"Keep it up and I won't make you a mocha for the ride home," Mo warned, but despite her words, she filled my insulated bottle with steaming coffee and made sure the cap was tight. The aroma alone warmed me.

"You love me too much to send me out into the cold dark night without sustenance."

Mo grew still for a moment, and I instantly regretted what I'd said. Mo and I met when I started working as a housekeeper for the Wentworths a month after I moved to Charbonneau. She insisted on being called Mo, joking that her mother should be charged with child abuse for naming her Maureen. I was immediately drawn to her quick wit and intelligence, but her red hair, worn short and spiky, and a galaxy of freckles didn't hurt, either.

We'd had an immediate attraction, but after four dates, I told her I couldn't continue. When she asked why, I had no answer for her. The real reason would have pretty much guaranteed that she'd want nothing to do with me, and I couldn't bear the thought. We'd somehow still managed to be friends, though some days the connection was fragile. And here I'd gone and put my big foot in it.

"Except for one little detail," Mo said, either ignoring what I'd said or choosing not to respond, "it's neither cold nor dark. Now get out of here before she sees you leaving early." She slid an insulated bag along the polished counter top toward me, and I caught it.

Outside, I put the bag into my bicycle basket and nestled the bottle holding my precious mocha into the holder attached to the bike frame. I walked the bike through the gate to the road. Late November weather could be cool and blustery, but rain had held off for the day. I stood over my bike while I put on my helmet and gloves, breathing in the late fall air with its aromas of damp leaves and evergreens.

The best part of my day was often the ride to and from the Wentworths' home. Almost ten miles from my little apartment in Charbonneau, their property sat alongside a two-lane paved road that meandered through old growth forest and past a few other stately homes on large swaths of acreage.

I relished the freedom of riding my bike, of moving along the road under my own power, just the bike, the road, and me. I loved the quiet swish of the narrow tires on the pavement, the clicking of the rear hub in the brief moments when I coasted, and the kerchunk of the chain when I changed gears. Cresting the steeper hills gave me a sense of accomplishment and descending on the other side made me whoop with delight. The songs of birds and the rustle of the breeze through the trees were my music. I called hello to horses and cows in their pastures as I rode by and waved to them if they lifted their heads from the grass to gaze in my direction.

My favorite sight was an old barn, gray and paintless, leaning with the weight of years. I liked to think about the people who built it, liked to think about their sense of accomplishment and pride of ownership in a time long past, when having such a structure meant shelter for their animals and perhaps a storehouse for their food. I'd never know who those people were, but they'd left a sense of their presence behind.

Forty-five minutes later, I collected the day's mail, added it to the bike basket next to the insulated dinner bag Mo'd given me, and rolled my bike into my tiny apartment.

"Shadow, where are you?"

I dropped the mail onto the kitchen table as my fluffy black cat came to a sliding stop near my feet. I picked him up and hugged him, briefly ignoring his struggles to get free. I filled his food dish and made sure he had fresh water.

"Now it's my turn."

I open the insulated bag Mo had given me to find half a roasted chicken, steamed broccoli, and mashed sweet potatoes liberally laced with butter. Seeing the food made me again regret what I'd said earlier. No matter what, she always looked out for me.

As I ate, I sorted through the mail until I came to an envelope with a return address that made me put my fork down with a thud. Wilson and Wyatt, Attorneys at Law.

"Hell and damnation, now what?"

I stared at the address for a long moment before dropping the unopened envelope onto the table. Whatever it was could damn well wait.

"Shadow, old man, want a bite?"

The cat jumped up to the table top to accept a morsel of chicken and sat on the offending letter.

"Yeah, that's how I feel about it, too."

I'd almost finished eating, sharing bits with Shadow, when my phone buzzed. Seeing Sharon's name on the caller ID lifted my spirits.

"Hey, chickie." She always sounded upbeat and tended to take me with her. "How's things?"

"Not too bad. I got home early today. Shadow's been mooching my dinner, so I'm having my usual wild time in great metropolitan Charbonneau."

"How'd you escape? I thought Number Four would make you stay to serve dinner again."

The current Mrs. Wentworth was the doctor's fourth wife. The joke was that he changed wives so often it was easier to number them than to learn their names.

"Mo told me they're having a smaller party than usual tonight, and the doctor wants everything done family style. You know, big bowls of stuff on the table and roast on a platter to pass around. The house was ready, so he sent us cleaning folks home early."

"I'll bet that toasted her buttons," Sharon said, laughing. "You know how she loves to play lady of the manor. I'd pay good money to see her passing the gravy boat while trying to remain above it all. Hey, got any plans for tomorrow?"

My plans for Thanksgiving included a frozen turkey pot pie and watching football on the telly with Shadow. And ignoring the Wilson and Wyatt envelope.

"No, why?"

"Do you know Ada and Hal Brownlee?"

"The names sound familiar, but I don't think I've met them."

"Yeah, in a town this size, you hear everyone's name sooner or later. Here's the thing. Ada had hip surgery recently, so she's in a wheelchair while she recovers. Hal's a great guy, but he's the typical mid-century man, which means he's totally useless in the kitchen. I want to surprise her tomorrow with a good home-cooked Thanksgiving dinner. Hal's on board. He was happy to be a co-conspirator once I told him his reward was turkey and dressing. What do you say?" She paused for a moment. "Please say yes. I've already been to the store, which I have to tell you is no fun at all the day before Thanksgiving. They're great folks. You'll love them."

How could I refuse? "Sure, it sounds like fun. Certainly more fun than watching football with my cat."

And opening that damn envelope.

The next morning, Sharon and I carried four heavy grocery bags up the front steps of a tidy Craftsman-style bungalow. Before we could ring the bell, the door opened to reveal a short stocky woman with blue eyes, a head full of sparkling white hair, and a questioning expression on her face. She leaned on a cane held in her right hand.

"Sharon, honey, what's all of this? And who's your friend?"

"Let me put this down somewhere," Sharon said, hefting her two bags, "and all will be revealed."

Ada took a careful step back to let us enter and closed the door behind us.

"Ada May Brownlee," a gruff male voice emanated from inside the house, "what the hell are you doing? Get back in your chair. Doc Wentworth will have your hide."

"Shut up, old man," Ada called back in an equally stern voice. She gave us a little wink. "I ain't crippled, you know."

Moments later, a man who looked remarkably like his wife came around the corner pushing an empty wheelchair. He was taller than Ada, but just as round and just as white-haired. I couldn't resist the thought that, had they been carved from wood, they'd have made perfect Matryoshka dolls.

"Don't argue with me," he said. The amusement on his face belied his attempts to sound commanding.

"I'll argue with you all I want," she retorted, but she eased into the wheelchair anyway and handed him the cane.

"Ada, Hal," Sharon said, "this is my friend, Annie. We're making Thanksgiving dinner for you. We have all of the fixins right here."

"And you're not going to argue with us about it, got it, old woman?" Hal tried again to be stern, but gave up after a few moments.

"No," Ada said, "I certainly will not." She took one of Sharon's hands in her own. "Thank you, dearie. How nice of you. And you, too, Annie."

Two hours later, the aromas of roasting turkey and sage dressing perfumed the air. A pumpkin pie sat cooling on the countertop, a pot of peeled potatoes was simmering on the stove, vegetables were prepped and waiting, and a large colorful salad was cooling in the fridge.

I scanned the kitchen. "What's next?"

"Ladies," Ada said, "why don't you sit down and rest and let the turkey cook? I think you've done plenty. Hal, don't we have some iced tea made? Or would you gals rather have coffee?"

"Tea sounds good to me," I said, which the others echoed.

Once we settled around the kitchen table, iced tea in hand, I asked, "How do you three know each other?"

Ada chuckled. "I think my great-grandmother was Sharon's grandmother's second cousin, or something like that. Small town like this, we're probably all related in one way or another. How about you two?" She turned to me. "You're new here, aren't you?"

"Moved here about five months ago. I've always liked driving in the mountains between Portland and the coast, so I decided to take a drive to see where I'd wind up. I stopped here for a bathroom break and met Sharon by chance over by the park."

"Yeah," Sharon chimed in. "I was watching the kids play and she asked if I'd recommend somewhere to have lunch."

"And you sent her to Freddy's," Ada said.

"Of course. Where else?"

"When I moved here in July, I needed a job, and lucky for me, I ran into Sharon again. She told me about a couple of people who needed a housekeeper. And here I am."

"I know we just met," Ada said, "and I don't mean to be rude, but I have to ask."

"All right," I said, unable to anticipate what she might want to know.

"How is it that you have dark hair and olive skin, but such bright blue eyes?" Ada put her fingers to her lips and spoke through them. "Am I being too nosy?"

"Of course, you are," Hal said.

"Not at all," I said, relieved and with a quick smile for Hal. "My dad was born in Mexico and my mother's family was Scandinavian, mostly Swedish. The luck of the genetic draw."

"You are beautiful," Ada said.

"Thank you," I said, but my face grew warm.

Ada saved me from further embarrassment by announcing in a business-like voice, "Let's talk housekeeping. See this rig?" She indicated the wheelchair. "I'll probably be stuck with it for a while. These old bones don't heal like they used to, and this old man is about as useful around the house as tits on a bull. Think you could help me out now and then?"

Somehow, I managed not to laugh at Hal's feeble protest. "I'd be happy to."

She grasped my hand and pulled me to my feet. "Then let me give you the nickel tour."

Shortly before nine on the Monday morning after Thanksgiving, I rode my bicycle through the gates guarding the Wentworths' driveway. Unlike most days, the morning's ride had been less about enjoying the scenery and fresh air on my way to work and more about working off anxiety and anger. I'd pounded the pedals with a vengeance, with "damn it, damn it, damn it" keeping time with each revolution of my feet.

Until I'd opened the letter from Wilson and Wyatt, I'd had a truly enjoyable Thanksgiving holiday. After Sharon left to celebrate the holiday with her husband and kids, Ada and Hal insisted I stay to eat with them, and they were delightful company. Their bickering was endearing. I went home with enough leftovers to keep Shadow and me in turkey and sweet potatoes for the foreseeable future.

But I could ignore reality for only so long. By Sunday afternoon, the Wilson and Wyatt letter had stared at me for four days, so I gave up and opened it. The envelope contained a routine accounting form and a note from Patrick Wyatt, scrawled in pencil on the firm's beautiful off-white stationery.

"Annie, here's the most recent trust account statement. Natalie replenished it for us, as usual. When Beth calls you, pick up. She gets annoyed when she can't reach you and takes it out on me. She's the best detective in Portland, so it's in your best interests to stay on her good side. You don't make my job any easier by avoiding her." He hadn't bothered to sign it, but since we'd been friends since second grade, no signature was necessary.

I hated that he was right. I'd been avoiding talking with the Portland homicide detective, even though all I had to do was refer her to Patrick. She knew I didn't have to talk with her without my attorney present. She did have good reason to want to know my whereabouts but understanding her rationale didn't make me like it any better. My own stubbornness sometimes caused more problems than it solved. I grabbed the phone and jabbed the speed dial button for his office, getting all the more annoyed because my call went straight to his voicemail.

"Patrick, it's Annie. Got your note. What's with you being on first name terms with that cop? You're supposed to be on my side. Okay fine, if I'm not working when she calls, I'll answer the damn phone, but I'm not talking with her without you on the line."

If I'd had one of those old solid black phones with the separate receiver, I'd have slammed it down. Poking the "end" button wasn't nearly as satisfactory. Giving a piece of my mind to a recording and downing three beers in quick succession hadn't helped, either.

Fortunately, Patrick called before I left for work and, as he'd done so many times, talked me down off the ledge. Despite his efforts, I still harbored enough residual anger to get me to work ten minutes faster than usual.

When I arrived at the Wentworth home, I dismounted and wheeled my bike toward the garage. I'd entered the code to open the door when a black and silver sedan with a blue and red light bar on the roof and the Charbonneau Police Department logo painted down the side pulled up and stopped nearby.

My first, almost overwhelming, impulse was to get on my bike and ride away as fast as I could. I gripped the handlebars hard while my breath escaped me and the world seemed to sway in my vision, but then I saw the two officers get out of the car and walk toward the front door. They rang the bell and were ushered inside.

They weren't looking for me.

I waited until my pulse calmed and I could breathe fairly normally. Of course they weren't looking for me. Even though I'd moved to Charbonneau, I'd made sure that the Portland police knew where I was and how to reach me, and Patrick, as my attorney, kept tabs on me. Logically, I knew the Charbonneau police had no reason to want to see me at my workplace, but the sight of the police cruiser sent me spinning anyway. I wondered if I'd ever truly believe that I wasn't on anyone's Most Wanted list.

I parked my bike in the garage and went through the connecting door to the kitchen. Mo was there with Lupe, the other housekeeper, and Orlando, the Wentworths' surly gardener. They were huddled next to the prep island, talking in low worried voices.

I sidled up to Mo. "What's going on? I saw a police car outside."

Mo pulled me closer and spoke in a low voice. "Elise says some of her jewelry was stolen this weekend. She ordered us into the kitchen and called the cops. She's carrying on like an overwrought three year old, throwing things and screaming."

Lupe held a damp cloth against the left side of her face. "She hit me with her coffee cup." She showed me a laceration under her eye. The skin was reddened around and below the oozing blood. A brown stain covered the shoulder and side of her white uniform shirt. "All I did was offer her a scone."

"What's going to happen?" Orlando fidgeted where he stood. "Are we just supposed to wait here?"

Hearing Orlando speak in a soft accent reminded me of my father. The gardener wasn't a very friendly man, but I liked him, and of course, I had a soft spot on my heart for Mexican men of my dad's age.

"What do you think they'll do?" Lupe lowered the damp cloth from her brow but replaced it when the cut on her face kept bleeding. "I want to go home."

"Hold on," I said. "Unless they find evidence that one of us took the jewelry, they probably only want to talk with us, do some basic information gathering. I can't imagine they'll do anything right away." I hoped they didn't ask how I'd know. Maybe they'd think I watched too many cop shows.

"Easy for you to say," Mo said. "You weren't here this weekend."

"True, but I know the entry codes to the house, same as you. And not all of you were here the whole weekend, either, were you?"

"Just me," Mo said.

"I thought you had the weekend off."

"Best laid plans, my friend," she dropped her voice to a whisper again, "in a world ruled by Number Four."

Doctor Wentworth came into the kitchen, accompanied by two men wearing Charbonneau police uniforms. He looked tired, with lines around his eyes, and his voice was flat. "This is Sergeant Baker and Officer Harrison. They want to talk with you for a few minutes, and then you should all go home."

As the doctor turned to leave, Elise Wentworth stormed into the kitchen. She was barefoot and wore only a short nightgown made of thin fabric. She'd put a silky robe on over it, but the robe had slipped off one shoulder. Her hair was a tangle and her face so red it was almost purple. She glared at everyone in the room and, pointing an accusing finger at each of us in turn, fairly shrieked. "Someone here took my necklace. Whoever did is going to prison."

"Elise, honey." The doctor laid a calming hand on her shoulder, but she shook him off.

"And you're fired, all of you. If you ever come back into this house, I'll have you arrested for trespassing." She yanked ineffectively at the shoulder of her robe and left as abruptly as she'd arrived.

The doctor let out a weary sigh. "I'll take care of her, Sergeant, let's talk again after you're done here."

After the doctor had gone, Sergeant Baker focused on Mo. "Doc Wentworth said there's an office here?" When she pointed to the door at the back of the kitchen, he said, "All we're going to do today is spend a few minutes with each of you and then you can go." He consulted a sheet of paper in his hand and turned to Lupe, who still held the blood-stained cloth to her face. "What's your name?" he asked.

"Lupe Quezada." Her voice was almost a whisper. "Guadalupe, I mean."

"Okay, Ms. Quezada, I want to take a couple pictures of your face, and Officer Harrison here will take you down to the clinic and get you fixed up, okay?" He held his hand out to the younger officer. "You got the camera on you?"

Lupe protested, "But I can't afford—"

"Don't you worry about that," Baker said. "We'll take care of it. You need to have your face looked at. That cut might need stitches."

Officer Harrison said, "Hey, the doc's right upstairs, Sarge."

"Take her to the clinic," Baker said. "Can't have any conflict of interest."

Over the next ten minutes, Baker spoke with Lupe and Orlando. Once freed from the kitchen office, they quickly escaped out the side door. Only Mo and I remained.

"Annie Velasquez? Please come in."

He closed the door behind us. I perched on the edge of the chair opposite him.

"I'm sorry about this, Ms. Velasquez. The missing jewelry is quite valuable, so I have to ask these questions. I hope you understand."

I relaxed my grip on the arms of the chair and expelled a breath. Though I'd had time to recover from the initial surprise of seeing the police car outside, I was still on edge.

"How long have you worked for the Wentworths?" He held a pen above a notebook.

"Almost five months, since early July."

"And you work upstairs, in the master suite? As a housekeeper?"

"Sometimes, yes. Our assignments change, so I've also worked in the rest of the house."

He wrote for a few moments, then glanced up. "Did you work this weekend?"

"No. The doctor gave me the weekend off and let me go home early on Wednesday." Baker must have known that, because he didn't write it down.

"But you can always get into the house, right?"

"But I didn't." Note to self: don't argue with the cop.

"Okay. Where were you from Wednesday night until this morning?"

I gave him a rundown of the weekend, dinner at the Brownlees, a drive into Portland to visit my grandmother and a couple of friends. He didn't ask for their contact information. I didn't offer it.

"Had any guests arrived before you left for the weekend?"

"The doctor's oldest son and his family got here on Tuesday. I think they live in Seattle."

"Anyone else?"

"Not that I know of, but Mo would have the list."

He made a note. "Did you see anyone in the master suite who shouldn't have been there?"

"No. As far as I know, any deliveries are handled downstairs here. The doc's kids and their families have the run of the house when they visit. The wives do, too, even though it's not their home any longer."

"The wives?"

"The current Mrs. Wentworth is the doctor's fourth wife. It's amazing, but somehow he's on good terms with all of his exes. One of them still lives in town, and she's here fairly often. The others visit for holidays and birthdays and such."

"He's a better man than I am, Ms. Velasquez," he said with a low laugh. He put his notebook aside and stretched his back for a long moment. "I'm sorry about your job. I hope you can find another one."

"Oh, we're not fired, Sergeant."

"No?" He raised an eyebrow in surprise. "She sounded serious to me."

"It's a rare day she doesn't fire at least one of us. The doc always manages to calm her down somehow. Between you and me, she probably won't remember she said it."

"Tough way to make a living."

"It pays the bills."

"I suppose." He wrote down my address and phone number. "I'll be in touch."

He walked with me to the door, where Mo was pacing back and forth in the kitchen. She followed him into the office, and I headed for the garage.

Later, in a comfortable booth at the Charbonneau Diner, Sharon and I discussed the day's events.

"You know, I feel a little sorry for her." I stopped with my sandwich halfway to my mouth at the surprised expression on Sharon's face. "I do." I took a bite, savoring Freddy's house-made pastrami, the tang of the sauerkraut and mustard. "Damn, this is good."

"You're either insane or you have no idea how to tell a joke." She stopped with her soup spoon in the air, as if she'd forgotten she held it. "Tell me you don't really feel bad for that little diva. I've never met her, but she sounds insufferable."

I swallowed. "She's obviously unhappy. I mean, wouldn't you be, in her shoes?"

"For starters, I'd never be in her shoes. I never see her that she's not wearing those ridiculous six-inch stilettos. I think she does it so she'll have weapons handy." Sharon made an overhand stabbing motion with her spoon. "You could take out an eye easy with those things."

"Very funny. You know what I mean. I keep hearing that the doc has been seeing someone on the side. Who knows if it's true, though." I took another bite of my sandwich and tried not to close my eyes in bliss.

"That's the other thing. Did she really think he'd change his ways for her? She's his fourth wife, for pity's sake. I hear he's a nice guy, and I know he's a good doctor, but his track record in the marriage department is hardly a secret."

I took a sip of Freddy's excellent coffee. "What I can't figure out is why women keep marrying him."

Sharon rubbed her thumb against her fingers in the time-honored gesture for money.

"Yeah, I know," I said. "But that can't be everything. He's attractive enough, and he does have a great personality, but I don't know—" I shook my head. "I'll never understand some women."

"Now that's just sad." Sharon said with a low laugh. "I'd have thought one of the perks of being a lesbian was understanding women."

I couldn't help but grin. "I have an easier time deciphering my cat."

"Coffee, ladies? How's your lunch?"

"Freddy, my friend," I said as she refilled my cup, "I'd pay good money for your pastrami recipe."

"Not a chance, little girl," Freddy said with a smirk. "You keep paying for the sandwiches, and I'll keep making them for you. That's as close as you're getting to my secret recipe."

"I had to try."

We'd exchanged the same banter so many times it was a regular part of my visits to the diner. And try as I might, I could never get her to explain why her name tag read "Fred" when Sharon told me the diner owner's real name was Louise. Whenever I asked, she'd draw a finger across her lips, as if to zip them closed, with a twinkle in her eyes. We both understood I'd ask again. She'd told me she started working at the diner as a dishwasher when she was fifteen, worked her way up, waiting tables and cooking, and eventually bought the place. The Charbonneau Diner, known to the locals as Freddy's, was the sort of eatery the Charbonneau residents knew about, but visitors wouldn't notice. We liked it fine that way.

"Ladies," Freddy said, "I'd try to entice you with some pie for dessert, but the Charbonneau Bakery had a fire in the kitchen a few days ago and they're closed for repairs. I can make pastrami and burgers—"

"Fantastic pickles," I said.

"Yep, pickles and whatnot, but I can't bake to save my substantial ass, so we're out of pastries. I do have ice cream, though, so let me know if you want some."

Freddy moved on with her coffee pot to nearby tables.

"Pickles?" Sharon asked.

"Oh my God, yes. Do you mean to tell me you've never tried her kosher dills? They're heavenly."

"I'm not a big fan of pickles." Sharon tilted her chin toward the front of the diner. "The wives are here."

Three well-dressed women stood inside the diner's door, scanning the room for an available table. A casual observer could think they were sisters, but a closer look revealed differences in age that belied a first impression. They were each tall and slender, with light brown hair. Much to the amusement of some and the puzzlement of others, the doctor's former wives had become friends and were seen together frequently enough to have been dubbed "the wives."

Sharon said, "The doc sure has a type, doesn't he?"

Just then one of the wives waved to Sharon.

"You know her?" I asked.

"Melissa's my cousin. Third wife. My uncle wasn't happy at all when his daughter married the doc. They were together for seven years or so, and when they divorced, he gave her a house and a pile of cash. He's apparently a better ex-husband than a husband, and they have a terrific friendship. Oh, and get this. A few months ago, he bought her a new Mercedes. From what I heard, Number Four almost popped a blood vessel."

"Speaking of which, I gotta go. There's another party at the Wentworths tonight, and the lady of the house wants me to dress up and serve dinner." I checked the ticket Freddy left on the table and pulled a few bills from my wallet. "It's nice to make more money, but I'll be glad when these holiday parties are over."

Chapter Two

Accompanied only by the ticking sound of the cooling engine and the patter of rain on the roof, I sat in my truck, clutching a sodden tissue as tears streamed down my face. I'd parked under the trees at the far end of the lot, where nobody would see me staring at the charred building and crying. Not for the first time, I was grateful for the fence separating what remained of my dad's bike shop from the gas station next door.

No matter how many times I went there, I never got used to what I saw. The wood building was old when Dad bought it, but where others saw a shack, he'd seen opportunity. He shored up the structure and added a brick façade with large display windows on either side of the centrally located door. When I was small, I'd fancied the windows as eyes and the door a nose, and I'd giggle at the thought of walking in through the store's nostrils. Dad laughed and hugged me and said, "*Muy graciosa, niña.*" Very funny, little girl.

He'd hand-carved the sign that hung above the door for decades. The top line read "Velasquez Cycles," but below that, the signed proclaimed, in much larger letters, "Bikes." That was Dad, direct to a fault. A recent immigrant, he'd painted the sign in the green, white, and red colors of the Mexican flag. But his favorite part of the design was visible only to those who knew it was there. Down in the bottom right corner, he'd carved "M. Velasquez, Proprietor" in tiny letters. He knew it was old fashioned, but he was proud of moving to a new country, opening his own store, and providing for his family and the community doing something he loved.

If only I'd left the house earlier that morning, he might still be alive.

The sign was gone, the windows were shattered, and the blond bricks he'd so carefully mortared were blackened now, scarred by a fire that destroyed nearly everything. The plywood that we'd nailed across the doors and windows was missing and the sign declaring the building as unsafe was lying in the mud, apparent testament to the misguided optimism of someone who thought there was something left to steal. A remnant of crime scene tape flapped in the late November wind, left behind when the rest had been torn away. The bright yellow stood out against the charred brick.

I mopped my face. As I reached for the ignition key, I was startled by a tapping sound. Outside the driver's side window, a slender man with dark skin rode a bicycle in a tight circle, coming back to tap the window and wave at me before spinning again. I rolled the window down, squinting against the rain.

"Joe, what the hell are you doing? Don't tell me you've been out riding in this weather."

He rolled up next to my truck and stepped off his bike with one foot. His cycling shorts revealed that his left leg ended below his knee at a prosthesis. He'd had one made just for riding. The shining metal framework included a special attachment for his bike pedal. I was sure that anyone who saw him riding would be startled and impressed at the same time.

"A little birdie told me I'd probably find you here." He leaned forward and gave me a smooch on the cheek. Rainwater ran off his bicycle helmet onto my face. I wiped futilely at it with my soggy tissue.

"Patrick needs to mind his own business," I said, but we both knew I didn't mean it. We'd all known each other for far too long. "Aren't you freezing in that getup?"

"This?" He ran a hand down his jersey-clad chest, obviously soaked through. "Nah. I just finished about sixty miles out to the Gorge, up and over Mount Tabor and back. I'm toasty warm. A tad damp, though." He wiped water off his face and laughed. He'd always had a positive outlook, one that losing a leg had dampened only temporarily. His laugh was infectious, but in that moment, I was immune. "Are you going to Grandma Natalie's?"

I ignored his question. "Damn it, Joe. How am I supposed to sit here and feel sorry for myself if you're so fucking happy all the time?"

"You're not, sis. That's the point. I figure my goal in life is to give you perspective."

"I hate perspective." I tried to scowl but noticed something on his cycling jersey. "Team Three and a Half? What's that?"

He laughed again. "With your issues about perspective, maybe I shouldn't tell you." He made another circle, stopped again by my window, staying on the pedals and balancing himself with one hand on the truck roof. "I wouldn't want to lift your spirits or anything." He winked at me.

"Come on, tell me."

"Okay, but don't say I didn't warn you. Remember the relay race we have here in Oregon every year?"

"Sure. Dad liked to be one of the sponsors. Isn't it something like four hundred miles?"

"Yeah." He beamed with pride. "But each team member rides fifty-mile segments. This year, it started in Bend and wound up through the Cascades. I got together with three of the guys from my unit, and we rode it this year."

"Wow." I realized my mouth was hanging open and shut it. "You can't be serious."

"True enough, but we really did do it."

"And the name?" I knew that, after a rough time, Joe had recovered remarkably well from his injuries in Iraq, but I still struggled to get my head around this news. A one-legged cyclist in a four-hundred-mile race?

"You've met Brad, right?"

"Once or twice."

"He lost a leg like I did, only above the knee. Eddie lost his lower right leg and his left forearm. And Ryan lost both legs above the knee, so he rides a hand cycle. After a few beers one night, we figured we had about three-and-a-half people on our team. And you know what? We kicked ass." He gave a whoop of glee and made another circle of the parking lot.

"I wish you'd told me, you big doofus. I would've crewed for you." From my dad's days as a race sponsor, I knew that each team needed a support vehicle to provide food, mechanical support, and a place for the riders to rest and prepare for their next leg of the race. A four-hundred-mile relay could easily last over twenty-four hours, so a support crew was critical.

"Thanks, sis. We got a few other guys from the unit to do it. It was great to get them all together again." He rolled his bike back and forth a few inches. "Are you going to Grandma Natalie's or not?"

"Yes. Why?" His persistence made me suspicious.

"No reason," he said, trying—and failing—to look innocent. "But another little birdie told me you should go see her."

"Okay." I drew the word out, realizing I'd been ambushed by my family. "Throw your bike in the back and come with me."

"No way am I putting my beautiful ride in your skanky old truck, but I'll race you there." With that, he pushed off and sped out of the parking lot.

To those who didn't know her, Grandma Natalie seemed like a stereotypical grandmother. She kept her silver-gray hair neatly trimmed. She wore light blue jeans and flowered blouses and low-heeled shoes. She was often seen wearing an apron with "Kiss the Cook" embroidered across the front. Her blue eyes sparkled behind wire-rimmed glasses. Her countenance was kindly and caring. People meeting her for the first time often seemed to expect a hug and a plate of cookies.

They could not have been more wrong.

I pulled into her driveway and Joe wheeled in right behind me. Before I could shut the engine off, Grandma Natalie came barreling out her open garage door, waving her arms and shouting. I rolled the window down.

"You're not parking that chop shop reject in my driveway. Get your miserable hunk of junk away from my beautiful bike." She stood with her hands on her hips, glaring at me, until I put my truck into reverse.

She and I had different ideas about what made a beautiful bike. Mine had red handlebar tape, a saddle that fit me perfectly, and clipless pedals. Hers had a powerful engine, a swept back windshield, and cruise control. Yes, at sixty-two years old, my grandmother was a Harley Davidson aficionado. At the moment, her 2005 Road Glide was parked inside the open garage, behind her aging car.

I humored her and parked on the street, but in truth, I hadn't been anywhere near her beloved Harley. Joe wheeled his bicycle into the garage and stood with her, he dripping wet and looking as if he knew something I didn't, and she standing with a smug expression on her face.

"You both look like the proverbial cat," I said, as I joined them. "What's going on?"

Grandma Natalie tried for nonchalance and failed miserably. "Not a thing," she said, though she did hug me. "Come on in. I made coffee, and I got Voodoo doughnuts."

"Did you get me the bacon one?" Joe's favorite was the famous maple bar with a strip of bacon on top.

"Of course. But you're not parking your soggy butt on my chair. Go change your clothes."

Joe kept clothes at Grandma Natalie's house, did he? A conspiracy was definitely afoot.

We were seated at the table with our mugs of hot coffee and Grandma's expertly selected sweets when the kitchen door opened and Patrick came in, impeccably dressed, as usual, in a suit that had to cost more than half a year's rent for my apartment. No doubt about it, they were all up to no good. Grandma Natalie got him a mug of coffee, and he settled into the chair next to me.

"When are you guys going to tell me what's going on here?" I favored each of them with a suspicious glare. "For one thing, it's a weekday, Patrick. We all know that you don't leave the office without very good reason, so spill it."

"You went to the shop again, didn't you?" Patrick took a bite of his chocolate éclair. Of course, Grandma Natalie had bought his favorite, too. Clear evidence of premeditation.

"So what if I did?" I tried not to sigh and resigned myself to finding out whatever plot these three had hatched only when they were ready to let me in on it.

"I don't know why you keep going over there, Annie. You can't do anything about it, and all you do is get yourself upset."

"I'm not upset," I snapped back. "I'm angry, especially at Nicky. If she wasn't already dead, I'd want to kill her myself for what she did." That wasn't all I felt, of course. I'd loved Nicky more than I thought it was possible to love any woman. She and I had talked about marriage, buying our own home, maybe even adopting a kid or two. I was angry with her, but I was also heartbroken.

Patrick said, "Not a good thing for you to say, considering the circumstances."

"I have attorney-client privilege."

"Which is waived when you speak in front of third parties."

I stuck my tongue out at him. "They're on my side."

He held his coffee mug in both hands and gave me an appraising look. "Okay, fine, you win. I'll let it pass this time."

He rubbed my shoulder in that reassuring way he had. He'd always been a comforting presence in my life, even in the worst of times. I often considered how fortunate I was to have two brothers—what was the phrase? A brother from another mother?—who stood by me, no matter what happened.

"I don't know why I go over to the shop," I said. "It's hard, you're right about that, but I can't quite make myself stay away."

Grandma Natalie sat next to me and held my hand. "Maybe it's part of the grieving process."

"Maybe." I wiped a tear away and turned back to Patrick. "If nothing else, the place looks better. At least the crime scene tape is gone."

Patrick said, "The worst of the hazardous stuff, the chemicals, has been cleaned out, but the building might be a total loss."

I stared into my coffee, unable to speak for a moment, willing away the tears threatening to flow.

Patrick put his arm around my shoulders and gave me a squeeze. "It's okay, Annie. If you want, I can get it taken care of."

"But it's not okay." I knew I sounded petulant. "It was Dad's shop. He built his life, our lives, with it. He taught people to love bikes. He helped kids in the neighborhood learn to ride." I wiped my nose with a paper napkin.

"He gave me my first bike," Joe said in a sad voice.

I squeezed his hand, remembering the skinny black boy with ratty shoes who'd stood outside the shop, day after day, his eyes focused on a scratched and dented red bike someone had used as a trade-in. Dad saw him, too, and after a while, he couldn't take it any longer. He invited the youngster in and asked his name. After checking with the boy's mother, Dad gave him the red bike. Joe's life had never been the same, and neither had ours, because not long after, Joe's mother died. When Dad learned the young boy had no relatives who could be found, he applied to be Joe's foster parent. Joe moved in with us and instantly became my little brother, less than a year my junior.

"Whatever happened to that old bike?" I picked icing off my cinnamon roll and took a bite of the fragrant pastry.

Joe leaned back in his chair in a nostalgic moment. "I fixed it up and gave it to a neighbor kid a few years ago. Now he's on his college bike racing team and wants to go pro. Dad said 'bikes change lives' so often that he should have had it tattooed on his chest."

"Or at least put it on his business card," I said, remembering.

Just then, I heard the sound of an engine outside. Grandma Natalie rose from her chair and went through the kitchen door out into the garage. Curious, we all followed her. The rain had let up and the clouds had parted to show patches of blue sky.

A young man dressed in jeans and a dark jacket with a logo above the breast pocket emerged from a shiny green Subaru wagon occupying the spot in the driveway where I'd tried to park earlier. He carried a clipboard with a stack of papers attached.

"Natalie Lindberg?"

Grandma met him near his driver's side door, where they spoke briefly. She accepted the pen he held out and signed her name where he indicated. He handed her the sheaf of papers and a key fob and they shook hands. He got into a different car that pulled across the end of the driveway and left. Patrick, Joe, and I watched all of this, but I was sure I was the only one who had no idea what was happening.

"You bought a new car, Grandma?" I asked.

She handed me the key fob. "Go take a look. It's only a couple of years old, low miles, in great condition."

I slid into the driver's seat and sighed. Compared to my little truck, the Outback was luxurious. Scanning the dashboard, I saw controls for air conditioning, a navigation screen, and miracle of miracles, heated seats. I started the engine and relaxed in bliss as the sweet sounds of soft jazz filled the car.

After a few moments, I was embarrassed to see my grandmother, Joe, and Patrick lined up in front of the car, watching my every move. I shut the engine off and got out.

"Didn't anyone ever teach you that staring is rude?" I tried to sound miffed, but the comfort of my grandmother's new car hadn't yet worn off. "Grandma Natalie, you're going to love this car." I held the key fob out to her.

She didn't take it. "No, I won't. It's yours, not mine."

I blinked. "What?" This did not compute. "What are you talking about?"

"It's yours," she repeated. "Not mine."

"But—" My brain refused to engage. "I can't afford this—"

"It's a gift, you moron." Patrick had always had a way with words, in the courtroom and out. "Get it?"

I stood there, mouth agape, unable to speak for a long moment.

"No. How? What—"

Grandma Natalie saved me from my mindless jabbering. "Annie, your little truck is old and worn out and not reliable anymore." Her tone was gentle and her hand on my arm was reassuring. "I worry about you every time you make the drive into town, that it might break down and strand you somewhere."

"I know, but—" Tears ran down my face for the second time, but now they were tears of happiness. "But it's too much, Grandma. I can't accept it."

"Sure you can. Think of it as keeping me from worrying about you." She gave me an unconvincing sad look. "It's not nice to make old ladies worry, you know."

Leave it to Grandma Natalie to make me laugh in spite of my tears.

"See," Joe added. "A different perspective."

"I hate perspective." I wrapped my grandmother in a big hug. "Thank you," I whispered. "I don't know how I'll ever repay you."

She put her hands on my shoulders and held me at arm's length, tears in her eyes. "You can't," she said. "You'll owe me big time forever." She let go of me. "Now let's get into this fancy rig and go get something to eat. You're buying."

The next Thursday morning, I walked through the Wentworths' side door and came face to face with the lady of the house.

"You're late." She stood in my way, arms akimbo, glaring.

"I'm an hour early," I said. "You have a lot of company coming, so I thought—"

"Oh, so you're padding the bill?"

I was silent for a moment. "I'll come back." I stepped away from her and grabbed the door handle.

"Never mind. Go check the assignment board and get to work. Do the guest suite first. They're coming in a day ahead of the others."

After she'd gone, I went into the kitchen. Mo was leaning against the counter, trying not to laugh. "That woman could give a person whiplash. Go left. Go right. Sit down. Stand up." She mimicked Elise's voice well.

"Stop," I said in a stage whisper. "She'll hear you."

I checked the white board where Elise wrote the daily schedule. She was an imperious little diva, but an organized one. Each staff member had a column showing the day's assignments. Sure enough, the guest suite was written under my name, along with other tasks. The list was longer than usual, making me wish I'd come even earlier.

"How much of the clan will be here?"

"Mary isn't coming," Mo said. "but all three kids will bring their families."

"Mary?" I still had trouble now and then keeping track of everyone.

"First wife. She and her husband are going to Tahiti or somewhere with sun and sand, but Carl the Third and the twins will be here with their families, so I count twelve people, if everyone shows up. Carl and his wife and kids are driving down from Seattle later today."

Carl was the oldest of the doctor's offspring. He'd visited a few times before, and I'd gotten used to hearing him called Carl the Third, as if he were royalty. The twins were his sisters, younger by two years.

"Hence the rush order on the guest suite."

"Theresa, second wife, and her husband and daughter and the daughter's fiancé will get here tomorrow. Melissa lives here in town." She counted on her fingers. "Eighteen? And that's if nobody else tags along. No wonder Number Four's in a tizzy."

I reread my list on the white board, then focused on Mo. "Can you imagine all of your husband's former wives and their kids showing up at the same time? It'd be a miracle if she wasn't tense."

Mo snorted. "Don't tell me you feel sorry for her. She's raised tension to an art form. I'm pretty sure she's worried about being on next year's invitation list when she'd much rather hold court as lady of the manor." She turned back to the vegetables she was prepping and chopped onions at lightning speed.

I jotted down the day's assignment on a scrap of note paper. Nobody would say Elise Wentworth wasn't difficult, but I sensed something desperate in her demeanor, an underlying insecurity she couldn't quite hide.

"I thought I told you to start on the guest suite."

She also had a talent for appearing as if by magic.

"On my way," I said, intentionally not looking Mo's direction.

I spent the rest of the day on the upper floor of the big house. The suite had two bedrooms, two bathrooms, and a central seating area with a wet bar. I opened windows, despite the early December cold, to clear musty air from rooms that saw little use. I put fresh linens on the beds and towels in the bathrooms, cleaned and dusted every surface, and swept and vacuumed every floor. Lupe came in with vases of cut flowers and baskets of fruit and candies, which made the suite feel festive.

After the guest suite, Lupe and I gave the same treatment to half a dozen other bedrooms and four other bathrooms. We vacuumed hallways and stairs. We pursued each mote of dust with laser focus, knowing Elise would find every missed speck. We put more vases of flowers and fruit baskets in each room and candles and other decorations on the accent tables decorating the upstairs halls.

"Damn, Lupe," I said, when we took a lunch break in the kitchen. "When did this house get so big?"

She gave a weary sigh. "I'm glad Christmas is only once a year. I mean, I think it's nice of Doctor Wentworth to get his family together at the holidays, but my feet hurt, and we still have the downstairs to do."

"At least you don't have to cook three meals a day and snacks for half the known universe," Mo said. She put big mugs of hot coffee on the table for Lupe and me, followed by thick turkey sandwiches. She sat down across from us with a sandwich and coffee for herself.

"As if you don't love it," I said.

Mo laughed. "True, but it can be exhausting. The good news is that most of the dishes the doc and Elise asked for can be made ahead, so it's not so bad."

"Let me know if you want help, okay?" I said. "I know my way around a kitchen."

She beetled her eyebrows at me. "You actually think I'm letting you touch my knives? No way. Off limits. Not happening."

"Hey, I can wash dishes or something." I tried to look offended, but I must have failed because Mo and Lupe both laughed out loud. "But you're cooking for a lot of people for what—three days? I'm offering to help."

"Fine, fine. I'll put you to work scrubbing floors. That," she said, "I know you know how to do."

Lupe and I spent the rest of the day dusting and vacuuming the already spotless lower floor of the big house. We'd finished putting the cleaning stuff away when the doctor's son and his family arrived.

Carl the Third was in his late thirties, a doctor in Seattle. He was taller than his father and had broader shoulders, but there was no mistaking the resemblance. I couldn't decide if his overweening attitude was the cause or the result of his work as a surgeon. His wife was also a doctor, a pediatrician, and they had two teenage boys who gave off a studied air of disaffected youth.

The doc and Elise met them at the door, and Lupe showed them to the guest suite and adjacent rooms. Mo had prepared a platter of light snacks, and the doc opened his liquor cabinet for the adults.

When the long day was over, I stopped by the kitchen on my way out.

"Need a hand with anything?" Just for fun, I extended a finger toward Mo's knife block, as if to touch one of the shining implements, only to retract it when she favored me with a mock glare.

"No, hon. I have it under control, for tonight anyway. Are you serving this weekend?"

"No," I said. "Just cleaning up after the crowds. I think Lupe is on laundry duty. But once everyone is here, if you need help setting tables or plating or whatever, call me."

She surprised me by giving me a long hug.

"I will. As I said before, I think it'll be okay, but if Number Four spins out of control and decides to change the menu or something, I might take you up on that. The doc let me bring in two students from the culinary school in Portland to help while the whole gang is here." She handed me a travel mug from which the aroma of her excellent coffee wafted. "See you tomorrow."

By the time I arrived at the Wentworths' the next day, chaos reigned. The rest of the doc's family had arrived. Cars were parked haphazardly in the driveway and on the front lawn. The gardener, Orlando, who was surly on his good days, was almost comically purple in the face as he marched around the grounds with his fists clenched, glaring at the tire tracks on his otherwise pristine lawn. I was glad to see he wasn't armed. I hoped it never occurred to him that he had ready access to hedge clippers and all manner of other sharp tools that could make short work of the tires currently wreaking havoc on his meticulously groomed landscaping.

I went inside through the side door, as usual, and detoured through the kitchen to check the assignment board. Mo had prepared lunch for what sounded like a thousand people. She waved hello and got back to work, instructing the two culinary students who had been pressed into serving duty. She put scoops of raspberry and lemon sorbet into dessert dishes and garnished the perfect orbs with edible flowers. Each sorbet dish went onto a plate, to which she added three shortbread cookies, cut into wreath shapes. The students took the beautiful desserts to the dining room as fast as Mo could prepare them.

I said, "That would go faster if you'd let them help you."

"No way," she said, once the servers had left the kitchen. "Presentation is everything. I'm not about to let amateurs mess up my homemade sorbets and beautiful little cookies." She handed me a cookie and made shooing motions with her hands. "Now beat it. I imagine there's all kinds of messes waiting for you."

My assignment for the day was general cleaning, so I went into the dining room to make sure the guests had what they needed.

"Annie!" Doctor Wentworth greeted me as if I were an old friend, rather than the part-time cleaner of toilets and organizer of closets. "Come in and meet the family."

He stood at the head of the dining table, holding a glass of iced tea. He lofted it in the general direction of the crowd in the room. "Hey, everyone," he called out, "come and meet Annie." He drew me into the room by my elbow. "Be extra nice to her while you're here. She'd never say it, but she's the one who keeps this place going."

I protested, sure my face was as red as the holiday poinsettias on the dining table, but he ignored me. A barrage of introductions ensued. Fortunately, I'd either met or seen most of the doc's extended family before, but I still hoped there wouldn't be a pop quiz when he was finished.

Once I escaped the gaze of everyone in the room, I busied myself tidying the table and filling water glasses. A nearby sideboard held pitchers of cold drinks, an ice bucket, and a large coffee urn, along with a canister of sugar and a pitcher of cream to replenish the table.

"Annie?" The doctor's second wife, Theresa, added two used plates to the stack I'd collected from the table. "Need a hand?"

"Thanks, but I think we're all set." I was as impressed as I was surprised by her offer. After all, she was a guest, but I saw a considerable intelligence and a good sense of humor in her eyes. "Besides, I'm supposed to take care of you, remember? Can't have the doc think I'm slacking."

She squeezed my arm for a moment. "No," she said in a conspiratorial tone, "that wouldn't do at all."

As they ate dessert, swooning over the fruity sorbet and delectable cookies, almost everyone, the adults, anyway, seemed to go out of their way to call me by name and thank me whenever I refilled a coffee cup or offered some small service. For the most part, the teenagers kept to themselves, especially Carl the Third's two boys. People could say what they liked about the doctor's predilection for serial monogamy, but he did know how to surround himself with intelligent, pleasant people.

When I had a moment to stand back and observe the room, I was struck by the incongruity of it all. In his home, the doctor had two former wives—one of whom was accompanied by her current husband—and their several offspring and his newest wife for what he considered a family event. I was impressed by his ability to pull it off and even more impressed at his apparent lack of self-consciousness about it.

The real surprise was Elise. She was charming and outgoing and made sure to speak to everyone. She was thoughtful in her requests of the serving staff and of me. At first, I thought perhaps I was seeing the Elise the doctor met and married, but every once in a while, she'd purse her lips or shoot a withering glance. She somehow managed to maintain the façade after someone asked whether her jewelry had been found.

"No," she said with a sorrowful face. "The police said they're working on it, but the detective they assigned doesn't really care. Fortunately, it's insured, but Carl had it made for me." With that, she gave her husband a sad smile that, to me, seemed contrived. "I'd much rather have it back than collect the insurance money."

After lunch, I helped clear away the dessert dishes and clean up the dining room. Once the room was in order, the doc and his son hauled an enormous fir tree into the living room and positioned it in a corner near the windows. Over the next two hours, the doc and his extended family decorated the tree and drank hot chocolate. More than once, the doc insisted that I add a glass ball or a strand of tinsel to the tree. I was a little embarrassed to crash the family event, but I enjoyed participating. Shadow instantly turned any holiday decorations in my apartment into cat toys, so I had to get my Christmas tree fix from others.

After the tree was finished and the multi-colored lights were twinkling, the guests all disappeared to other parts of the house. The quiet was a relief that allowed me to work in peace.

"Where'd everyone go?" In the kitchen I slid a tray of hot chocolate mugs onto the counter near the dishwasher. "I didn't think that many people could vanish so quickly."

"They're with the master of grand gestures," Mo said with a laugh. "The doc rented a bus, if you can believe it, one of those big cruise coaches, and he's taking everyone out to the beach later this afternoon. It might be December, but darned if he isn't show off the Oregon coast to anyone he can. I think they're touring Cannon Beach this time, or maybe Tillamook."

"Yeah, but aren't they from here? It's not as if they haven't been out there before."

Mo lifted her hands as if to say "I don't get it, either" and turned back to rinsing dishes and loading them into the washer. "You'd better enjoy the quiet while you can. They'll be back in time for dinner, or at least the doc said they'd be." She stretched her back and yawned. "It's been a long day, and we're nowhere near done. How was it in there?"

"Surreal, actually. The doc introduced me as if I were part of the family instead of the help. He always finds ways to surprise me. And get this. Theresa asked if she could lend a hand. She seems nice."

"She's a good person," Mo said. "I was sorry to see her go when they divorced, but when she visits, she always comes in to chat."

"She was the second wife, right? I almost need a wall chart to keep track of everyone."

Mo snickered and I said, "What?"

She checked to make sure the coast was clear. "You know how we call Elise Number Four?"

I got it. "Oh, no, they don't call her Number Two, do they?"

We looked at each other and the giggles set in, followed by uncontrollable laughter. I had tears running down my face and Mo was gasping for air.

"Oh, that would be so wrong," she was finally able to say, trying to catch her breath.

I grabbed a tissue from a nearby box and dried my face, little hiccups of laughter still bubbling up. I hadn't laughed like that since before the explosion and fire at my dad's shop. It felt damn good.

Chapter Three

The rest of the weekend was a blur of family meals and house-cleaning, keeping up with the Wentworths. Lupe and I cleaned bathrooms and changed linens and joked that we almost wore the vacuum cleaner out. In between meals, Doctor Wentworth provided excursions and entertainment for his family, including special events for the younger set. I was amazed at how much he could cram into one weekend, and everyone seemed to be having a good time.

Mo was right; the days were long. Every night when I went home, I was awake scarcely long enough to apologize to my cat, check the mail, and eat the dinner Mo sent home with me.

My other clients had been kind enough to let me adjust their cleaning schedules around the doc's family gathering, but I still stopped by the Brownlees' home on Saturday and Sunday mornings to vacuum and dust and try to teach Hal how to load the dishwasher.

Ada was still using her wheelchair some of the time, and Hal still nattered at her whenever she walked instead, even though she was careful and used her cane. What she was not allowed to do was clean her home or do much cooking. She liked it that way, which was fine with me. I was no great shakes in the cooking department, but I could prepare vegetables and make a salad and pop a chicken or a roast into the oven without too much fuss. I organized sandwich fixings for them and made sure there were cans of soup or chili to heat in the microwave. I enjoyed the Brownlees immensely. Their good-natured bickering was exactly the antidote I needed to counteract Elise's demeanor, which could vary without warning from icy to enraged.

On the last day of the Wentworth shindig, I arrived during lunch to find Mo, obviously exhausted, sitting in the corner of the kitchen with a coffee mug nearby.

"Remind me never to have company, okay?" She took a drink of coffee.

"You live here," I said, happy to tease her a little. "You always have company."

She groaned. "Don't remind me. Actually, it's not too bad. Having rooms above the garage means I have a quiet place to escape to." She stood, stretching her back and yawning. "After this weekend, I might not come out until January. They don't need me to cook. Let 'em eat cake. Hey, that reminds me," she said with renewed energy, "want to see tonight's dessert?"

She motioned me to follow her to one corner of the kitchen where a covered cake plate sat safely out of the way. With a dramatic wave, she lifted the stainless steel dome from off the plate to reveal a fourteen-inch round three-layer cake. The top was decorated with candied pecans and tiny flowers and leaves painstakingly made from colored icing. The aroma of cream cheese frosting made my mouth water.

"Mo, it's beautiful. It's a work of art. Please don't tell me it's carrot cake, because I'm already drooling."

"Sorry, hon, it's carrot cake, complete with pineapple bits and walnuts," she said, not sounding sorry at all. "All three layers." She replaced the dome. "Want to hear the sad part?"

I raised an eyebrow. "What could possibly be sad about carrot cake?"

"She wants it cut into squares two inches on a side."

"What—"

"Yep, she wants my lovely round cake cut into squares too small for the layers to stand up. Heaven forfend that we cut it into wedges like normal people."

"Forfend? What's with you and the ten-dollar words lately, huh?" I gave her a playful push with my shoulder.

She laughed and nudged me back. "I have a vocabulary and I'm not afraid to use it. Know what? I'm going to make like I didn't remember and cut it the right way." She gave me sly look. "Oops."

I laughed. "Oops is right." I glanced at the clock. "Better get going before the crowd gets back."

The rest of the day flew by. I cleaned the dining room to ready it for dinner. Lupe had gotten the table linens washed and ironed and ready to go. She and I worked our way through all of the guest rooms, making beds and cleaning bathrooms. We had enough time for a snack before it was time to set the table for dinner.

For the last night of the gathering, Mo prepared a festive holiday dinner with an enormous rib roast that filled the house with enticing aromas. She accompanied it with side dishes from different parts of the world, including Yorkshire pudding, rice pilaf, and curried vegetables smelling of ginger and turmeric.

"An unconventional dinner," she said. "For an unconventional family."

I resumed my duties in the dining room, offering coffee and iced tea, and refilling water glasses, while Doctor Wentworth opened wine from his cellar. We'd made room on the sideboard for Mo's cake, which rested under its dome, eliciting inquiries about what delights were to come.

Elise was playing the lady of the manor again, almost simpering at some moments, and yet I'd occasionally see her eyes narrow as if she were displeased. Almost everyone seemed to have a good time, and food disappeared at a satisfying rate. At one point, Doctor Wentworth called Mo into the dining room for a round of compliments that made her blush to the roots of her red hair.

One of those present who hadn't entered into the spirit of the evening was Eric, the younger son of Carl the Third. I'd noticed before that he seemed to keep to himself a lot of the time. He didn't say much to the other people at the table. On the other hand, it was clear the young man enjoyed his food. Unlike his father and brother, he had blond hair, and in what appeared to be an act of deliberate nonconformity, he wore it long with the front part combed forward over his eyes, almost to his nose. When I spoke to him, he was distant, but he met my eyes through his fringe of hair. I had the impression he was a kind young man.

When I went to the sideboard to start the coffee maker, Eric approached me.

"Annie?" He was tentative, almost shy. Up close, I realized he'd tinted part of his hair a pale blue. I wondered what Carl the Third had said to him about it. Eric's dad didn't strike me as the diplomatic type.

"Hi Eric. What can I get for you?"

He blushed. "Nothing." He leaned toward me slightly, as if he wanted a co-conspirator, and he whispered, "What's under there?" He indicated the silver cloche that occupied the center of the sideboard.

I went with it.

"Cake," I whispered back. "Carrot cake with luscious cream cheese frosting. And if I know Mo's baking, it'll be amazing."

Even through his hair, I saw good humor in his eyes. I took a chance.

"You aren't having a good time, are you?"

His sadness reappeared and his shoulders sagged.

"Because it seems as if you'd rather be somewhere else." I hope I hadn't overstepped. The sadness in his eyes made me want to protect him.

"More like *anywhere* else," he said in a low tone. "She doesn't like me."

I didn't have to ask who "she" was. I'd seen Elise throw more than one withering glance in Eric's direction.

"I'm sorry." I wanted to say more, but Doctor Wentworth called my name.

"Annie, while you're over there, will you grab me a clean napkin, please? I've made a mess of this one." He held it up as proof.

"Sure." I turned back to Eric and kept my voice low. "Tell you what, if you want to escape, go see Mo. I'm sure she'll fix you a dessert plate that you can take up to your room."

The relief on his face couldn't have been more obvious. "But what about Dad?"

"You go on. If your father complains, I'll sic your grandfather on him. Take this." I handed him one of the ice buckets. "It'll give you an excuse to leave."

He flashed a grateful smile and headed in the direction of the kitchen.

"Where are you going, Eric?" Carl the Third hadn't paid any attention to his son until then. When Eric ignored his father and kept walking, he turned to me. "Where's he going?"

I handed a fresh napkin to the doctor. "He saw I was busy and offered to refill the ice bucket for me. Such a thoughtful young man."

Doc Wentworth caught my eye and gave me an almost imperceptible nod.

The rest of the dinner was pleasant, with the guests complimenting Mo's cooking and Elise's holiday decorations. When they were ready for dessert, Mo came in to cut the cake and served it with the cinnamon ice cream she'd made. She put a generous wedge of cake onto the first plate.

"Mo," Elise said. "Are you sure that's right?"

Mo turned to her with a look of perfect innocence. "Yes, ma'am," she said and resumed cutting. I made myself busy with the coffee so I could hide the amusement on my face.

Elise raised her hand and opened her mouth as if to object but must have thought better of it. Her pleasant expression, which had seemed pasted on anyway, became fixed.

Mo finished cutting the cake and scooping ice cream. I delivered the plates to the guests and listened to their compliments as they ate. Elise seemed to enjoy the two bites she took of her dessert. Everyone else cleaned their plates, and a couple of the teenagers asked for another piece. Nobody commented on Eric's absence.

After everyone had eaten their fill, Lupe and I cleared the table and readied the dining room for the next meal. As I carried the leftover cake to the kitchen, I passed the doctor's home office. The door was open a couple of inches, and the lights were on. I started to knock, to see if he wanted anything from the kitchen when I heard Elise's angry voice.

"—little fag isn't welcome in my home."

Shocked at what I'd heard, I stepped to one side of the door where I couldn't be seen.

"Elise, please." The doctor's voice was tense. "We've had this conversation before. He's my grandson, and he's welcome here any time he wants to visit."

"Not in my house, he's not." Each word was accompanied by a thud, as if she were pounding her fist on the desk. "I won't have that little pervert in my home."

"Now listen here." The doc's voice grated with barely controlled rage. "This is also my home." He spoke with deliberate spaces between his words. "You do not get to dictate who is welcome here. Nor do you have any right to malign my grandson. He's gay. That's all. He's a kind, intelligent young man who happens to be gay. He is not a pervert. Don't you dare ever say that again in my presence. And if you ever say it within Eric's hearing or to anyone else in the family, I'll have your bags packed before you take another breath." He took a deep breath and blew it out. "Jesus, Elise, grow the fuck up. I don't care what you say, my grandson is welcome in my home at any time, and you *will* make him feel welcome. If you don't like it, you can leave."

Elise gave a frustrated shriek. "You'd like that, wouldn't you, you bastard. Don't think I don't know you're already planning to get rid of me. Everyone in town says so."

"I think you're the one planning to go. I know what you've been up to. His wife knows, too."

"She doesn't know fuck all about anything, and neither do you. I'm not going anywhere. As far as I'm concerned, you're stuck with me until you're dead.

As old as you are, I'm sure it won't be long until I don't have to put up with this bullshit."

The sound of angry footsteps brought me back to awareness. I fled down the hall to the kitchen.

Mo took one look at me and did a double-take. "You okay?" She took the cake plate from me. I'd almost forgotten I held it.

"No, I don't think so." I tried to clear Elise's hostile words from my ears. "I heard Doc and Number Four arguing when I went by his office."

"About Eric." Mo made it a statement, not a question.

Surprised, I perched on a nearby stool. "How'd you know that?"

"They have the same argument about him every single time he's here. Turns out our little Elise is a raging homophobe." She handed me a glass of ice water.

"That's no joke." I took a sip and looked at Mo's spiky hair and multiple earrings and androgynous clothing. "But . . ." I waved vaguely in her direction.

Mo laughed. "I know. I'm about as obvious as can be, short of carrying a neon sign saying 'dyke here.' I don't think she'd know about Eric if the doc hadn't told her. She's got a hateful side, but she's also clueless. We could hold our own Pride parade in the driveway, and I don't think she'd get it."

For a moment, I enjoyed the mental image of Mo, Eric, and me swathed in rainbow flags, marching around the Wentworths' property.

"Did he come down to see you?"

"Yeah. I fixed him a plate, and he took it up to his room. Poor kid. He must be counting the days until he can escape to college. His dad isn't much better than Elise in the tolerance department. I think Eric comes to these shindigs only to please his mother. And he does love his grandpa. They get along great."

"Yeah, I'm pretty sure the doc saw me give him a reason to escape the party, and I think he was relieved. I need to get home," I said, sliding off the stool onto my weary feet. "I'm so glad to have a few days away from here."

Mo handed me an insulated bag. "Here's some dinner. And a little gift." She gave me a quick hug and I headed out to my car.

Late the next morning, I stopped by the diner on my way to Portland. As usual, Freddy was behind the counter, greeting customers from the open kitchen. She waved when I came through the door.

"Hey, Freddy, got a sec?"

She scanned the flattop where half a dozen burgers sizzled. She flipped a couple of them and rested her spatula on a nearby plate.

"What's up, hon?"

I handed her the foil-wrapped parcel. "A little present."

She gave me a suspicious look and unwrapped it carefully, revealing a generous wedge of Mo's carrot cake. She inhaled the aromas of cinnamon and ginger and gave a sigh of contentment.

"I love it already." She got a fork from under the counter and took a bite, careful to include a dollop of the cream cheese frosting. Her eyes closed for a long moment until she swallowed. "Did you make it?"

"No way. A boxed cake mix is beyond my abilities most days."

"Says she who wants my pastrami recipe." She took another bite. "Damn, this is good. Who's the baking genius behind this beautiful cake?"

"A friend of mine. She doesn't know I'm doing this, but since you told me the bakery's out of commission—"

"And out a customer, if this is typical of your friend's talents."

"—I thought I'd see if you'd like to talk with her."

"As if you'd have to ask," she said through another mouthful of cake.

I promised to pass the word along and headed for my car.

The drive to Portland usually put me into a meditative state, but not this time. The passing scenery of dense forest and serene farmland failed to ease my mind. I'd been dreading this day ever since Patrick told me that the new detective on Nicky's case asked to talk with me. Meeting with police officers was not my idea of a good time, even if Patrick would be there.

The closer I got to town, the more stressed I felt.

I pulled into the parking lot at Patrick's office building and backed into a spot near the exit. I might not have been able to avoid this meeting, but nothing would keep me from leaving as quickly as possible afterward.

When I passed the reception desk, the young woman seated there said, "They're waiting for you." I gave her a half-hearted wave. She and I had seen too much of each other of late.

The hallway to the conference room got longer every time I was there. In truth, I passed only three offices on one side and floor-to-ceiling windows on the other, but I couldn't shake the feeling that disaster loomed on the other side of the tall oak door at the far end of the passage.

Patrick emerged from the conference room and let the heavy door close behind him. He met me halfway.

"Now, remember what I told you," he said in a near-whisper, as we walked together toward the conference room. "Beth is one of the good ones. She's doing us a huge favor meeting here instead of asking us to go to the precinct, so behave yourself. She can't say so officially, but I think she believes you're innocent."

I took a deep breath to calm myself. "I don't get it, Patrick. Haven't I told the police all about this before? Why do I have to do it again?" My voice was quavering, and a tear ran down my face.

He handed me a tissue. Of course, he had tissues with him. He knew me too well.

"She's new to the case, Annie. She's being thorough, doing interviews, and examining the evidence herself instead of relying on what others have done. She also has a lot more experience as a detective than the others we've talked with."

"But—"

"I know what you're going to say. Yes, you have to tell it again. And I'm sorry about that, I really am. But give her a chance, please."

He opened the door for me and followed me into the room. "Be nice," he whispered, and I gave him a glare.

Wilson and Wyatt's meeting room looked like any law firm conference room in any movie ever made. Their long oak conference table appeared solid enough to withstand a tsunami. It was surrounded by black leather chairs with tall backs and padded arms. Bookshelves and cabinets lined two walls, with the third occupied by a credenza holding a coffee maker and cups. The fourth wall was a continuation of the expansive windows I'd passed in the hall.

The detective had taken a chair at one side of the table near the far end. When we entered, she was turned away from the door, reaching into a briefcase sitting on the floor alongside her chair. She straightened and put a short stack of file folders on the table alongside a pad of paper and a cup of coffee.

When she saw us, she stood and moved toward us, right hand extended. Patrick made the introductions.

"You want any coffee, Annie?" he asked.

"I'll get it." I picked up a cup and went through the motions of filling it with hot coffee and adding a dollop of creamer. I didn't want coffee. I needed a distraction, a few moments to recover my balance.

Not only did I have to recount, for what felt like the millionth time, the most devastating events of my life, but I had to do it for a woman who could easily look at home on any movie set in the world. Why couldn't this superstar homicide detective in Portland have been a sixty-year-old overweight man with a five o'clock shadow and a nicotine habit? No, I had to look at platinum blond hair pulled back into a business-like ponytail and chocolate brown eyes set into a heart-shaped face on a woman whose smooth muscles were visible through the silk blouse she wore. Patrick was clearly overdue for a lesson in karma for not warning me.

I inhaled deeply to calm myself and took a seat across from her at the table. Patrick sat to my right. I favored him with another glare. He gazed back at me serenely.

"Okay," I said. "What do you want to know, Detective? I'm sure you know from your stack of files that I've been over this several times already."

"I'm sure you have." She picked up a pen. "First, please call me Beth. We might be spending a lot of time together, and I try to avoid feeling as if my name is 'detective.'" She assumed a professional tone. "I know how difficult this must be for you, but—"

"I doubt that." My tone was harsher than I'd intended. Patrick put a calming hand on my arm.

She looked contrite. "I'm sorry. I misspoke. What I'm trying to say is, though it's hard for you to go over this again, it's important for me to hear it fresh. I was assigned to your case only last week, so I've barely had time to read these files, much less analyze their contents." She tapped them with her pen. "Maybe the easiest way to start is for you to tell me what happened."

I took a drink of the coffee I hadn't wanted, grateful now to have it so I could collect my thoughts.

I told her about Dad's bicycle shop, how he'd started with a shack of a building and turned it into a thriving business. "I worked there summers during college, and after I graduated, I helped out now and then."

"Pretty busy place?"

"Sometimes. And after it'd been open for a while and word got around, it turned into a gathering place. Dad sponsored organized rides once or twice a year, and local riding groups used the shop as their meeting spot. The neighborhood kids would bring their bikes in, and he'd show them how to air up their tires and do minor repairs for free."

I thought again of Joe peering through the window at the battered red bike and the joy on his face when Dad gave it to him. Beth brought me back to reality.

"And Nichole Fleming? When did you meet her?"

A leaden feeling spread in my chest. I pushed my coffee cup aside. "I met Nicky at Oregon State my junior year. She was a year behind me. She came home with me for a visit when her sophomore year ended. Her family is from Bend. About a year after she graduated, she moved to Portland for a job. We'd stayed in touch off and on, and we started dating after she moved here."

Grandma Natalie and my dad had both liked Nicky from the start, so when we moved in together after dating for almost a year, they were supportive.

"Is that when she started spending time at the shop?"

"She'd come by once or twice a week to hang out with me and Dad, eat with us, have a beer or two." I reflected at the memory for a few seconds. "One day, he asked her to help us in the store, stock shelves, put things into the shed out back, stuff like that. He joked that he was tired of her freeloading so he decided to put her to work, but I know he liked having her around."

"Did you have any idea that she'd set up a meth lab in the shed?"

"None. No clue at all. I never would have suspected her of having anything to do with drugs." I paused for a moment. Even now, with the proof that we'd found, I still couldn't reconcile the thought of Nicky making or selling meth with anything I thought I knew about her. "If I had, I'd have confronted her. If Dad had known, I'm sure he would have called the police. I know he'd have banned her from the shop and our home. He didn't let anyone or anything endanger his family."

"And you didn't notice any strange odors, chemical smells, stuff like that?"

"Have you been to the shop yet?"

"Not yet," she said. "I'm hoping to get over there this week. Why?"

"It was on a corner with a gas station next door. An auto body shop was behind us, but it closed, too, damaged by the fire. Dad had solvents and cleaners and sometimes paint in the store. There were enough chemical odors around that I don't think anyone noticed anything unusual coming from the shed. I know I didn't."

"What about strangers hanging around where they shouldn't have been? Any break-ins or vandalism?"

"No," I said. "The shed was visible from the street, so anyone could have gone back there, especially at night. Dad was too trusting to put up security cameras or a fence. He didn't even bother to put a padlock on the door. That old shed was stuffed to the rafters with junk Dad collected over the years. Nothing worth saving, really, but he tended to be a packrat. Nicky told us she'd organized it all. We only found out later—" I stopped, my throat suddenly constricting.

"After the fire," Beth prompted.

Patrick handed me a bottle of water and I took a long drink, grateful for the cold liquid.

"After the fire, we found that she'd gotten rid of most of the stuff in the shed to make room for her meth lab."

"Okay, let's shift gears a little."

I took a deep breath, relieved to talk about anything except my father's death but knowing what was next.

Beth consulted one of the files. "The fire was on April third. When did you last see Nicky?"

"That morning. She had an early meeting, so she left around seven. I had a temp job at a veterinary clinic. I didn't have to be there until ten, but I left the house a little after eight. The shop was on my way, so I liked to stop in and say hi to Dad on my way to work. When I got there, the shop was on fire."

All of a sudden, I couldn't breathe. I stared down at the table, only vaguely aware of Patrick's soothing hand on my back. After a long moment, I cleared my throat and took another sip of water. "I called 9-1-1." Tears were running freely down my face. "Dad's car was in the lot"—I choked on the words—"but the fire—I couldn't get inside." Patrick gave me another tissue and I wiped my tears away.

Beth didn't speak for a few minutes. I fought to get my emotions under control and focused on trying to breathe. I'd never forget standing outside the shop, screaming for my dad, forced back by the flames, hoping against hope that he wasn't inside. Cursing myself for not getting there sooner.

"When did you see Nicky next?" Beth's tone was soft, gently bringing me out of my painful reverie.

I took a deep breath. "I didn't. I called her cell phone several times that day to tell her what happened, but she didn't answer. I figured she was busy. When she didn't come home, I left more voicemails over the next few days, but she never called me back. The fire investigators told us about the meth lab in the shed. They figured that some of the chemicals had exploded and started the fire."

She sorted through the files for a moment and extracted one, opened it, and handed me a sheet of paper. "When did you receive this?"

I didn't have to read it. The words Nicky had written still haunted me.

*Annie, I know you can never forgive me, but I had no choice.
I never would have hurt Dad. I hope you know that. I'm so sorry.
I love you. Nicky.*

I handed the note back to the detective, tears welling in my eyes. "I got it in the mail a few days after the fire. I figured she learned about Dad from the news."

"Did you hear from her after that?"

"No."

"What about her family?"

"They'd always been nice to me, and I talked with them a few times after Nicky disappeared. They hadn't heard from her, either. After she was found, they stopped returning my calls and answering my emails. They told me to stay away from her funeral." Grief at the memory formed a lump in my throat. A drink of cold water helped only slightly.

"And when did you learn she was dead?"

I dabbed at my eyes with the tissue that Patrick provided. "The detective we worked with before—" I fumbled for his name.

"Aikawa?"

"Yes, Detective Aikawa called me on May tenth." I took a deep breath and blew it out. "He said that her—he told us she'd been found somewhere in downtown Portland."

"What details did he give you?"

"Not much. He only said she'd been found in Old Town, in the alley behind one of the bars, and she'd been shot." I looked directly into her eyes and stated with emphasis, "And I've been the focus of the investigation ever since."

She put her pen down and closed the files.

"I know you have, but you're not the only person of interest. From an investigator's perspective, you appear to have the strongest motive. I hope you understand that we have to examine every possible explanation."

I started to protest, but she waved me into silence.

"We're also interviewing all of her friends and family and searching for her drug connections. If she was making meth, or involved in distribution or selling, she must have had contacts. So yes, we have to consider you a person of interest, perhaps a suspect, but trust me, you're not the only one."

After a few more questions, the detective collected her files, gave me her card, and left. I stood and turned on Patrick, towering over him for a moment until he pushed his chair back and stood.

"You bastard. Why didn't you tell me?"

"I don't know what you're talking about." He attempted an innocent expression but failed.

"You could have let me know this oh-so-wonderful detective could pass for a super model on her worst day. You're my damn lawyer, and you let me trip all over myself like an adolescent school girl. Did you get your law license out of a Cracker Jack box?"

"It gets better." He was practically dancing with glee.

"Oh?"

"She's family. Your family, that is. Didn't you notice she didn't hesitate at all to talk about Nicky as your partner?"

"Fuck you, Patrick," I said, but my words were less insult than reflex.

"As you've reminded me many times, I'm not your type. She is, though."

I leaned against the table, too weary to continue arguing. "I don't have a type anymore. Do you really think she believes me? That I didn't kill Nicky?"

"I do." He was finally being serious. "Having her working this case is the best thing that could happen. She's an excellent detective. She used to work on narcotics cases, so she might have helpful connections. Give her a chance." He stepped a few paces away from me and from a safe distance said, "And hey, maybe an invitation for coffee, once this is all done."

Over the next two weeks, I immersed myself in work. Ada Brownlee was still in her wheelchair, at least when Hal was home, so I went by their home every few days to dust and vacuum and do the laundry. The Brownlees referred me to a couple of their friends, so my client list grew. All of them asked for additional cleanings in preparation for holiday visitors. The Wentworths' party schedule was also full. I didn't mind the long days. Working kept my mind off my visit to Patrick's office and the Portland detective who might arrest me for murdering Nicky.

When I wasn't working, I was out on my bike. Nothing cleared my mind quite like a hard ride in the cold and rain. My favorite route was a twenty-mile loop through Oregon's wine country and up into the steep hills to the west.

I arrived home from a ride feeling that kind of satisfying weariness that comes from hard physical exertion. I was also soaked to the skin from the winter rain, but that was no matter because I felt calmer than I had in weeks. I'd just parked my bike inside the apartment when my phone buzzed.

"Hey, chickie," Sharon said. "Got time for lunch?"

An hour later, freshly showered and dressed, I met her at the diner.

"You look like something the cat wouldn't drag in," she said in greeting.

"It's nice to know I can always count on your support. I've been having insomnia lately, so I went out for a ride."

"In this weather? Now I know you're nuts."

We settled into a corner booth and took menus from the metal bracket at the end of the table. I turned my coffee cup right side up in the time-honored signal for "coffee, please." I'd had a good ride, but the hot shower afterwards hadn't quite banished the December chill from my bones.

"I don't know why I'm reading the menu," I said. "I always get the same thing."

Sharon agreed, and we continued to examine the menus as if we hadn't seen them before.

All of a sudden, I felt a presence near my shoulder and in my ear, someone said, "Okay, spill it."

Startled, I looked up to find Freddy staring me in the eyes from four inches away. I leaned back to get her into focus. "Spill what?" Of course, I knew what she wanted.

She filled my coffee cup, plunked the pot down on the table, and slid onto the booth bench next to me.

"Who baked that cake?"

From the corner of my eye, I saw Sharon's amused expression. I'd told her what I'd done, sharing Mo's cake with Freddy, but even Sharon didn't know the identity of the master baker who'd created it.

"I'll trade you information for your pastrami recipe," I said, mentally crossing my fingers. It was true; I'd have no idea how to make pastrami from scratch, but it was worth a shot.

She called my bluff. "Not a chance. I have a reputation to protect. How about you come across with a name, and I won't ban you from my diner."

My answer must have shown on my face because she grinned in triumph.

"Fine. Her name is Maureen." I slid the menu into the metal bracket at the head of the table. "I'll have the pastrami."

Five days before Christmas, I parked my car at the Wentworths' home and sat for several minutes in the morning gloom, mentally preparing for another long day. I didn't want to be there. In the three weeks since the Wentworth family gathering, Elise had been on a worse tear than usual, preparing for the last holiday party of the season, and she'd asked me to come in extra early to make sure the house was ready. I fully expected to mop spotless floors, dust shining furniture, and vacuum carpet that hadn't seen a footprint since the last cleaning.

As much as I needed the work, I'd developed an intense dislike for Number Four. Always before, I'd tried to keep the peace. If I couldn't agree with her, at least I could keep my head down and do my work. She was my employer, not my friend. But her treatment of Eric and her hostility toward gay people had put an end to any attempts I might have made toward understanding. Unfortunately, my tight budget didn't give me the freedom to ditch my most financially rewarding client.

Sighing, I pulled the hood up on my jacket and got out of my car. The morning was dark with heavy clouds that had been pouring rain nonstop for hours. I locked the car and, head down to protect against the rain, went into the house through the side door as I always did. The house seemed cold, so I kept my jacket on while I checked the white board for my assignments. I shivered as I read the list, not from the length of it, but from the chill in the air. I hadn't been to the Wentworths' home so early before, and I wondered if they turned the heat down at night.

Lights from the kitchen shone through to where I stood. Perhaps Mo was working early, too, prepping food for the big bash.

"Mo, you up already?"

All of the kitchen lights were on, but Mo wasn't in sight. Two pots sat on the stove, and the kitchen reeked of hot metal. One of the pots sat a little crooked on a lit gas burner, but when I straightened it, it felt light. I lifted the lid and saw that it was empty and discolored from the heat. Starting to worry, I turned the burner off. Mo would never have been that careless.

Concerned, I looked around more carefully. Vegetables were piled near the butcher block cutting board. An onion and several carrots littered the floor. A chicken with one leg and a thigh piece cut away lay on the board, the skin drying at the edges.

"Mo, are you back there?"

I checked the pantry at the far side of the kitchen to no avail. One of the tall stools she kept near the cupboards lay on its side. The wood knife block was pushed out of its usual spot on the counter, and several of the knife handles were askew.

Something was definitely wrong.

I called her name again but got no response.

I scanned the utility room near the kitchen. No luck. When I went back out into the hallway, a cold draft made me shiver and pull my jacket tighter around me. The air currents seemed to come from the back of house, so I walked down the passageway, flipping on the light as I went.

The back door was halfway open.

"Well, no wonder," I muttered, and started to push it closed.

The light from the hall illuminated a narrow strip of the back porch and the lawn beyond. An odd brown shape on the grass caught my eye, so I pulled the door open. Elise would never stand for litter in the yard when she was having a party. I pulled the hood of my jacket up and went down the steps to collect the offending object.

I found a sodden leather slipper.

"What on earth?" How did a slipper get out into the yard?

I turned back toward the door when, through the pouring rain and in the dim December light, I saw a dark shape on the grass to the left of the porch. Reaching back through the door into the house, I switched on the outside light.

Doctor Wentworth lay motionless on the cold ground.

"Doc?" I knelt down beside him, called his name. His body was cold and wet from the rain. His open eyes were cloudy. Only then did I see that blood had made a gruesome trail down his neck and shoulder from beneath his dark robe.

"Oh, no, Doc." Illogically, I put my hand on his shoulder and called his name again, despite knowing at some level that he couldn't respond. I rushed back into the kitchen.

"Help! Mo! Is anyone here? Anyone? Mo?" I grabbed the kitchen phone and called 9-1-1.

"Please help," I said when the operator answered. "I don't know what to do. I don't know what to do."

"Calm down, ma'am," the operator said, which made me realize I was sobbing. "I can't understand you."

I wiped tears from my face and tried to take a deep breath, but couldn't stop crying.

"He's dead, the doc is dead. Please," I said through my sobs, "send everybody to Doctor Wentworth's house on Old Pine Road."

I dropped the phone onto the counter, ignoring the clatter it made when it slid off the slick surface and onto the floor. I made my way down the hall and stood in the open doorway, frozen with my hands on both sides of the doorjamb, unable to move further. The light above the back porch made the doc's body seem surreal. I couldn't take my eyes off him, even though I was shivering from both shock and the chill in the air.

Somewhere between seconds and eternity, the police and an ambulance crew arrived, lights flashing, sirens blaring. My cries had awakened the gardener, whose room was close by, and he alerted Elise. She rushed to the door, and when she saw the still form of her husband on the ground, she fainted. Orlando caught her as she fell. For a split second, I wondered if she were faking, but I chastised myself for thinking so. Even someone as selfish as Elise Wentworth was capable of honest reactions to a shocking sight.

Mo still hadn't appeared. Even in the chaos, I worried. Something wasn't right.

The police officers I'd met when Elise's necklace went missing arrived first, and after they made a quick examination of the doctor's body, they asked me how I'd found him and what I might have touched or moved. They told me to stick around, then left me alone. They had time to take photographs of the scene before the paramedics arrived, followed by the county medical examiner.

About the time the paramedics were putting the doctor's body onto a gurney, a tall, dark-haired man dressed in jeans and a plaid shirt arrived. Though dressed casually, he had an air of authority about him. He consulted with the police officers, who asked everyone to meet in the living room. He waited until we were all seated.

"I'm Dean Jarrett. I'm a detective on the Charbonneau police force. Is everyone here?"

I scanned the room. Elise was pale and trembling, tears wetting her face. She was wrapped in a blanket clearly failing to provide warmth or comfort. Orlando, the gardener, perched on the edge of the sofa, his face revealing nothing. I sat to one side, near the massive Christmas tree with its multi-colored decorations, sparkling lights, and cascading tinsel that now seemed obscenely cheerful.

"Our live-in chef isn't here," Elise said quietly. "Her rooms are above the garage. Maybe she's there. We have one other housekeeper, but she's not scheduled to come in until later. We have no guests at the moment, though we're expecting—" She stopped speaking for a long moment and took a deep breath. "We're expecting Carlton's family to arrive tomorrow." She gazed down at her hands and let tears flow down her face.

Jarrett sent one of the uniformed officers to check Mo's rooms. "When the call came in, the chief asked me to come out. I don't believe I've met any of you before now, but I only moved here from Portland a few months ago. I was a homicide detective there for several years, so I have experience in these cases."

He scanned each of our faces, as if searching for answers. I had the feeling he seldom missed a detail. Fine for the Wentworth family, but I wasn't so sure it would bode well for me over time.

He waited until Elise looked up at him and spoke quietly to her. "I'm sorry for your loss."

She didn't speak, and he turned to Orlando and me in turn. "And the same to you. I heard Doctor Wentworth was a good man." He spoke to Elise again. "First we need to search the house. Do we have your permission?"

When she agreed, he had her sign a form that he'd brought along, and asked Orlando and me to give our contact information to the officer who stood near the door.

Jarrett said to Orlando, "Sir, we'll be in touch with you over the next few days. Please go home after you've talked with Officer Harrison here."

Orlando shuffled toward Harrison looking every bit as stunned as I felt.

Jarrett turned to me. "You found him?"

"Yes." My voice was barely a whisper.

"Please come with me."

I followed him into the doc's office. The house already felt wrong with the knowledge that Doctor Wentworth was dead, and being in his office made it worse.

Jarrett sat behind the doc's desk and gestured for me to take a seat opposite him. He asked my name and jotted it down, along with my phone number and address. I recounted for him how I'd found the doctor's body, including the disarray in the kitchen and the open door. I'd just finished when there was a knock and the door opened.

"Hey, boss?" Officer Harrison leaned into the room. "Sorry for the interruption, but I thought you'd want to know that we've finished an initial search of the house. We didn't find the chef. Her car's gone, too."

"Thanks, Jimmy. Make sure the kitchen, the porch, and the yard are cordoned off and that Mrs. Wentworth and the house staff understands those areas are off limits until we get all of the evidence collected and the crime scene documented."

The officer gave a half salute and left the office, closing the door again.

Startled, I turned to the detective. "Mo's car is gone?"

Jarrett gave me a keen look. "Mo?"

"The chef. Her name is Maureen Shaughnessy, but she prefers to be called Mo. She's been the chef here for the past four or five years. Something must have happened to her, Detective. She wouldn't leave a mess like that in the kitchen."

"You know her pretty well?"

"We've been friends for a few months. She's conscientious to a fault about the cleanliness of the kitchen. But I had to turn a stove burner off this morning. The pot had boiled dry. She'd never leave a pot like that."

He sat back in the chair and looked at me, obviously thinking through what I said.

"Did she have any disputes with Doctor Wentworth? Could they have been having an affair?"

"No. No disputes. There's no way they were having an affair."

"No? Why not?"

"Mo's a lesbian."

"She told you this?"

"She didn't have to." I paused for a moment. "She and I dated a few times when I first moved to Charbonneau." I watched to see how he'd respond, but all he did was jot down another note.

"No disputes with him? No resentments you know of?"

"No. They always seemed more like brother and sister than employer and employee. He protected her from the worst of Elise's tantrums, and she made him special desserts and favorite dishes Elise wouldn't let him eat."

"And how was your relationship with him? Any problems I should know about?"

For a long moment, I was at a loss for words. Only two days ago, I'd sat across a conference room table from a police detective who considered me a suspect in a murder and who had the power to arrest me if she saw fit. How was it possible that I might be having the same experience again?

"No, none at all," I said. "We got along fine. I didn't see him very frequently since I'm mostly here while he was working. Elise manages the house staff But he always treated me well, sometimes better than I would have expected."

"Such as?"

"Little things. Making sure I had time off for Thanksgiving, for instance. Interceding once in a while with Elise. He looks out—I mean, looked out for us, the house staff. He was almost fatherly to me." My voice broke and I shut up, willing myself not to burst into tears.

Jarrett glanced at the door, making sure it was closed. He peered at me closely, as if trying to decide what to say next. His next words surprised me, and didn't, at the same time.

"Tell me about Elise."

I was right about Jarrett. He'd been in the house only a short time, and he'd apparently already decided he needed to know more about the doctor's widow.

He leaned forward in his chair and in a near-whisper said, "Is it true that people call her Number Four?"

I couldn't help it. A short yelp of laughter escaped me before I was able to clap a hand over my mouth. "How did you hear about that?" I glanced at the door, remembering her tendency to appear without warning. "Yes, it's true. She's the doc's fourth wife. He liked to trade in for younger models every few years."

Amusement showed on his face for a moment, but then he grew serious again. "I'm getting the feeling she can be difficult."

"True. My friends think I'm crazy, but I think she's insecure. She married a man who had three divorces behind him and who was thirty years older. This is a small town, Detective, and word has gone around that he was planning to leave her for someone else. I don't know how true it was, but nobody would have been surprised by it. She must have heard the rumors."

"And she took it out, this insecurity, if that's what it is, on the house staff?"

"And sometimes the doc's family members, when she could get away with it," I said, remembering Eric.

"What about her friends?"

"I'm not sure she has any. I've never seen her have anyone over, but she does go into Portland fairly often, so maybe she meets friends there. I don't know."

I scrubbed my face with my hands and ran my fingers through my hair. Less than an hour had passed since I'd seen Doctor Wentworth's clouded eyes, but it felt like weeks. My exhaustion felt bone deep.

Jarrett put his pen down and reached across the desk to shake my hand.

"Thank you for your help, Miss Velasquez. Why don't you go home and get some rest. We'll be in touch if we have more questions. And please call me if you hear from the chef or if you think of anything else."

He slid his business card to me, and I left.

Chapter Four

The news of the doctor's death spread quickly across Charbonneau. Despite his history of what people called "serial monogamy," Doctor Wentworth was respected as a physician and well liked as a man. Almost everyone in town had some connection to him or his family, which had been among Charbonneau's early settlers.

The story led on Portland's local evening news. The perky twenty-something news anchor reported in breathless tones about the murder of a local physician, but everything she said was long on drama and short on details. Sharon told me later that she saw one of the news vans parked near the diner.

When Grandma Natalie saw the news, she called me to demand I leave Charbonneau immediately. I tried to tell her there was nothing to worry about, but she proved yet again that she was the genetic source of my own stubbornness. So I packed a bag, put Shadow into his cat carrier against his better wishes, and drove to Portland. I'd never have admitted it, especially not to Grandma Natalie, but being coddled and watched over was exactly what I needed. Even Joe and Patrick were also solicitous, though Patrick did corner me in the kitchen apart from the others long enough to make a feeble joke.

He said, "Just what you need, another murder to deal with."

In return, I smacked him with a spatula, but he pulled me to him in a bear hug and whispered, "I wish you hadn't seen his body."

I wrapped my arms around Patrick and buried my face against his chest. Seeing the doc's cloudy eyes brought back haunting memories. I'd tried hard to forget the sight of my own father's eyes, but I doubted that I ever would.

I'd arrived at the bike shop to find smoke pouring from shattered windows. I'd called 9-1-1 in a panic, and then my family, who stood with me while the firefighters poured water on the smoldering remains of the building. We watched from the parking lot, Joe with his arm around my shoulders and Grandma Natalie holding my hand, while the firefighters wielded the heavy hoses, extinguishing flames and saturating spots that kept smoking. An ambulance crew waited nearby, since I was sure that my dad was inside. They had a gurney standing ready. When the last hose was shut off, I tore away from Joe and into the shop, ignoring his protests and the shouts of the firefighters.

Since then, I'd wished a million times I hadn't been so impulsive, but I'd do it again in the same circumstances.

Dad was lying face down on the floor in front of the beat-up old recliner he kept at the back of the shop in between shelves of bike parts and tools. The wall to his right was caved in and he was covered in debris. His face and clothes were blackened with soot. He wasn't burned, but he wasn't moving, either. With one glance, I knew he'd never move again. His eyes were partially open, the dark brown irises already starting to dull.

I collapsed onto the floor and had to be carried out. I spent the next several days at Grandma Natalie's home, not talking, not sleeping, refusing to eat. Only when she, along with Joe and Patrick, threatened to have me hospitalized did I start to come around, and then only with great effort. In the seven months since the fire, I'd gotten most of the way back to my normal self, but there'd always be a scar where my daddy lived in my heart.

And now I'd seen the doc's eyes, and what few defenses I'd built against the deaths of people I cared about were gone. Here I was again, living through another terrible loss. Though I wasn't anywhere near as close to the doc as I was to my father, the old terrors and nightmares and sadness all came back.

The first two nights at Grandma Natalie's, I dreamed of Dad and of the fire. More than once during those nights, I got up to wander the house, try to read, watch a little television. More than once, Grandma Natalie rose from bed to comfort me. She switched on her Christmas tree lights, at least the ones that Shadow hadn't turned into cat toys, and made me lie on the sofa and use her lap for a pillow. She put a blanket over me, stroked my hair, and we talked and admired the twinkling lights until the sky lightened. I felt as if I were a child again, insecure about my absent mother, fearful that something would happen to my dad, too. As I grew up, I occasionally wondered why I never worried that misfortune would befall Grandma Natalie. She was my rock.

I also wondered if that's why I had always been reluctant to ask her about my mother. All I knew was that Natalie's only child, my mother, had been absent from my life since I was young, too young to remember her as anything except a blonde blur. The times I asked, my grandmother stiffened, her jaw set and her lips a pale line, and all she'd say was "she's been gone for a long time, Annie dear. There's nothing to tell." After a couple of attempts in my teens, I stopped asking.

Sharon called to check on me and also to give updates, which were mostly that she had nothing to report. Others had called to offer me condolences and assistance. Lupe told me the party was cancelled, of course. Carl the Third and his family had arrived, and Lupe was more than happy to stay away from the drama their family posed.

Elise had maintained the cleaning schedule on the whiteboard. When I called Lupe to apologize for leaving her with all the work, she reassured me that she understood why I had to be away for a few days.

"Do you believe it," she said in a near whisper, "that cold bitch cares more about the house being ready for guests than the doc's death."

"I wish you didn't have to deal with her yourself. I'll be home in a day or two."

The next time my phone rang, the caller ID screen read simply "Jarrett." Damn cops. He was making me regret breaking my old habit of leaving my cell phone in the car.

"Hello, Detective."

"Ms. Velasquez, do you have time to talk? I tried to see you at your apartment a couple of times, but I keep missing you."

"Sorry about that. I'm in Portland with my family. What can I do for you?"

"Have you heard from Ms. Shaughnessy?"

The heaviness of worry I'd felt in my chest since I saw the mess in the kitchen solidified into a mass of lead.

"No, I haven't. And it sounds as if you haven't either. You think she might have had something to do with the doc's death, don't you? There's no way it can be true."

He was silent for a moment. "When are you coming back to town?"

"Tomorrow, maybe, or the day after. Why?"

"Give me a call when you're home. I have more questions, and it's best if we meet in person."

I didn't have to ask who it was best for.

A day after Christmas, Shadow let me know it was time to go home by standing on my head and pulling my hair when I tried to sleep. His message was reinforced at breakfast when Grandma Natalie asked me why I had claw marks on my forehead.

"Goofy cat plays all night long. I think it's time to pack him up and take him home. I've imposed on you long enough." I poured a cup of coffee and sprinkled cinnamon sugar on my buttered toast.

"Nonsense," she said. "I wish you'd come back and live here with me. You're too far away in that little Podunk town."

I'd wondered how long it would take for her to bring that up. We'd had the same conversation more times than I could remember in the six months since I decided a change of scenery would do me good.

"You're stubborn, aren't you?" I winked at her over my coffee cup.

"Yes, I am," she said with pride. "You're my favorite granddaughter, and I want you here with me."

"I'm your only granddaughter."

"Details, details." She waved my words away with a laugh before growing serious again. "Look, hon, don't tell me that finding the doctor's body didn't throw you for a loop. You've been having nightmares about your father again. I might be getting older, and I might be stubborn, but I'm not blind or stupid. It's not good for you to be alone and so far away." She spoke over my protests. "Now, you're all grown up and you're as bullheaded as I am, so you'll decide for yourself, but I want you to know my opinion."

"As if I didn't already, Gram." I got up and kissed her on the cheek. "But it's time for me to go home. Nightmares or not, I found him, so the police want to talk with me. I can't avoid it. I promise I'll think about moving back, but I have to deal with this first." I headed out of the kitchen to pack and find Shadow.

"At least call Patrick before you go." She was silent for a moment and spoke with reluctance. "I'm worried what might happen if the Charbonneau police discover your connection with Nicky."

"Me, too." I paused for a moment at the door. "I mean, what are the odds a suspect in one murder would find the body of another murder victim?" I gazed out the kitchen window at the gray December sky, my thoughts roiling, before meeting her eyes again. "I expect they'll figure it out. The detective in charge of the doc's case used to be a Portland homicide detective. Hell, for all I know, he's friends with the Portland detective who was recently assigned to Nicky's case." I sighed heavily. "I must have really pissed someone off in a past life to have karma like this."

A few minutes after nine the next morning, I made my reluctant way through the doors of the Charbonneau Police Department to the front desk. The receptionist was a woman about the same age as Grandma Natalie. She was on the phone, but raised her eyebrows in an obvious inquiry.

I gave her my name and said, "I have an appointment to see Dean Jarrett."

Still cradling the phone receiver between her shoulder and chin, she whispered, "I'll let him know you're here." She went back to her call.

I wandered around the reception area, too nervous to sit on one of the plastic chairs lining the wall. Photos of past Charbonneau police chiefs and of the building decorated the drab walls. The department had evidently been in one place for a long time.

"Miss Velasquez?"

I turned to find a young officer, whose name escaped me, waiting next to the reception desk. We shook hands.

"I'm Jimmy Harrison. Dean—er—Detective Jarrett asked me to come out and see you. He has someone in his office right now. Uh, Shirley?" He addressed the receptionist who was just hanging up the phone. "Is there anywhere else we can talk?"

"The chief's office is busy, too." She thought for a moment. Sounding doubtful, she said, "What about the library?"

Harrison frowned. "I don't think he'd like that."

"It's that, or whispering out here, I guess." She turned back to me. "We don't have much extra room. The department outgrew this old building a long time ago, but there's no money for a new one."

"Okay," Harrison said. "The library it is."

I followed him down a narrow hallway, wondering what kind of library a police department would have. Law books, maybe, or case files. I'd certainly never heard of a police library before now.

Harrison stopped in front of a solid-looking metal door and pulled a key ring from his belt. The door had a window about twelve inches square in the upper third with wire mesh embedded in the glass. These cops were certainly protective of their library.

He unlocked the door. Before he opened it, he said, "Maybe he'll take you down to his office instead. In the meantime, make yourself comfortable, if you can."

He pushed the door open and I went in.

The Charbonneau Police Department "library" was a small room, maybe ten feet square, windowless except for the one in the door. It was devoid of books. The cell-like space had been painted an institutional color—maybe yellow?—so long ago that any pigment remaining on the scarred walls was mostly dingy gray. The fluorescent ceiling light distorted what little color there was in the room. An ancient tape recorder sat toward one end of the rectangular table alongside a pad of yellow legal paper and a plastic ashtray that didn't appear to have been used since the state legislature banned smoking in public buildings. Maybe the officers thought its presence gave them an edge when a suspect who was also a smoker was denied its use. Two plastic chairs sat opposite each other at the table.

I was in an interrogation room.

I turned to the officer with what must have been a look of incredulity. The expression on his face said "sorry about that," and left, the heavy door closing behind him with a sigh and a click.

"Unbelievable."

I peered out the window in the door at the empty hall. Resigned, I settled into one of the chairs and pulled my phone from my jacket pocket. I could always play solitaire while I was in solitary. I smiled at my own silly humor.

After a few minutes, the door whooshed open and Dean Jarrett came in carrying a flat oblong box and two bottles of water. He set one in front of me and took the other chair.

"The library? You call your interrogation room the library?" I opened the bottle he'd given me and took a drink.

He looked embarrassed for a moment. "Not my idea. I didn't intend to meet with you in here anyway. Last minute meeting. Sorry for the wait."

"But why is this called the library?"

He opened his own bottle of water. "The joke is that this is where criminals get the book thrown at them. Doesn't make much sense, does it?"

"Yeah, that's what happens in courtrooms, right?" I was surprised that I was relaxed enough to make light conversation with a police officer.

"Exactly." His sat up straighter and his professional persona reappeared. "I thought you might like an update, and then I have a few questions."

"Okay."

"You probably know that Doctor Wentworth's funeral is Friday afternoon."

"Yes, I'm planning to go."

"I thought you might. The investigation is ongoing, of course. We're talking again with all of the family members, past and present, as well as everyone who was in the house and anyone who worked for him. We'll probably want to talk with you more about the household, so it's good you're back in town."

"And Mo? Maureen, I mean. The chef. The last I heard, she was still missing."

"And unfortunately, it's still true. Which leads me to why I asked you to come in, rather than talking on the phone."

He picked up the box he'd brought with him, lifted the lid, and removed an object contained in a plastic bag. He set the object on the table in front of me, and when I saw what I was, I had trouble getting my breath.

"Do you recognize this?"

"Of course." I picked the bag up carefully, knowing the edge would be razor sharp. I examined it through the clear plastic. "It's Mo's chef's knife." I put it down, realization dawning that I might have the murder weapon in my hand. I looked into the detective's eyes. "Why do you have it?"

"How can you be certain it's hers?"

I picked it up again and held it out toward him. "See right here, right where the blade meets the handle?"

"Uh huh."

"It's hard to see, but if you get it in the right angle, you'll see where she had her initials engraved."

He took it from me, glanced up at the ceiling light, and tilted the knife until he saw the tiny letters. "How did you know about this? I'm not sure I'd have seen it if you hadn't shown me."

"She received a new set of knives about the time I started working for the Wentworths. She was so proud of them that she got them all engraved. Good knives aren't cheap, and the doc bought her the best. She wouldn't let anyone touch them. Come to think of it, this is the first time I've held one."

The thought of Mo zealously guarding the tools of her trade would have ordinarily been amusing, but these weren't ordinary times. "And you still haven't said why you have it here."

"When you found the body, you said you saw blood."

I dreaded what was sure to come next.

"The autopsy showed Doctor Wentworth was stabbed twice, once in the abdomen and once in the back, and this"—he indicated the knife—"this is the most likely weapon. We're still waiting for the forensics report, but it fits the wounds."

I sat back in my chair, closed my eyes, and mentally surveyed both the kitchen and the area around the doctor's body. "I don't remember seeing a knife. Mo's knife block—the wood knife holder—was out of place, but the kitchen was a mess. Maybe I missed it."

"When we searched the kitchen, we found this knife in the dishwasher. Someone had put it in there and turned it on, probably thinking to wash any evidence away."

I stared at him in disbelief for a long moment. "That confirms what I've been telling you." I got up, too agitated to sit any longer. I turned to him and, leaning my fists on the table, I spoke at a deliberate pace. "No way in hell would Mo put her knife in the dishwasher. She's not the killer. No way." I felt the need to move, to release nervous energy, but the room was too small to let me pace, so I circled the table. Still on my feet, I faced Dean and took another drink of water, my mind racing.

"How can you be so sure?" He sounded genuinely puzzled.

I dropped into my chair. "Mo told me there's not a decently trained chef in the world who would put a knife like this one in a dishwasher. They're too important and too expensive. The only thing a good chef would do with a knife such as this"—I picked it up again—"would be to wash it after every single use, and by that I mean, after almost every ingredient, and when she was done, dry it carefully, and put it back in the block. It's even poor practice to put a knife into the sink for washing later, because of the injury risk. Do you have any idea—" I stopped, realizing what I was about to say and carefully laid the knife back into its box.

"Any idea about what?"

I sighed. "I was going to ask if you have any idea how sharp a knife like this can be." I looked into his eyes. "But if this proves to be the murder weapon, I guess you do."

Chapter Five

Doctor Carlton Wentworth's funeral was as understated as the man had been. The memorial service was held in the Charbonneau high school gym, which was still not big enough to seat everyone who attended. At least a hundred people were obliged to stand under the basketball hoops at each end of the gymnasium. If the occasion hadn't been so somber, I'd have found it amusing to see elegantly dressed women in heels and men in expensive suits clambering up and down the bleachers.

Doc hadn't been a religious man, so after the funeral director said a few consoling words, friends and family members came forward to speak. Most of them lauded the doctor's finer qualities: his compassion for his patients, his charitable work, and his kindness to others. A few lightened the mood, such as Hal Brownlee, who thanked the departed doctor for making Ada stay in her wheelchair long enough for her hip to heal properly.

A former colleague, who had worked for the doc many years earlier, regaled us with a tale of being fired repeatedly.

"I'd do something he didn't like, such as taping a dressing the wrong way. He'd get all wound up and fire me. Of course, I'd go back to work the next day. Most of the time, he'd have forgotten all about it, but now and then, he'd say, 'Didn't I fire you?' I would agree that yes, he had, but I knew he didn't mean it, and we'd get back to work." The man paused for a moment, eyes lowered. "He made me a better doctor than I'd ever have been without him." He paused for a moment and when he spoke next, his voice was constricted. "Bon voyage, Carl."

After the service ended, I met Sharon and Lupe at the diner. When I arrived, I found a line of people out to the street. Obviously most had been to the memorial service. Not many of Freddy's usual customers wore silk suits and designer dresses. I'd almost despaired of finding my friends, but Freddy waved me through the door and pointed to a corner booth where Sharon and Lupe were sipping coffee and getting acquainted.

"What I don't understand," I said as I slid into the booth next to Lupe. "is why they didn't have the doc's service somewhere nice in Portland."

"Hello to you, too," Sharon said.

Lupe said, "I heard Number Four talking about it. He made his funeral arrangements a long time ago and said he wanted everything done here. In a town this size, there's nowhere bigger than the high school gym." She sipped her coffee. "Number Four was none too happy about that."

That made sense, given what I knew about the doc. He might have come from a well-to-do pioneer family, but he'd always been down to earth.

"How was it at the house while I was away?"

Lupe rolled her eyes. "The whole situation was insane and sad, all at once. All of the wives and their families came down, of course, and there were a few friends. The house was packed. We had to put up a couple of people in—" Her gaze dropped to her hands.

"Up in Mo's room," I said.

She looked back up at me uncertainly. "There wasn't anywhere else. Elise brought in a couple of temps to clean up, but I'm glad you're back."

"I'm sorry I took off." I put my arm around her shoulders and gave her a hug. "I owe you big time."

"Hey, you found the poor man's body," Sharon said. "That had to be horrible for you. I'd have gone into hiding forever after that."

I gazed down at the table. She didn't need to know that the doc's wasn't the first dead body I'd seen in my life. "Yeah, it was bad."

A young woman I didn't recognize came to the table. She took our orders and poured more coffee, leaving the pot on the table. The crowd in the diner had grown. The connection between death and food seemed a universal constant. After my dad's death, well-wishers brought casseroles and soups and trays of cookies and fruit baskets until Grandma Natalie asked them to stop. She still had some of the platters and baking dishes since she'd been unable to identify their owners.

We tried to talk about anything but the doctor's death, but our conversation was halting. Fortunately, our food arrived, providing a welcome distraction. Unfortunately, Freddy's excellent pastrami couldn't erase worries about my missing friend.

"I wish I knew where Mo went," I said, finally voicing what was foremost in my mind. "The cops seem to think she killed the doc and took off . I don't buy it."

"Whenever I saw them together, they seemed to get along fine." Lupe looked despondent. "I wonder what will happen now."

Over the next few days, the Wentworth household tried in vain to return to normal. The doc was gone, and his moderating influence on Elise died with him. In some respects, she seemed more calm than usual. Lupe and I speculated that perhaps it was because she was no longer worried about being replaced. She was, after all, the last Mrs. Carlton Wentworth, Jr. In other ways, though, she was more out of control than ever. Her tone with us was sharper. She demanded more work in less time and carped about every little flaw. On the days I worked for her, I went home exhausted. The only good news, if it could be called that, was the cancellation of the New Year's Eve party. Even Elise couldn't muster the energy to pretend to celebrate.

The kitchen was no longer my refuge, the place where I could find a sympathetic word or a snarky joke about servitude under Number Four. Mo was still missing. Her car hadn't been found, either. Elise hired a new chef, a mousy little woman named Kate. I couldn't picture her cutting a cake in wedges when she'd been told otherwise or serving anything except the minuscule portions the lady of the house demanded.

Had my budget permitted, I would have quit. Instead, I asked the Brownlees and my other clients to let me know if they heard about anyone who needed a part-time housekeeper.

As we all tried to establish a routine despite the changed circumstances, I couldn't shake the nagging sensation I was forgetting something. I searched my memory, trying to identify it, but without success. After a time, I told myself it must be nothing, but the feeling persisted. I tried to ignore the troubling sense of déjà vu and went about my work.

Though Ada Brownlee's hip was no longer keeping her in a wheelchair, she still liked to have me come in twice a week to dust and vacuum. Hal and Ada's friendly squabbling, the sort that only well-matched couples who've been together for decades can do, kept me entertained.

A week after the doc's funeral, I was putting the vacuum cleaner away when Hal came in from the garage with grocery bags in each hand. Ada went to help him, but he shooed her away.

"I'm fine, old woman." He stopped long enough to plant a kiss on her cheek. "Now get out of my way."

He deposited the bags on the counter and refused to let her help with the groceries. "Go visit with Annie," he said.

"All righty then." Ada turned to me. "Coffee?"

We took our cups to the kitchen table and were getting comfortable when Hal deposited a bakery box in front of us without saying a word. Ada opened it to reveal two enormous cinnamon rolls, one with icing and one without.

"Hal," I said. "You're a man after my own heart."

He returned to the table with two plates and utensils. On impulse, I jumped up and kissed him on the cheek. His face turned a deep red, and Ada laughed in delight. I put one roll on each plate and heated both of them in the microwave. I served Ada the iced roll and took the other one for myself. The warm cinnamon roll paired with Ada's excellent coffee could almost make me forget the ugliness I'd have to confront at some point.

"How are you doing, dearie?" Ada ate a bit of the icing melting off her cinnamon roll.

"I'm okay."

Hal snorted. "I doubt that very much."

Ada shot him a glare, but said to me, "He's right, isn't he?"

"It is what it is, Ada. I was the first one to the house that morning, and I found him. That's bad enough, but my friend is missing and the cops think she killed him. I haven't been able to convince them otherwise."

"Your friend, she was the chef?"

"Yes. She and the doc were buddies. It's not possible that she'd hurt him. Something has happened to her. I can't sleep, worrying about her."

Ada patted my hand and reminded me to drink my coffee before it got cold. I'd long since realized that spending time with Ada and Hal let me miss Grandma Natalie a little less. Maybe I needed to give serious consideration to moving back to Portland after all.

"Are you going to ask her, or do I have to do it for you?" Hal plopped down in the chair next to Ada, his own coffee cup in hand.

Ada scowled at him. "Shut up, old man. I don't need your help."

"Ask me what?" I peered suspiciously at each of them in turn. "What are you two up to now?"

"Nothing, dearie," Ada said. "I have a doctor's appointment in Portland next week, and this useless hunk of humanity"—she poked Hal's shoulder with a finger—"has decided he doesn't like driving there."

"It's not that at all," Hal said.

"Yes, it is. So Annie, would you mind taking me? It's next Wednesday at ten."

"Of course I'll take you. I usually visit with my grandmother on Wednesdays anyway, so it's no imposition at all. In fact, it'll be fun. Maybe we can go to lunch with Grandma Natalie."

Ada gave Hal a look as if to say "so there," and he laughed.

"Hey, Annie, I'm fine driving. You have a nice new car, and I thought you might like to show it off, that's all." He made a show of giving me an exaggerated wink, pretending Ada didn't see it and laughed again. "Besides, now I'll get some peace and quiet in the house for a change."

On Wednesday morning, I arrived at the Brownlees' home in time for breakfast. Ada insisted on feeding me in return for driving her to Portland. Since I was never one to turn down a homemade meal, I presented myself at the door at eight o'clock on the dot.

Breakfast was made all the better by the resident sideshow. Their friendly bickering was endlessly amusing. Even before they met, I knew Ada and Grandma Natalie were going to get along fine.

When it was time to go, Hal helped Ada into her jacket and reached to button it.

"Leave me alone, old man." She patted his hands out of her way. "I can dress myself."

"Yes, but when you do, I'm not sure I want to be seen with you in public. The last time you put this jacket on, you buttoned it all wrong. You looked like an escapee from the loony bin."

"I was. I escaped from you." She stepped away from him and fastened the top button.

"We'd better go," I said. "Don't want to be late."

Ada gave Hal a smooch. "You behave yourself today, okay? We're having lunch with Annie's grandmother, so I won't be home until later."

"I'll be fine. Call me and tell me what the doctor says, okay? Now get out of here. The locksmith is due to arrive at any moment."

"Okay, hon. Good luck finding a new wife." She gave him a peck on the cheek and we headed to the car.

As we pulled away from the house, I said, "Locksmith? New wife?"

Ada laughed, a hearty sound that always lifted my spirits. "Hal likes to joke that he's going to change the locks when I'm not home. He actually did it once, just to be funny, so I never know when he might do it again."

"Must have been an expensive joke."

"True, and it was forever before we got the keys right. The big doofus loves to pull pranks. I go along with it just for fun, and every once in a while, I get him back. He's better at it than I am, though. For all I know, the house will be purple with pink polka dots by the time I get home today." She laughed again and put a hand on my arm, leaning toward me slightly despite the seat belt across her shoulder. "One time, he built a fence around the front yard and filled it with goats—mamas and kids. There must have been thirty of them."

"Goats? Where did he get goats?"

"He borrowed them, if you can believe it. Somehow, he managed to convince one of the farmers outside town to lend him a herd of goats for the day. You should have seen Hal and that poor farmer trying to round them up. Baby goats can bounce in five directions at once. I laughed until my sides hurt."

"Maybe that was his payback, having to catch them."

For the rest of the drive to Portland, we chatted about inconsequential things. We were both avoiding any talk about the doctor's murder and Mo's disappearance. Neither topic was ever far from my mind. Ada provided a welcome respite from the stress of those events.

After Ada's appointment, where the orthopedic surgeon released her from any restrictions on her activities, we drove to Grandma Natalie's house. On the way, Ada called Hal to tell him the doctor insisted that she take things slow, that she still had some healing to do. She gave me a conspiratorial look and held her fingers to her lips while she talked to her husband. The fun never stopped with those two.

Grandma Natalie met us at the door, but she wasn't alone. Ada was getting the full family treatment.

"Ada Brownlee, this is my grandmother, Natalie Lindberg."

They exchanged greetings, and I could see them already making a connection. They were of an age, each with a good sense of humor, and it showed. Somewhat belatedly, I realized that I might have started something I'd regret later.

"And this is my brother, Joe." I saw the involuntary quirk of Ada's eyebrow when I introduced the tall black man beside Grandma Natalie. He grinned, having also seen her reaction. We'd had a lot of different responses from people over the years, so we were used to it. I went on to explain. "You know how it is, Ada. He showed up at the door, Grandma Natalie fed him, and now we can't get rid of him."

Ada laughed out loud and clapped a hand over her mouth. "I'm so sorry," she said, tears of laughter in her eyes.

"No need to be sorry," Joe said. He wrapped her in a bear hug, which she returned with enthusiasm.

When he released her, I said, "And this is our friend, Patrick. We've known each other since elementary school." No need to tell her that he was also my attorney.

Grandma Natalie invited Ada into the kitchen for coffee. "No formal living room stuff for us."

As we walked toward the kitchen table, I noticed Joe limping a little. I caught him by the arm.

"Is your leg bothering you?"

"Some. The new one still needs a little adjusting. It'll be fine."

"New one?" Ada pulled out a chair and made herself comfortable.

"I lost my lower leg in Iraq," Joe said. He pulled his pant leg up to show the bottom part of the metal framework of his prosthesis. He took the chair next to her.

"I'm so sorry," she said quietly. "You're okay otherwise?"

"Don't give him any sympathy, Ada," I said. "He was probably limping to get attention." I caught the wadded-up napkin Joe threw at me. I knew better than to think he was milking his disability for attention, but being a good sister, I took every available opportunity to tweak him.

Joe said, "Do you see what I have to put up with? First she calls me a stray, and then she calls me a cripple." He tried to look sorrowful, but the humor in his eyes gave him away. "And all I've done is try to be a good brother."

"A cripple?" I turned to Ada. "This so-called cripple rode in a four-hundred-mile bike race recently."

"You did?" Ada's eyes were wide with astonishment.

"Well," he said, trying to sound modest, "the event was a relay, so I only rode a hundred miles of it, but yeah, three buddies and I did it."

While we drank our coffee, Joe regaled Ada with stories from the relay race. I was sure that most of them were fiction, but she seemed to enjoy every minute. I did my best to interject a bit of reality into the conversation, but Joe was on a roll. Once he started spinning tales, there was no stopping him.

"Okay, enough." Grandma Natalie had watched us with amusement while Patrick rolled his eyes and stayed out of the fray. "If we're going to lunch, we'd better get a move on, or we'll be having dinner instead."

On our way back to Charbonneau after lunch, Ada was uncharacteristically quiet.

"You okay?" I wondered if she'd eaten something that disagreed with her. She'd been enthusiastic about having Thai food for lunch, but maybe it'd been too spicy. We'd all carefully avoided talking about Doctor Wentworth's murder, so I wasn't concerned that she was upset by our mealtime conversation. Still, for chatty Ada to remain quiet this long was disconcerting.

She didn't respond at first, but after a few moments, she turned to me with a big smile on her face. "I've made up my mind. I'm doing it," she declared.

"Doing what?" With women like Ada and my Grandma Natalie in my life, I'd long since learned to be suspicious. There was no telling what plot they'd hatched.

"I'm calling Natalie to accept her invitation."

I'd been anticipating this ever since we'd walked out of the kitchen and through the garage, with a stop to admire the Harley, on our way to Happy Thai.

"What will Hal think?"

"Who cares?" She did a wrist flip that would've done a drag queen proud. "He's my husband, not my nanny. I don't need his permission. If I want to take a ride with Natalie on her motorcycle, that's exactly what I'll do." She thought for a moment, and then looked a little sheepish. "Maybe I won't tell him until after."

Two days later, I was at the Wentworth home again. After the doc's memorial service, I'd expected life at the big house to calm down, but I couldn't have been more wrong. A constant flow of guests poured in and out of the place.

Every day, it seemed that someone new arrived. Some paid only short visits to offer condolences, but most had travelled far enough that they stayed over a night, sometimes two, sometimes more. Lupe and I were kept busy every day, cleaning guest rooms, preparing the dining room for meals, and keeping track of the guest list.

The new cook also struggled to keep up. She was young and clearly lacked experience, especially since Elise demanded meals that could have passed for offerings from five-star restaurants. Elise also hired two kitchen helpers, which Mo hadn't needed, so things had definitely changed.

All of the former wives and their families came and went as if they still lived there. I hoped they didn't see Elise's pursed lips and stony glare every time they arrived. When Carl the Third and his family visited, I kept a particular eye out for Eric, knowing that with the doc's death, the grief-stricken young man was deprived of his grandfather's protection.

The doc's friends and colleagues from medical school and his years practicing medicine mingled with family members, talking about what a good man and doctor he'd been. Inevitably, the conversation turned to how he'd died and whether anyone had been arrested. To my dismay, Mo's name came up far too often. Everyone seemed to assume that, because her knife had been confirmed as the murder weapon and because she was missing, she'd killed Doctor Wentworth.

At those times, I did my best to make myself scarce. I wasn't sure I could conceal my feelings when talk turned to Mo's presumed guilt. With every passing day, I was more certain that whoever killed him had also hurt her. So I kept my head down and did my work and was glad to escape at the end of the day.

On one of those days, we finished mopping the floors in the kitchen and bathrooms, and Lupe left for home. I checked the schedule yet again, though these days, it was always the same. Long days of keeping the guests happy and doing all I could to avoid provoking Elise. No wonder I was exhausted.

"Annie?" The new cook came around the corner from the kitchen. "You okay?"

"As much as I can be. Did you know Doctor Wentworth?"

"No, sorry. I moved here for the job, but I heard what happened. How awful for all of you. I've heard he was very kind."

"He was. And I suppose you know that the previous chef and I were friends?

She looked thoughtful for a moment. To my surprise, she said, "I hope they're wrong about her. From what I've heard, she was a good person."

"She is," I said, emphasizing the present tense. "She's a great person. She's also a good friend and I'm worried something bad has happened to her." I read the schedule board again, unwilling to look into the eyes of the sympathetic young woman. Tears threatened to well up.

To my relief, she changed the subject. "I still haven't quite adjusted to Mrs. Wentworth's menu preferences, so I have a ton of food left from lunch. I don't want it to go to waste. Want to take something home for dinner?"

A tear rolled down my face. Mo almost always sent me home with some of her excellent cooking. I wiped the tear away and on impulse hugged the new cook.

"Thank you, that would be nice," I said.

While I stood by the schedule board for another minute, waiting for her to bring me her dinner offering, my gaze turned to the back door. I looked at it for a long moment, remembering the morning I'd found it standing open to the cold December air.

Without thinking, I went to the door, opened it, and stepped outside. I hadn't put my jacket on yet, but the cool breeze was refreshing. I walked down to the grass and stood where I'd found the doctor's body. No traces were left to show that a man died there. Winter rain had washed away the blood, and the lawn, always so carefully tended, showed no evidence of having been disturbed.

The lack of any sign of the doctor's passing bothered me. Surely a person's death, especially a violent death, should leave an impression.

I shivered in the cold air and turned to go back inside, but something caught my eye.

Above and to the left of the door, tucked back under the eaves in a corner and aimed toward the back door and the adjacent yard, was a security camera.

I'd seen other cameras on the house. Two out front were positioned to show the driveway and the gate near the road, and another aimed at the front door. Cameras on each side of the house covered the lower floor windows. None of the them were monitored. I'd only seen a recording checked once before, when the gardener had reported damage to one of his flower beds. Elise had suspected vandalism and demanded an investigation. She'd been proved right in one respect: a marauding deer had made a meal of the recently blooming nasturtiums. Mo and I had thought the whole episode was hilarious.

Surely the police would have asked if there were security cameras and an alarm system here. After all, the Wentworths were wealthy by anyone's standards. Their large home sat on several acres of land with the trees and grounds well-tended, including a copse of apple trees not far from the back door, all bare now in the winter wind. But this camera, tucked as it was into a dark corner, would be easy to miss.

I dismissed my worried thoughts. Charbonneau might have a small police department, but the detective was an experienced investigator. I had no reason to doubt him.

"Annie? Aren't you cold?" The cook stood in the doorway, a concerned expression on her face. She held up an insulated bag, the same one Mo had handed to me many times. "Here's something for your dinner and a muffin for tomorrow morning. Come back inside. If you like, I'll make you some coffee for the road."

The next few days followed the same pattern. Guests in, guests out, Elise murmuring thanks for the sympathy and condolences she received. And of course, the constant speculation about why the chef, such a lovely person, they all said, would do such a terrible thing. Lupe and I could only glance at each other in disbelief and do our jobs.

I arrived home one night physically tired from another long day on my feet and emotionally exhausted from worrying about Mo and wondering who had killed the doc. I took a long shower and settled down in front of the television with my dinner and my cat and pulled my lap blanket over my legs. Of course, the phone rang.

"Go away," I mumbled at it through a bite of mashed potatoes. "Whatever it is, I'm not interested."

Curiosity got the better of me and I checked the screen.

"Hell and damnation." I jabbed the button on the phone and said the first thing that came to mind. "What do you want? Don't you know it's dinner time?"

There was a short pause. "I'm sorry, should I call back tomorrow?"

I let myself enjoy the moment. I didn't often get to embarrass a cop, and this one was trying to pin a murder on my friend.

"No, it's okay, Dean. I'm just really tired. What's up? Did you find Mo?"

"Sorry, no. Not her car, either. I'm sorry to have to say it, but all evidence points to her killing the doctor and leaving town."

"Not possible." I shook my head as if he could see me. "I don't know how to convince you that you're wrong, but you are. My cat is about to eat my dinner, so if you didn't find her, why did you call?"

"Would you have time to come in to see me sometime in the next day or two? I need to talk with you about something."

"Another visit to the library?" I took a big bite of mashed potatoes.

He actually laughed a little. "You didn't like the ambiance? Personally, I think it has all the charm of an unfinished basement, but if you like it . . ."

The next morning, I met Dean at the reception desk of the Charbonneau Police Department. I was relieved when he told me the library was already in use and we'd talk in his office. When we passed the interrogation room, I heard the murmur of voices. On our way down the hall, Dean paused long enough to grab two bottles of water from a refrigerator.

His office wasn't much of an improvement, though. Maybe eight feet square, it was at the corner of the building. The outer two walls were almost entirely taken up by windows. The open feel the windows provided was the room's only good point. A battered gray metal desk occupied most of the floor space, and a bank of file cabinets took up one wall. The wall behind the desk was bare of paint where the top of the chair had scarred it over the years.

Dean gestured for me to settle into the chair beside his desk. He sat behind the desk and leaned back, thumping his head on the wall. He sat forward again, looking chagrined.

I tried not to smile when he rubbed the back of his head. "How many times a day do you do that?"

"More times than I care to admit. Being six-six in a tiny room isn't nearly as much fun as you'd think."

I opened the water bottle he'd given me and waited.

After a moment, he cleared his throat. "Okay, I know you don't think that Maureen killed the doctor—"

"I know she didn't."

"—but I have to investigate every possibility and follow the evidence."

I waited.

He sat back again, careful to avoid the wall. "How much do you know about her family?"

"Not a lot. She doesn't talk about them much." I thought for a moment. "She's been estranged from her parents for a long time. They're religious, and when she came out to them, they abandoned her, kicked her out of the house, when she was maybe fifteen? Or sixteen? I'm not sure."

Concerned, Dean sat forward and leaned his elbows on the desk. "Where did she go? Another family member? Grandparents?"

"She never said, but I had the impression she was on the streets for a while. Somehow, she found a way to go to culinary school, but I don't know how. Anyway, she said something once about a brother, I think." Thinking, I looked down at my hands for a moment and then met Dean's eyes. "That's about all I know. She's a pretty private person in a lot of ways."

He made a few notes. "What about her friends? Do you know any of them?"

"I think most of her friends live in Portland." I gave him the few names I knew. "I don't have any of their addresses, but from what Mo's said in the past about where they get together, they must be in the Sellwood or Hollywood areas, maybe Mount Tabor."

He made another note as he muttered, "That covers a lot of territory east of the river."

"I know, sorry."

"We'll figure it out. Do you know anything about her finances, whether she has any problems with money?"

"No. She lives at the Wentworths' and she drives a reasonably decent car, but nothing fancy. I suspect Doctor Wentworth paid her well. He was generous with all of us. But it wasn't something we talked about. Why do you ask?"

He paused for a moment. "Just gathering information."

But I had a feeling there was more to his inquiries. "You could have asked me these questions on the phone last night. What do you really want?"

"You don't miss much, do you?" He picked up a pencil and tapped the eraser end on the desk until I thought I'd have to take it away from him. The look on his face told me he was struggling with a decision. I let him struggle. Far be it from me to interfere with deep thought.

"It's been busy at the Wentworths' home, hasn't it? Lots of guests?"

"Yes, but don't you already know that?"

"I imagine they talk about what happened."

"All the time." I was willing to go along with whatever snowball he had rolling downhill in his mind, at least for the time being.

"Do they talk with you about it?"

"No, but why would they? I'm there to clean the house and occasionally serve dinner. Lupe and I talk about it, of course, but privately, not in front of the family or guests. What's your point?"

"But they talk in your presence?" He wasn't going to let me disturb his train of thought, but I was getting an inkling of where he was going.

"Sure, sometimes."

"I don't mean this the way it'll sound, but they do that—talk in front of you, I mean—because you're essentially—" He stopped, searching for a word.

I supplied it. "Invisible."

"I'm sorry, but yes."

"Nothing to be sorry for. Most of my more affluent clients give the help no more mind than they could a corner table. Doctor Wentworth was an exception. It used to bother me, but not now. Sometimes it works to my advantage because I can get my work done faster. Not a lot of distractions."

"Have you heard anything you think sounds off, that sounds as if it might help us figure out who killed the doctor?"

"No, I haven't, but I wouldn't expect to. I mean, those people are his family members and friends. All three former wives and their families have visited more than once, and I swear he knew every doctor, nurse, orderly, pharmacist, and hospital administrator west of the Mississippi."

"Okay, I guess that makes sense. But if you do hear anything that doesn't sound right to you, no matter how minor it might seem, I'd appreciate it if you'd let me know." He took a business card from the desk drawer and wrote on it before sliding it across the desk to me. "That's my cell number. Call or text me any time. Would you be willing to do that?"

I picked the card up and read it, my mind churning. Patrick was right; the last thing I needed was involvement in another murder case. At least this time, I wasn't a suspect, but there was nothing I could do to extricate myself. I was already involved, had been since I stepped outside the back door and saw the doctor's body lying on the grass.

I glanced up from the card to find Dean peering at me closely.

"You have something on your mind?" he asked.

My stomach clenched. Here it was, the perfect opportunity to tell the detective about my problems in Portland. I couldn't do it. I knew I should, it was the right thing to do, but I was already emotionally raw after finding the doc's body. I couldn't bring myself to talk about my father, not today. I didn't have the strength.

I tucked Dean's card into my pocket. "Okay, I'll keep you up to date, but only on two conditions."

He raised an eyebrow. "Oh?" He leaned his elbows on the desk and gave me another suspicious look. "Let's hear it."

"First, try to keep an open mind about Mo. I'm telling you I'm right. Something has happened to her."

He opened his mouth to speak, but I waved him off.

"Yes, I know, you have to follow the evidence, and I'm not asking you not to, but I *am* asking you to consider that perhaps the evidence isn't telling the whole story yet."

He hesitated. "And the second condition?"

"To the extent you can, I want you to share with me everything you find out about Mo. I can't begin to tell you how worried I am about her, and maybe I can help."

He sat back in his chair and peered at me through halfway squinted eyes.

"You don't scare easy, do you?" he finally said. "I've been a cop for almost twenty years, including ten as a detective, and I've never once had anyone give me conditions for cooperation."

"Maybe that should tell you how much I believe in my friend."

Chapter Six

Are you out of your fucking mind?"

I hadn't thought Patrick would like the agreement I'd made with Dean, but the intensity of his reaction surprised me. "Patrick, let me—"

"Let you what? Explain?" He dropped into the chair opposite me at Grandma Natalie's kitchen table. "Oh, please do. Explain to me how you're planning to feed information to the cops. Do tell me what a wonderful idea this is." He leaned back in his chair and spread his arms wide, as if to say "go on."

After my meeting with Dean, I'd gone to Portland for my regular visit with Grandma Natalie. As frequently happened, Joe was there, too, and I told them about Dean's request. Over my protests, he called Patrick. I was outnumbered.

"All he wants me to do is tell him if I overhear anything that might help him find out who killed the doctor. That's all. What's so terrible about that?" I regretted that last line the moment I said it.

"What's terrible? Okay, let me see. First, does he have any idea he's asking a woman who is a suspect in a murder to help him investigate a different murder?"

"No, it's not relevant. The cases are not related."

"Not relevant. Not related." His tone had calmed, but still carried an undercurrent of incredulity. "So, let's say you do hear something that might be important."

"That's the idea."

"And then let's say that he asks you who said what and you tell him, and it turns out to be critical to solving the case." He went from disbelieving to sarcastic.

"That's a good thing, right?"

"And then, to add to the fun, let's say you turn out to be an important witness."

"Patrick, he's not asking me to testify."

"Yeah," Joe spoke up, "whatever she'd report that someone else said would be heresy, wouldn't it?"

"Hearsay, you moron," Patrick said. "Not heresy."

"Pardon me for trying to lighten the mood." Joe took a pitcher of lemonade from the fridge and poured some for himself and Grandma Natalie.

"But what *is* heresy," Patrick said, "is that you have any notion you should be involved in this at all. I get it, you want to find out who killed the doctor and you want to help your friend. But you're not the right person to do it."

"Why not? I'm in the house all the time. They talk about anything and everything as if I'm not there. Who knows what I could overhear that might be helpful? What I do know is Mo didn't do it. Something happened to her, I just know it. She's missing and everyone assumes she killed the doc and took off. She would never do that. All Dean Jarrett asked me to do is tell him if I hear anything that doesn't seem right."

"But you didn't come clean and tell him about Nicky."

"No. I tell you it's not relevant." I crossed my arms and glared at him, my stubborn streak asserting itself.

"He's going to find out, Annie. He's an experienced homicide cop with several years on the Portland force. He knows everyone, probably including Beth O'Brien. He'll find out, and when he does, he'll blow a cork." Patrick got up and paced. "And he'll be justified because your status as a person of interest could very well scuttle his case."

"I don't see how."

"No?" He stopped pacing and leaned on the table across from me, using his height to advantage.

"If they call you as a witness, how much credibility do you think you'd have if it came out in court that you're involved in a different murder case? Credibility is all witnesses have, Annie, and yours would be nonexistent. And it would be worse if the defense brought it up in court, and nobody else knew about it." He ran his hands through his hair in frustration. "And then, what if he and the prosecutor talk about how you concealed information and they decide you're a likely suspect? You said it yourself—you're always in the house. You're friends with the chef, which means you've been in the kitchen, and you know where the knives are kept. You get my drift?"

I couldn't speak.

Grandma Natalie rapped a knuckle on the table top. "You need to quit that job now and move back here." Her tone was severe. "You have no business getting involved."

"I'm already involved, Grandma. I found the doc's body. I can't walk away."

"Yes, you can. You move back here pronto, and if they need you to testify about how you found that poor man, you can do that. But you have all of us and yourself to look out for. Mo sounds like a good person, and I'm sorry she's missing, but you're not alone in this world. Your family counts, too." She'd pursed her lips into a white line, a sign I'd long recognized as meaning she wouldn't tolerate any disagreement.

Patrick finally sat down again. He reached across the table and took my hand. When he spoke, his tone was conciliatory.

"She's right, Annie."

"Of course, I am." Grandma Natalie fairly radiated disapproval.

"You need to remember the big picture here." He released my hand. "I'm doing everything I can to keep your ass out of prison for a murder you didn't commit. Don't make my job any harder by galloping off to be a hero and then getting roped into a conviction."

"I'm not galloping anywhere. I'll do my work and keep my eyes and ears open." Now my turn came to rise and pace the length of the kitchen. "Has it occurred to any of you that having him on my side might be a good thing? If he knows Beth and if I help him with his case, maybe he'll put in a good word for me with her. How could it hurt?"

"Maybe." Patrick's tone was grudging. "But not if you hide important information from him. And I don't care if you say it's irrelevant. Right or wrong, and yes, it's wrong, you're a suspect in a murder. And whether you like it or not, the evidence as it exists right now points to you, that you shot Nicky in retaliation for the fire that killed your dad."

"Then why hasn't Detective O'Brien arrested me?"

"Because she's cautious and good at what she does. She doesn't believe the investigation is complete, so she's continuing to work it. She won't do anything to compromise the case. Making an arrest too soon is not good police work, and as I told you, she's one of the best."

"Annie, sit down." Grandma Natalie caught my hand and drew me into the chair next to her. "Move home, hon. Please. You're not a cop, and you're in no position to act like one. For all you know, someone in that house killed the doctor, so you might be in danger. Have you thought about that?"

I had to admit I hadn't, and it gave me pause. "Okay, Gram. I'll move back, but"—I held up a hand to forestall the happy celebration I saw in her eyes—"after the case is closed. I have to make sure Mo is okay." I took both of her hands in mine. "I'll be extra careful, I promise. I'll keep my phone with me all the time."

"No more leaving it in the car?"

"I won't leave it anywhere, so you can call me whenever you want. And the moment Mo is found and the cops figure out who killed the doc, I'll pack up and move in here, and then you'll regret it, because Shadow sheds like there's no tomorrow."

She smiled with tears in her eyes and hugged me.

I turned to Patrick. "And I'll come clean with Dean the next time I see him. Good enough?"

I had no difficulty keeping my promise to Patrick because Dean and I kept in touch by phone, mostly a few text messages. After all, I'd said that I would tell Dean about Nicky's murder and the Portland investigation when I saw him, and I hadn't. Had Patrick asked, I could claim to have kept my promise. Patrick would be angry at my attempt to sidestep a promise, but it was the best I had at the moment.

As is common in the wake of a death, the initial outpouring of grief and support dwindled. After the first week, the doctor's friends and colleagues went home, saddened by their loss, but called by the demands of their lives to resume normal activities. The wives and their families were still an almost constant presence. Lupe wondered, only half joking, whether they'd set up a schedule, because no sooner would one group leave than another arrived.

"Maybe," Lupe mused, "they're hanging around to find out what the doc's will says."

"I'd imagine that the doc would have given them all copies anyway. It would have been typical of him, just because he was so generous. Maybe they're being supportive."

I'd been surprised to discover that my dad had a will. The only things of any value he owned were the bike shop and the house Grandma Natalie currently occupied. He'd bequeathed them in equal shares to Joe and me, but they were heavily mortgaged. When Grandma Natalie let me see his personal papers, I found that he'd also been thoughtful enough to carry life insurance. Joe and I were the beneficiaries in equal shares there, too, so we used the proceeds to pay off both mortgages. We liked knowing that Grandma Natalie would always have a home.

Elise still wanted the big house cleaned, but less frequently, which was a relief. Both Lupe and I had long since wearied of her imperious demands. With fewer people dropping by, she seemed more reasonable in her requests. The lists on the whiteboard were shorter and more mundane than before.

My schedule was cut to two days a week, which was fine with me. Being in the Wentworth house reminded me that Mo was still missing. After more than a month, I tried not to think of where she could be, but in my darkest moments, I wondered if she could possibly be dead.

Every few days, I'd get a text or a voicemail from Dean, but I had nothing to report. My abbreviated work schedule and the decline in visitors meant my deal with him was unlikely to yield any new information.

I was happy to have a lighter schedule. Once I wasn't in the Wentworth home every day, I recognized how heavily the doctor's murder weighed on me. For the first time in too long, I relaxed. I celebrated my extra free time by riding my bike more often, no matter how cold the early January weather was. A couple of times, Joe joined me. He was a lot faster than I was, but spending time with my free-spirited brother was a breath of fresh air I didn't know I needed.

At home in the evenings, reading a book or watching a movie with Shadow on my lap, I still felt I was missing something. I had a restless feeling I'd forgotten a detail, something I should remember that was half a memory out of reach. I tried to ignore the niggling in my head, but whenever I wasn't actively engaged in working or spending time with friends and family, there it was, making me restless and distracted.

A week after my argument with Patrick, I arrived home cold and wet from a long bike ride. The day had started out sunny, but clouds appeared, and when I was about fifteen miles from home, a light sprinkling turned into a soaking winter rain. I turned back and rode as hard as I could to try to stay warm, but I was still shivering by the time I got home.

I cursed my own stupidity and headed for the shower. Shadow sat on the dry side of the shower curtain and let me know in no uncertain terms what an idiot I'd been. Hypothermia was no joke, he said, and I wasn't about to argue.

And then it came to me.

I rinsed the shampoo from my hair and bolted from the shower, sending Shadow flying out of the room with a yowl. I grabbed my phone and called Dean.

"I just remembered something," I said when he answered. "It might not mean anything, but—" I was trying not to babble, but I was relieved to finally remember the thing that had been nudging me in the brain.

"Slow down, Annie. What is it?"

I told him about the argument I'd heard between the doctor and Number Four.

"She was livid about Eric, the doc's grandson, being there. He's gay and she doesn't want him in the house. Anyway, Doctor Wentworth told her he knew what she'd been doing and that someone's wife knew, too."

"Slow down. You're not making sense. Whose wife?"

"I don't know. He didn't say a name."

"And what did he say she was doing?"

"He didn't, but I thought it sounded as if Elise was cheating on him and he knew about it. The doc told her that Eric was welcome in the house, and she could leave if she didn't like it, and she said she wasn't going anywhere."

"Uh huh, go on."

I heard a pencil scratching in the background as Dean took notes.

"And then she said he was stuck with her until he died and she didn't think it would be much longer. I thought she was talking about him being so much older than she was, but given what happened, now I'm not so sure."

He was quiet. I could almost hear him thinking. "Did you tell anyone else about what you heard?"

"Yes, I told Mo."

"When?"

"Right then. I was headed home, and I went by the kitchen to say good night. I guess she saw I was unhappy or preoccupied or something, and she asked if I was okay. We talked about how much Elise hates gay people, which struck home for both of us, and I went home."

"What day did this happen?"

I grabbed a calendar and went through the events in my mind. "There was the weekend holiday thing for all of the wives and their families. So it would have been Sunday"—I ran my finger down the column—"the third."

I stopped, unable to speak, but Dean broke the silence. "And he was killed sometime during the night of the twentieth."

"Two and half weeks later."

Neither of us spoke, but my mind was churning. Could this be nothing more than an unfortunate coincidence?

"Uh, Dean—" I was reluctant to say what I was thinking.

"I know," he said. "Could be nothing, but thanks for telling me."

We didn't have much to say after that, but I lay awake most of the night, wondering.

The next day was a Saturday and the sun was out. I normally visited Grandma Natalie on Wednesdays, which was usually my day off, but I decided to go see her anyway. Ever since my argument with Patrick and her demand that I move back to Portland, she'd been distant, which worried me. I decided to talk with her in person, to let her know I'd keep my promise to her. I'd never been able to tolerate her being unhappy with me.

On my way, I went to Dad's shop, what was left of it. The shell of the building still stood. We all knew it would have to be demolished, but none of us had been able to face it. On the other hand, the new construction next door, where the auto body shop had been, was a hopeful sign that someone was willing to start anew, and I wondered what Joe and I could do with Dad's property. The space was, after all, a good-sized corner lot in a busy area of mixed residential, retail, and light industry. I decided to talk with him about it.

I pulled into Grandma Natalie's driveway to find the garage door closed and the curtains drawn. I'd left her a message earlier in the day that I wanted to see her, but maybe she'd gone out and missed my call. I used my key and went inside, but she wasn't home. Since she was probably the last human on the planet who would ever have a cell phone, there was no use trying to track her down.

I was heading back to my car when something near the garage caught my eye. When I saw what it was, I sighed. Subtle, she was not.

She'd gone to the moving place and bought what looked like thirty boxes, still flattened and tied with plastic bands. Taped to the top was a slip of paper with my name on it, written in my grandmother's lacy script.

"Message received," I muttered. I considered leaving them there, to let her know that I wouldn't be bullied, but I'd never won a battle of wills with Natalie Lindberg. I loaded the boxes into the back of my car and left.

I made a couple of stops on the way home. By the time I'd unloaded bags of groceries, including the all-important cat food and kitty litter and Grandma

Natalie's stack of boxes, I was ready for a hot bath and a beer. Shadow claimed the packing boxes as his own and sat on top as if he owned them. Typical cat.

I'd also stopped at the take-and-bake pizza place for my favorite pie. The oven was heating, and I was guarding the pie against Shadow's paws when the phone rang.

"You have a talent for calling at dinnertime," I said. "Are you sure you weren't a telemarketer in a previous life?"

As much as I disliked spending time around cops, I liked Dean and rather enjoyed teasing him. Patrick wouldn't have been at all amused.

"Do you want me to call back later?"

"No, I'm just giving you a hard time. I'm waiting for the oven to heat so I can put a pizza in."

"I'll be right over," he said, laughing.

"I thought cops only ate doughnuts. When I buy some, you're the first person I'll call, but you're not getting any of my double pepperoni and mushrooms." I nudged Shadow off the counter and, holding the phone between my chin and shoulder, slid the pizza into the oven. "What can I do for you? I haven't been to the Wentworths' for a few days now, so I don't have anything else to talk about."

"I do, though."

His voice went from light-hearted to serious in a moment, and a frisson of dread ran up my spine.

"What's going on? Did you find Mo?" I almost dreaded the answer.

"No, we didn't. But—" He paused too long for my comfort.

"But what?"

"We found her car."

I sat down at the kitchen table. "Where?"

"Portland airport, long term parking, way out at the far end of the lot."

I stared into space, seeing nothing.

"Looks like someone parked it and walked away, as if they had a plane to catch. No damage. Nothing unusual inside. Dirty windows and leaves on it, which you'd expect for a car parked for—"

"A month."

"I'm sorry, Annie. You asked me to keep an open mind about Mo, and I'm trying, but how else could her car be at the airport? I mean, sure, someone else could have driven it, but without any evidence to the contrary, I have to assume she parked there herself. We're checking for fingerprints other than hers, but she had a fabric steering wheel cover, so I don't expect much."

I took a deep breath. "Is there any way to find out if she took a flight?"

"We're checking on it. With almost twenty airlines and over two hundred flights out of PDX every day, it'll take time. And it's not just that. She could have taken the parking lot shuttle to the terminal and walked to one of the nearby hotels or taken transit away from the airport. She could be anywhere."

"Or someone else who drove her car could have done the same thing."

"True."

I'd been so sure about Mo's innocence but now doubts were creeping in. Maybe I didn't know her as well as I'd thought. "Thanks, Dean. I appreciate that you're keeping your part of our deal. I truly don't know what to think, but thank you for telling me."

"I wish I had better news."

"Me, too."

That night, I hardly slept at all. I couldn't bring myself to believe Mo was capable of stabbing a man, not once, but twice. On the other hand, I'd told Dean she was a private person. Maybe I wasn't the only one in the Wentworth house with secrets.

The morning brought sunshine. I scowled at the bright blue sky. How dare the world contradict my dark mood?

I tried calling Grandma Natalie again to no avail. I was definitely getting the electronic cold shoulder. She'd always been my greatest fan, but she knew how to pile on the disapproval when she felt it was warranted.

The stack of flattened packing boxes stared back at me in defiance.

I had to get out of the house.

I wheeled my bike out and rode away, not paying much attention to where I was going, wanting only to feel the cold breeze on my face.

I rode fast, head down, pedaling as hard as I could. I refused to gear down on the hills and crested the steepest one standing on the pedals. I cleared my mind of as much thought as possible, taking my grief and stress and anger out on the road. The sweat running down my back and face was my reward.

After a time, I looked around and realized I'd ridden most of the way to Portland. I laughed out loud for the first time in days. I was glad to have a bike computer that showed route and distance; otherwise, Joe would never believe I rode twenty miles in one direction.

I turned around and stopped on the side of the road for a drink of water. I took a deep breath, feeling the air expand my lungs in a way I hadn't felt since before I went out the back door of the Wentworth home and saw the doctor's inert form on the wet grass.

"Well, hell," I said out loud and laughed again. I'd never ridden more than twenty miles in one day. Maybe anger and insomnia were the motivators I needed.

Or maybe not. In my rush to leave the house, I'd neglected to grab my phone. I couldn't call Sharon or Lupe to rescue me. I'd always prided myself on being self-sufficient. Idiot.

After another few minutes and more pulls at the water bottle, I pushed off again.

On the ride back, though, I took my time. The hard push I'd made on my way out had taken its toll on my legs, so I set an easy pace on my way home. The sunshine was welcome and warm on my face. The breeze wasn't as cold, either. I made a point of admiring the scenery and calling out to the horses and cows occupying the occasional pasture. A dog barked at me from the shelter of his porch but couldn't be bothered to chase me. I listened to birds singing and dodged a particularly suicidal squirrel who ran across the road in front of my tires.

I was over halfway home, my pace lagging as my legs threatened to give out, when I realized I was on the road fronting the Wentworth home. I hadn't known it was also a route from Charbonneau to Portland.

As I went by the gate, I glanced up the driveway. For the first time since Doctor Wentworth's memorial service, I saw no cars that didn't belong to the occupants of the big house. Maybe things were calming down at last.

I paused long enough to drink the last of the water in my bottle and kept going. Now in familiar territory, I knew which horses would look up when I called out, I knew which hill was next and where I'd see the old barn, and I knew I was almost home.

Familiarity let me take my mind off my ride and consider my life instead. I decided to quit the Wentworth job right away. I had no desire to step foot in that house again. Elise and her Lady-of-the-Manor mood swings would have to find someone else to torment, and to hell with my budget. With everything that had happened, especially the murder of her husband, she still found time to whine about her missing necklace. How shallow could a person be?

I also had to find a way to get back into Grandma Natalie's good graces. Of course, the fastest way would be to show up in a car loaded with a grumpy black cat and boxes packed full of my household belongings. As much as I'd argued with her about helping to clear Mo's name, I had to admit she was right about the risks. So was Patrick.

I sighed.

I wanted to move back to Portland anyway, so what was I waiting for?

Sometimes being stubborn was a damn lot of work.

My musings got me home. I almost fell getting off my bike. Joe would have laughed at the bad case of rubber legs I had. Maybe he'd help me train for long rides once I moved home.

Home.

The word came to me unbidden, and its appearance decided the issue right then and there.

I parked my bike and made a beeline to the shower. When I came out, I made myself a mug of coffee and only then did I think to check my phone. The blinking light told me I'd missed a call, and when I checked, I found I'd missed more than a dozen calls.

"Annie, it's me." Joe's voice sounded strained. "Grandma Natalie's in the hospital. She was hit by a truck."

Chapter Seven

I'll never know how I made it to the hospital without acquiring any speeding tickets or running anyone over. More than once on the way, I thanked Grandma Natalie for the new car. My old truck would never have made the trip so quickly.

Joe was pacing the floor in the emergency department waiting area. I ran up to him and hugged him as hard as I could.

"What happened? How is she?" I heard my voice rise to a near shriek and made myself stop and take a deep breath.

He put an arm around my shoulders and drew me to a nearby chair.

"She's in surgery, Annie, and it's bad. She was out for a ride with a friend and some yahoo in a truck ran a red light. Totally broadsided them. The bastard kept going, but two guys chased him down. I heard they hauled his ass out of his truck and taught him a lesson in responsibility that involved several well-placed punches and maybe a broken nose." The smile he tried didn't reach his brown eyes, which looked worried enough for both of us.

I tried to digest this through the adrenalin making my head spin. "Where were they?"

"East Powell, I think. She said something about wanting to take her friend to a new restaurant she'd heard about. I called you a million times, Annie. Where were you?"

I rubbed my face with my hands, trying to think.

"I went for a ride. I forgot to take the phone with me. I'm so sorry." And then something clicked. "Who's the friend she was with?"

He hesitated for a moment as if he didn't want to tell me. "Ada Brownlee."

"Oh, no, not Ada." An image of her face came to mind, always cheerful and kind, and her defiance at having decided to step out and go for a motorcycle ride. "How is she? Please tell me she's all right. Does Hal know?"

"He's with her right now. She has a broken leg and scrapes and cuts. Somehow, Grandma Natalie turned the bike and protected Ada from the worst of it."

"She would. She always protects everyone." A sob escaped me, even though I made an effort to contain it, and Joe pulled me into a hug. After a long moment, I sat back in my chair and held Joe's gaze. "How long has she been in surgery?"

"Since I first started calling you, maybe three hours? She has internal bleeding and a bunch of broken bones. The docs didn't think she had any brain damage, but she was unconscious, so we won't know until she wakes up. Her helmet wasn't even scratched, which is a good sign."

Only when Joe handed me a tissue did I realize tears were running down my face.

"Where the heck did you ride? You're usually not gone for so long."

"What?" The mundane nature of his question caught me off guard. "I took off without thinking about it."

"Obviously, if you left your phone behind."

"I know." Another broken promise I was sure to hear more about. "I've been worried about my argument with Patrick and Grandma Natalie being mad at me, and all the stuff in Charbonneau with the doctor being dead and Mo missing, and the Portland police investigating me. I needed to get out and clear my head. You won't believe it, but I went almost twenty miles before I realized where I was. Talk about checked out."

"Did it help?"

"Yeah, it did, but I missed your calls. I should have been here a lot sooner." Another tear slid down my face. "Good thing I've decided to move back. I'm still worried about Mo, but I'm not doing her any more good in Charbonneau than I am here. Grandma Natalie was right."

"Patrick was, too."

"Yeah, but if you tell him I said that, I'll deny it."

"You can't. I heard it for myself." Patrick loomed over me and wrapped me in a bear hug. "How's she doing?"

Joe said, "we're waiting for the surgeon to come out and tell us. They said it could be a while."

We sat together for another hour, mostly staring into space or trying—and failing—to concentrate on whatever show was on the TV that was bolted to the wall. My stomach roiled from too much vending machine coffee. Every time the door between the waiting area and the emergency department opened, we all looked up, hoping for news. Finally a nurse stepped through the door and called for the family of Natalie Lindberg. I'm not sure what she thought when she was met by a woman who looked Hispanic but had blue eyes, a tall black man, and a white guy in a silk suit, but she seemed to take us in stride.

"Natalie is still in surgery. The surgeons said things are going well. Her internal injuries were worse than expected, so the surgery is taking longer than originally planned. But she's holding up fine. Her vital signs are good. She'll be in the intensive care unit after surgery. You might want to go home and get some rest and come back in the morning."

"Can we see her in the ICU?"

"Yes, for short visits, but the doctors might keep her sedated for a short time while she starts to heal. They do that sometimes for patients with serious trauma. The doctor will tell you more about that. You're still welcome to visit."

After she left, I was able to breathe a little better. "I'm not going home. It's too far. I'll stay at Grandma Natalie's until we know how she's doing." I called Lupe and told her what was happening and apologized for putting the burden of the Wentworth household on her. She assured me that she could handle Number Four and agreed to take care of Shadow in my absence.

After Joe and Patrick left, I went up to see Ada. Hal was sitting by her bed, holding her hand. Her right leg was encased in a plaster cast. She had bandages on one arm and bruises and scrapes on her face and forearms.

I tapped on the door, unsure of my welcome, but they waved me into the room when they saw me. Hal came to the door and gave me a hug and insisted I take his chair. Ada held out her hand for me to hold.

"I'm so sorry, Ada. I feel responsible."

"Nonsense," she said. "All you did was introduce me to a new friend. I decided to go for another ride with Natalie. It's not your fault at all."

"Another ride?" Hal was surprised.

"I don't have to tell you everything, old man," Ada said. "Once I'm back on my feet, I'm going motorcycle shopping."

With that, I knew she'd be fine.

She squeezed my hand. "How's Natalie?"

"Still in surgery, but the news so far is encouraging. How are you doing?"

"I have a bump or two, but I'm going to be fine. I think they'll send me home in a couple of days. Good thing I held on to that damn wheelchair, huh?"

On the verge of tears, all I could do was nod. Ada gave my hand another squeeze.

"Look, hon," she said. "Natalie will be fine. She saved me, did you know that? She saw that jerk run the light, and I don't know how, but she turned that big motorcycle or swerved or something, and she took the worst of the collision. I have a broken leg, that's all. It could have been a lot worse."

I took a deep breath and blew it out.

Hal said, "The cops told us a tow truck driver and another guy caught the driver who hit them, and they pretty much sat on him until the police arrived." He sounded pleased about that turn of events. "I saw him for a moment in the emergency room sporting a black eye and a bloody nose. The police had him in handcuffs. I'm not usually one for vigilantism, but anyone who can run down two old ladies and keep going needs a dose of his own medicine."

"Who are you calling an old lady?" Ada beamed at him with such love in her eyes that I felt that I was intruding on a private moment.

"I'll ask Patrick to check on him," I said, "to see if any charges will be filed. Having a lawyer for a friend can be useful sometimes."

Hal laughed and patted me on the back.

Just then, the nurse poked her head in the room and told us that visiting hours had ended. I gave Ada a careful hug and Hal a more vigorous one and left the room. On my way out, I checked with the surgery nurse, who told me Grandma Natalie was out of surgery and in the recovery room. Since it was late and we wouldn't be allowed to see her until morning, I breathed a sigh of relief and headed to her house for the night.

The next morning, I went back to the hospital. Grandma Natalie had been moved to the intensive care unit, so I went up there to check on her.

The ICU was laid out like a wagon wheel, with the nurse's station as the hub and each patient room the spokes. The walls facing the nurses' station were glass, so the medical staff could see into each room. Privacy could be had by pulling floor to ceiling curtains closed. Each room was set up for a single patient.

Grandma Natalie lay swathed in blankets, her head resting on a soft pillow. Clear IV lines snaked down to her arm from bags of fluids. She was surrounded by more beeping machines than I'd ever seen. One monitored her pulse and blood pressure, but I had no idea what the other devices did.

She was asleep or unconscious, I didn't know which. I pulled a chair to her bedside and held her hand, moving only to let the nurses hang new IV fluids or adjust the machines. When I arrived, they told me to keep my visit to fifteen minutes, but an hour later, they hadn't asked me to leave.

When Joe showed up, however, they did ask us to visit one at a time, so I stepped outside the room to let him sit with her. I watched from near the nurses' station and tried to stay out of the way. From that vantage point, I saw four other patients in their own rooms, also with visitors.

"Are you visiting Ms. Lindberg?"

A man who appeared to be in his fifties, dressed in hospital scrubs and wearing a white coat, approached me. He had dark brown skin, darker brown eyes, and black hair liberally laced with silver. His voice carried the pleasing lilt that people originally from India possessed.

"Yes, I'm her granddaughter."

"I'm Doctor Bhattacharya. I operated on your grandmother yesterday."

"How's she doing?"

"As well as can be expected at this point. She was seriously injured, mostly internal injuries, though she has a couple of broken ribs and a broken leg. We're keeping her sedated for a day or two, but I expect her to make a full recovery."

"That's a relief."

Joe joined us and I introduced them.

Joe said, "Yesterday, one of the emergency room nurses mentioned the possibility of a head injury."

"We didn't see any indication on x-rays or CT, but we won't know for sure until she wakes up. All signs are encouraging, though, so try not to worry too much." He paused for a moment. With a quizzical expression, he asked, "Is it true that she was riding a motorcycle? I mean, she's in her sixties. I saw the report, but I wasn't sure how accurate it was."

"Yes, she loves her Harley," Joe said, and I murmured my agreement. "She's ridden them her whole life. She was giving a ride to a friend, and from what we've been told, they were hit by a man who ran a light."

"I have a feeling your grandmother is a strong person, and barring any setbacks, I think she'll be fine."

Joe and I spent a little more time with our sleeping grandmother until the nurse in charge of her care insisted politely, but firmly, that we'd overstayed our welcome. We called Patrick with an update and bought sandwiches in the hospital cafeteria.

I said, "I think I'll go get Shadow this afternoon."

"And start packing?" Joe gave me a lopsided grin.

"I might as well. I'm going to stay here in Portland anyway. She'll need help when she goes home."

After lunch, I drove back to Charbonneau. Once I placated Shadow with treats and a new catnip toy, I called my clients to let them know I was leaving town. Most of them offered kind wishes for Grandma Natalie's recovery. I gave them Lupe's name and encouraged them to hire her. I contacted Elise Wentworth last.

I didn't feel the need to explain about my grandmother's collision and injuries. I informed her I wouldn't be coming out to clean for her any longer. Her reaction was not a surprise.

"What do you mean—you're quitting?"

For the first time, I said what I wanted, her feelings be damned. "It's a simple concept." I made no effort to conceal the disdain I felt for her. "Quitting means I won't work at your home again. I'm finished."

"But what about—"

"I don't care, Elise. I'm through listening to you bitch and moan about every little speck of dust. You're a spoiled diva with a superiority complex, when all you did was marry a wealthy doctor. He gave you anything you wanted, and you spit on everything he tried to do for you. He loved you, but I can't begin to fathom why. Nobody likes working for you. You might want to try changing your behavior before everyone quits. You'll have a hard time finding replacements, too, what with your reputation around town."

She was silent for a long moment. With a sigh, she said, "Okay, fine," and slammed the phone down.

I sat for a moment, feeling a little sheepish, thinking I'd been too harsh with her. And then I said aloud, "Damn, that felt good."

I had more calls to make, but I decided to pack a box or two first. I snipped the band around the cartons Grandma Natalie left for me. Shadow promptly claimed ownership of the plastic strip. I assembled a couple of the boxes and opened my closet door. Standing before the neatly folded sheets and blankets stored there, a feeling came over me that I'd made the right decision.

A couple of hours later, I'd packed half a dozen boxes. I decided to take a break and drove by the Charbonneau police station. Dean's car was in the lot, so

I parked and went inside. The receptionist phoned him and after a few moments, he led me past the infamous library and into his office.

"What can I do for you this fine day?" We sat opposite each other across his desk.

"I have a question first. Any news about Mo?"

"No, unfortunately. As I suspected, her car didn't reveal any evidence leading us to think someone else drove it to the airport. I'm sorry."

I spoke insistently. "It's been more than a month, Dean. I'd have bet my life she didn't have anything to do with the doctor's murder, but I don't know what to think any more. Either I'm wrong about her, or something terrible has happened to her."

He started to speak, but I waved his words away.

"The reason I came by is to let you know I'm moving back to Portland. My grandmother was injured in a bad crash, and she's going to need my help after she's out of the hospital. Truth to tell, though, I'd decided to move before this happened. I like it here, but I'm too far from my family."

"I have your phone number, Annie. I'll keep in touch if I hear anything about your friend. And if we ever find out who killed Doctor Wentworth and there's a trial, you might need to testify about finding his body."

"Thank you. I'll be willing to testify, of course." I tried to ignore the echo of Patrick's voice, warning me to come clean with Dean, which I'd avoided doing. Then I remembered something else. "I've been meaning to ask you something."

"Shoot."

"Didn't the security camera over the back door show anything? If nothing else, it should have shown the doc going out the door and falling, wouldn't it?"

"Someone at the house told one of the officers the camera didn't work." He picked up a coffee mug from his desk and took a drink.

"Sure it does."

He was still for a moment, coffee mug in his hand. "How do you know?"

"Last summer, not long after I started working there, Elise had a tantrum about the garden being vandalized. The recording from the camera showed a deer eating the flowers. If someone at the house said the camera was broken, they were wrong."

"Or lying." He put the mug down with a thud and reached for the phone. "Harrison," he barked, "get your ass in here, and bring your notebook."

Within moments, the young officer I'd first met when Elise's jewelry went missing was at the door.

"Yes, boss?" He sounded worried.

"Did you take the report about the Wentworths' security cameras when the doctor was killed?"

"Hold on." He riffled through the pages of his notebook. "Yes, I did. Why?"

"Who told you the camera outside the back door wasn't working?"

He riffled through the pages of his notebook and looked up with an embarrassed expression. "I forgot to write who said it."

Dean heaved a sigh. "You and Baker get out to that house and see if there are recordings from that camera. I want to know who told us it wasn't working."

"Yes, boss." Harrison headed for the door.

"And Jimmy, if it turns out the camera works, you and Baker better hope a recording still exists. Are we clear about that? And for god's sake, learn to take better notes, or I'll get your ass fired."

"Yes, boss," and this time, the young man escaped, calling for his partner as he hustled down the hallway.

"Damn it." Clearly annoyed, Dean drummed his fingers on the desk. Then he seemed to remember I was there. "Sorry about that. They should never have taken someone's word about that camera. It won't happen again, you can trust me on that."

He must have seen something in my eyes because he said, "What?"

"I'm wondering what else it might show," I said slowly. "Like whoever killed the doc? Or anyone else who might have gone out that door?" I didn't mention Mo, but I didn't have to. I got the sense Dean was on track with me.

"I suppose so, if it hasn't been recorded over."

"If I remember right, the cameras are motion activated, and there's usually not much activity out there, so fingers crossed."

Before I left, I gave him Grandma Natalie's address.

"It'll be a few days before I'm completely moved. I'll be at the hospital a lot, so if you need to reach me, call my cell."

He agreed and added his wishes for her recovery, and I went home to pack more boxes.

The next few days took on a sort of sad routine. I got up every morning and called the hospital for an update, hoping she'd regained consciousness, and every time, I was disappointed. The doctor was kind enough to call me and tell me I shouldn't worry, that she was still lightly sedated, but she was healing well after the surgery. I appreciated his efforts, but not worrying wasn't an option.

After that, I packed a few more boxes and loaded them into the car. Shadow alternated between hiding in the newly assembled boxes and leaping out at me in great delight.

Bit by bit, box by box, trip by trip, I got my stuff moved into Grandma Natalie's house. The stack of cartons grew slowly. Every time I lifted a box out of the car, I thanked my lucky stars I wasn't a packrat like Dad.

Of course, I left packing my books until last. I figured Joe would come in handy for that fun little task.

On the Monday after the crash, I was driving to Portland when my cell phone rang. I pressed the button on the steering wheel connecting my phone to the sound system in the car.

"Annie, where are you?" Patrick sounded annoyed.

"On my way to town. I'm stopping by Grandma's house to drop off boxes. Why? What's going on?"

"Have you heard anything new from the doctors?" His tone changed to one of concern. He hadn't had grandparents of his own, and Grandma Natalie took him in years ago as she had Joe and me, though his parents were alive and well. As far as Patrick was concerned, the sun rose and set on Grandma Natalie.

"No," I said. "I called again this morning, and she still wasn't awake. I'm going to see her anyway. Staying away feels wrong."

"I understand. When you're done, call me, okay?"

I agreed and we ended the call. I was worried that he'd sounded irritated at first, but maybe it wasn't about me for once.

At the hospital, I sat next to Grandma Natalie's bed and held her hand until the nurse evicted me. She'd let me stay long past the usual permitted time, and she sounded reluctant to make me leave.

"She's lucky to have you," the nurse said. "Some patients don't get visitors in here."

I moved out of her way while she changed the bag of IV fluid. We chatted for another minute, and I noticed the nurse stroking Grandma Natalie's hair. Even unconscious, she was making friends.

I made a detour through a fast food place on my way to the house and tried not to think about hardening arteries and antibiotic-laced meat while I devoured a burger and fries. After I ate, I unloaded boxes from the car.

In my grandmother's garage, I stood for a moment admiring the stack of cartons I'd made. Except for those I needed at my apartment, all of my sheets and towels were in there, along with most of my kitchen tools, bike accessories, and more cat toys than I cared to consider. A few more days, and my things would be completely moved. Except for the books. I still needed to call Joe about that.

Thinking about Joe reminded me to phone Patrick.

"Can you come to the office in about an hour?" He was back to sounding annoyed.

"I suppose so. Why?"

"Beth needs to talk with you again. And so do I." With that, he hung up.

Hell and damnation, what now?

I went into the empty house and tried not to think about what I was in trouble for this time. While I waited, I dusted and vacuumed and started the dishwasher. Keeping busy helped me to worry less about everything: my grandmother, whatever it was that Beth and Patrick wanted to talk about, Doctor Wentworth's murder, and my deep grief for my father. I stood back and surveyed the results of my efforts. No doubt about it, I needed a diversion, something fun to do.

At the appointed time, I made the long walk down the windowed hallway at Patrick's law offices. This time, the receptionist barely acknowledged my presence before waving me through.

I opened the conference room door to find Patrick standing near the coffee station and Beth at the table, this time without a stack of files before her. Neither of them responded to my greeting except to direct me to a chair.

Wary, I took a seat across from Beth. Patrick sat at the head of the table, not next to me as he had when we'd met here before. Neither of them spoke.

"Okay, I'm here. What's going on?"

"Do I understand correctly that you are somehow involved in the murder of a doctor in Charbonneau?" Beth's tone was icy.

So that was it.

"The word 'involved' isn't accurate. I didn't kill him, so no, I'm not *involved* in his murder. I found his body. That's all."

"That's not all," Patrick said. "Tell her the rest."

"What rest? I found the doctor's body and gave my report to the police."

"And?" He was using his lawyer voice on me, and I resented it.

"And I've given all the information I have to the detective there." I'd had enough. "For fuck's sake, Patrick, what do you want from me? Isn't it enough that I had the bad luck to find the doc's dead body? When I think about the doctor, you know what I see? I see my father's body with his shop burned down around him."

I couldn't sit still any longer. I rose and paced the length of the room while they both sat silently. After a few passes, I resumed my place at the table.

"Look," I said, trying to calm myself, "yes, I found him. Yes, I gave information to the detective. What else should I do?"

Beth finally spoke. "Have you told the Charbonneau detective about your father's death and your partner's murder?"

"No, I haven't." I ignored Patrick's snort of derision.

"Why not?" At least her tone was polite, if distant.

"It's not relevant, is it?"

"He might think otherwise."

"Why? How is the shooting death of a woman in Portland related to a stabbing of a doctor in Charbonneau? They have nothing in common."

"They have you in common."

I had no response to that.

"You're already a person of interest in a murder, Annie," Patrick said. "I don't believe for a moment that you killed Nicky, but someone else who doesn't know you, who has a different perspective, might disagree."

"And you," I said to Beth, "what do you think?"

She paused for a long moment before she answered. "I'm not drawing any conclusions yet. The investigation is ongoing. I can tell you that Nicky was working with a local gang notorious for violence. They've been linked to at least three killings in just the past year. But the other reality is that, as of today, the evidence still shows that you had what a lot of people would consider a strong motive to kill her. Her meth lab caused the explosion and fire that burned the bike shop and killed your father. In those circumstances, I might want to kill, too."

I opened my mouth to say, "I didn't kill her," but unexpectedly, my throat closed up and tears streamed down my face. I grabbed a handful of tissues from a box on the table. Her tone had been kind and understanding and caught me off guard. I took a deep breath and tried to control my emotions, but again, the image of my father's body hit me with unavoidable force. I wiped the tears away.

"I hope you realize," she said, "when Dean Jarrett learns that his most important witness is a person of interest in another homicide, he won't be happy."

"You know Dean?" I shouldn't have been surprised, but I was.

"He was a detective in Portland for several years. We didn't work together, but I know who he is. He's a good cop, Annie, the best, and you can trust him."

"But—" I stopped.

"But only if you're honest with him."

Just then, the phone rang and Patrick answered it. He replaced the receiver and turned to me.

"Remember when you promised to talk to Dean?"

I looked at him without speaking, dread growing.

"Did you do it?"

"No," I said in a low voice.

"Figured as much." He strode the length of the room and opened the conference room door.

That evening, I sat curled up in one corner of Grandma Natalie's white couch. I had a beer in my hand and a blanket pulled halfway up to my shoulders. Shadow pawed at the blanket, so I lifted the edge to let him settle in under it.

The television was on, but I had no idea what I was seeing. The angry silence I'd gotten from Dean and the lectures I'd endured from Beth and Patrick had me boiling with anger. I'd have thrown the bottle in my hand against the wall in frustration, but no matter how mad I might be, wasting good beer was not an option.

Truth was, I was angry because they were right.

"Fuck," I muttered, and took another drink.

Dean had come into the conference room, wondering why he'd been invited. As I told him about the fire at my dad's shop and the aftermath, including my status as a suspect in Nicky's death, I saw his expression go from friendly to unsure to enraged. I told him, as persuasively as I could, that I wasn't guilty and hadn't killed anyone, but all he could say was that his witness had lied to him and withheld important information.

And he was right.

He informed me in an icy tone that the district attorney would be in touch if my testimony about finding Doctor Wentworth's body was needed. He shook hands with Beth and Patrick and left without another word.

And then the fun really started. Beth and Patrick took turns informing me what a waste of space I was, that I'd set western civilization back a thousand years, that I was the best reason they'd ever seen for contraception, and that I was clearly in need of a chaperone. They didn't use those words, but they might as well have. I had retreated to Grandma's place feeling like a whipped dog.

I drained the bottle in my hand and got up to get another from the fridge. The phone rang.

"Go away," I said, slurring a little. Good thing I didn't have to drive anywhere. Still, I checked the screen and answered the call. "Hi Rachel."

"Annie? Are you drunk?"

"Working on it. Care to join me?"

Rachel and I had been friends since I did a temp job at the clinic where she worked as a veterinarian. She'd treated Shadow for me a time or two before I moved to Charbonneau.

"Have you had dinner?" she asked.

"Yes, carefully brewed by the fine artisans in Golden, Colorado."

"That's what I thought," she said, laughing. "Stay put. I'm taking you out for real food, and you can tell me what sorrows you're drowning this time."

An hour later, we were seated in a corner booth at a local restaurant known for serving breakfast twenty-four hours a day.

"Get pancakes," Rachel said over the top of the enormous laminated menu. "Soak up as much of the alcohol as possible."

"I *am* getting pancakes," I said in a snippy tone. "But only because I love pancakes."

"Whatever works." She went back to reading.

"Want some company?" A tall, muscular woman stood at the end of our table, a wide grin on her face.

"Sally!" I slid out of the booth and gave her a clumsy hug. "Sit. Have breakfast with us."

"You're right," Sally said to Rachel. "She's drunk again." She gave a mock sigh of frustration. "Whatever will we do with her?"

"Fuck you both," I said with a smile. Being with my friends again felt good.

Conversation waned as we decided what to eat. Once the server poured coffee and took our orders, they turned on me.

"Okay, Velasquez, spill it," Sally said.

"Yeah, we haven't heard from you in ages. Are you still living in that little hick town?"

I filled them in as best I could between the arrival of our food and visits by the server to refill coffee cups. They already knew about the fire and the details of my dad's death, especially Sally, who was one of the firefighters there that day. She'd helped to pull me away from his body and out of the still smoldering building. Rachel had known Nicky and was aware she'd been found shot to death.

They were both patiently sympathetic until I said, "But the other part is that the cops think I did it."

Their astonished protests felt good and made me regret having neglected our friendships when I ran away to Charbonneau. I waved them into silence.

"There's a new detective on the case, and Patrick thinks she's more on my side than the other cops. She won't say so outright, but I'm hoping."

"How is Patrick doing, anyway?" Rachel tried to sound casual, but she'd always had a crush on him, which he never seemed to notice.

"As much of a pain in the ass as ever," I said with a laugh. And then I grew serious. "Actually, none of us are too good right now."

I told them about Grandma Natalie's collision. Both of my friends had met her, and they loved her on sight just like everyone else did. Something about my motorcycle-riding grandmother drew people to her.

"And she's still unconscious?" With her background as an emergency medical technician, Sally knew enough to be concerned.

"They've been keeping her sedated. Her internal injuries were serious, but it's been three days, so I hope they'll let her wake up soon. She had a friend with her, but she was a lot luckier, with just a broken leg and a few scrapes and bruises."

"Wait." Sally put a hand on my arm. "I think I heard about this. Was it a hit and run, a guy in a truck?"

"Yes." I tried not to picture the crash, metal rending, bodies flying.

"I heard someone chased him down and held him until the police arrived."

"Two guys, and I guess they roughed him up when they caught him. I haven't met them, but I'd like to."

"No wonder you're in a funk," Rachel said. "Poor Natalie."

"Oh, that's not all." I told them about Doctor Wentworth's murder, how I'd found his body, how Mo was still missing, and all of the complications that followed, including the tongue-lashing I'd gotten earlier in the day.

"Jeez," Sally said, "no wonder you were drinking. After all that, I'd be at the nearest brewery with a funnel in my mouth."

We ate in companionable silence for a time. With all the talking, my eggs had gotten cold, but it didn't matter. I was with my friends.

"What are you going to do?" Rachel peered at me over the rim of her coffee mug.

"I'm almost moved in at Grandma Natalie's house. She kept asking me to move in, and now she'll need someone to take care of her while she recovers. After that, I'll find a job somewhere. I was thinking I could do housekeeping at a hotel or somewhere, have a regular paycheck for a change."

"I didn't mean it that way," Rachel said. She glanced at Sally, who chimed in.

"If the Charbonneau cop thinks your friend killed the good doctor, and you have good reason to believe he's wrong, what are you doing to help her?"

I sat back and looked at them in turn. "Didn't you hear me? The detective is seriously pissed off with me and certainly doesn't want my help any more. He thinks my problems here would taint his case, and I'm not sure he's wrong about that. I'm in no position to do anything."

Sally asked, "Does he still think Mo killed the doctor and absconded to parts unknown?"

"I think so."

"The question remains," Rachel said. "What are you going to do?"

Chapter Eight

The next morning, I drove to Charbonneau. I'd agreed to keep cleaning for the Brownlees during Ada's recuperation. She was getting around with crutches, but of course Hal wanted her to use the wheelchair. I was happy to help. They never failed to lift my spirits, which these days were, as my dad, a Mexican cowboy at heart, would have said, draggin' lower than a grasshopper's belly button. I was grateful for the work, too, since I'd quit the rest of my clients.

As I drove, I replayed the previous evening in my mind. Rachel and Sally were good friends, and I regretted not keeping in touch with them after I moved away. I had no excuse; I was in Portland frequently to see Grandma Natalie and spend time with Joe and Patrick. Sally and Rachel seemed to understand my need to grieve my father in relative solitude, which only confirmed in my mind they were friends worth keeping.

What had kept me awake most of the night was Rachel's question: *What are you going to do?*

What, indeed?

I was glad to see Ada doing well. She asked about Grandma Natalie, whether she had regained consciousness yet, and how the rest of us were holding up. Hal hovered over her like a nervous mother hen until she shooed him away.

"Leave me alone, old man. Can't you see I'm visiting with Annie? I swear, I'm getting you a puppy so you'll have someone to pester besides me." She beckoned to me when he wasn't looking and whispered, "Don't tell him I said so, but he's spoiling me rotten and I love it."

Just for fun, I said with exaggerated enthusiasm, "Hal, I know a breeder who has some Saint Bernard puppies due soon."

Hal looked worried until he saw I was joking.

After I'd vacuumed and dusted their home, I made lunch for them and prepared the ingredients they'd need for dinner. I wrote instructions for Hal so he could pop the pan into the oven, no muss, no fuss. I gave Ada a hug and Hal a smooch on the cheek and left to meet Lupe and Sharon at the diner.

Lunch with my friends was a good antidote for the stress I was carrying with me. Reconnecting with Lupe and Sharon was just as fun as my time with Rachel and Sally. We laughed and enjoyed each other's company and ganged up on Freddy when she refused yet again to give me her pastrami recipe.

"But Freddy," I said, giving her my best sad puppy face. "I'm moving away. You may never see me again. Don't you want to give me a goodbye present?"

"Bullshit," she retorted. "You'll only be forty minutes down the road, so quit acting as if you're falling off the edge of the planet."

"Spheres don't have edges, Freddy," Sharon said, which earned free chocolate ice cream for all of us.

Of course, our visit wasn't all fun and games. They asked about Grandma Natalie and said all the right things in response. They hadn't met her, but I knew they wished her well.

I tapped Lupe on the arm. "And how's life back at the ranch?" I was happy to never have to lay eyes on Number Four again, but I wanted to make sure that Lupe was doing well.

Lupe scooped up a bite of ice cream. "About the same, actually. No parties or anything, but the doc's kids still come around. She did buy herself a new car. You should see it, a fire-engine red sports car. The way she drives, she'll be lucky if she doesn't kill herself or someone else. And she goes into Portland several times a week." She shrugged one shoulder, as if to say "no accounting for rich folks."

"Kicking up her heels, is she?" I asked. "Maybe that's to be expected. I imagine she inherited the house and a pile of cash, so why not?"

"That's not what I heard. Word around the place is that the house and acreage have been in the family since Charbonneau was settled, and by family tradition, it has to pass to blood relatives. If that's true—"

"She'll be out," I finished. "Interesting. I hope he left the whole works to Eric. Lord knows he deserves it, the way she treated him."

After we parted, I went by the apartment for the last of my things. I'd decided the key to moving books was small boxes, but they were still cumbersome. I was surprised to find that I'd filled sixteen boxes with books. They filled the entire back of my car, making me even more grateful to my grandmother for her generous gift. After giving my keys to the landlord, I headed home.

I took the road fronting the Wentworth property, simply because it was more scenic than my usual route. I also wanted to see the old barn and contemplate yet again the unknown family who had built it.

I was almost to the Wentworth property when a red car flew out the gate and turned toward Portland. The sports car had to be Elise's newest toy. I could see what Lupe meant about how she drove. She hadn't appeared to check for traffic before she emerged from between the massive stone pillars supporting the front gates, and though I was driving faster than the posted speed limit, she left me behind, disappearing around a curve with a wisp of smoke from her tires.

"Never a cop around when you need one," I said aloud, and laughed at myself. My dealings with the police recently hadn't been pleasant, but the old saying came to me automatically anyway.

I was almost to the city limits when my phone rang. I pressed the steering wheel button to activate the hands-free connection.

"Hey Joe, what's up?"

"Where are you?"

"On my way home from Charbonneau with the last of my stuff. Hey, I thought you were going to help me load books." Then the tone of his voice sunk in. "Wait a sec, you sound stressed. Is Grandma Natalie okay?"

"Get a move on, Annie. She's waking up."

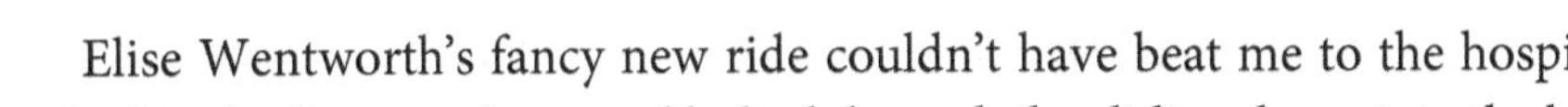

Elise Wentworth's fancy new ride couldn't have beat me to the hospital. I parked in the first spot I saw and bolted through the sliding doors into the lobby.

Too impatient to wait for an elevator, I ran up three flights of stairs to the ICU. Patrick and Joe were standing outside Grandma Natalie's room, accompanied by the doctor we'd spoken with before. I joined them and tried to catch my breath.

"Okay, what's happening?" I asked.

Doctor Bhattacharya turned to me. "I'm glad you made it. Remember we said we'd be reducing Natalie's sedation?"

I held my breath, anticipating his next words.

"It took a little longer than we'd hoped, but she's starting to come around. It's good you're here because she'll probably be somewhat disoriented, and familiar voices will help."

Just then, a nurse came out of her room and said, "It might be best if you went in one at a time and only for a few minutes. Leave the curtains pulled closed for now, to keep things quiet."

I didn't hesitate. "Me first."

Treading as lightly as I could, I slipped through the opening between the heavy drapes and went into the room. I pulled a chair close and sat in my usual spot next to her bed and took her hand. At first, she didn't respond, but I'd grown accustomed to sitting with her like that.

After a few moments, her fingers twitched and her head turned slightly toward me, her eyes still closed. I rose to my feet, still holding her hand between both of my own.

"Grandma?" I whispered. "Can you hear me?"

Her jaw worked, as if she were thirsty, but her eyes remained closed. I dabbed her lips with the foam applicators that the nurses gave me. In response, her tongue licked at the moisture.

I held my breath, afraid to break the spell.

Her eyes opened, slits at first and then wider. She scanned the room, and then she looked directly at me.

"Annie?" Her voice was hoarse.

"Yes, Grandma, I'm here." My own voice broke as I tried not to cry, but a tear slipped down my face nonetheless.

"My Annie." It was a statement this time. She closed her eyes again but gripped my hand tightly to her heart.

I stood still for a long moment, loath to take my hand away, and let the happiest tears I'd ever cried run down my face.

Doctor Bhattacharya entered the room, followed by Joe and Patrick. My brother took up his position on the opposite side of the bed and held her other hand. Patrick stood next to him.

After a few moments, the doctor asked us to step outside, and we gathered around him after the door was closed.

I spoke first. "She's okay, isn't she?"

"I think she'll be fine. She's still facing a long recovery, but she obviously has wonderful family support."

"And her head?" I was still worried about the possibility of brain damage after such a severe collision.

"We haven't seen any signs that worry us, but we'll do another CT scan while she's recovering. I doubt there's anything to be concerned about, but we'll do what we can to make sure."

He left to check on other patients. The nurse, the same one who had stroked Grandma Natalie's hair not long ago, came in and warned us not to stay too long. "Your grandmother needs to rest."

We stood like that, not talking, not moving, for a long moment, until Grandma Natalie opened her eyes again. She tried to smile when she saw us, but then she looked worried.

"How's Ada?" She said. "Was she hurt?"

"She's doing fine, Grandma," I said. "Her worst injury was a broken leg. She's home tormenting Hal now. You saved her, you know."

She took a deep breath and relaxed. "I'm glad she's okay." Her eyes closed for a moment, and then popped wide open. She grabbed my arm. "Wait! How's my bike?"

That's when we knew Grandma Natalie would be fine.

Over the next few days, my grandmother's strength grew. She was soon moved from the ICU to a regular patient room. Her roommate was a woman about her age, also recovering from surgery. After the first day, the nursing staff dubbed it the Party Room, since the occupants seemed to have a grand time keeping each other entertained. The other woman's family members were concerned that she wasn't getting enough rest, but before long, they'd joined in the fun.

I visited Grandma Natalie the afternoon she was moved to the new room. Someone had brought in an old boombox, which was playing Elvis Presley tunes. What appeared to be twenty helium balloons hovered near the ceiling.

"Annie," she called when she saw me. "Come on in and say hi to Liz. She's nice, even if she is short a uterus these days."

"Hey," Liz said. "At least I didn't leave my guts all over the street."

Grandma Natalie stuck her tongue out at her new friend, as a child would, and they both cracked up laughing. I stood there, dumbstruck. Was this the same woman who'd been unconscious for four days? Were the doctors positive she didn't have brain damage from the collision?

"Grandma, you're supposed to be resting. Where did all of these balloons come from?"

"It's the funniest thing. I commented to one of the aides how much I like balloons, and pretty soon, all of the nurses and the aides and a few of the ladies who bring us food showed up with bunches of them. Doctor Bhattacharya brought the purple one. Aren't they fun? And Liz's grandson brought music to listen to, though I wish he'd brought some Maroon Five instead. Elvis is for old folks, right, Liz?"

One of the nurses came into the room to check on its occupants. She rolled her eyes as if to say, "What am I supposed to do?"

"Natalie," the nurse said, "have you been out for a walk yet this morning?"

"Not yet. Liz and I are planning to do that in a little bit."

"You're going to walk, right? That's all?" The nurse gave her a warning look.

"Sure, you bet." Her attempt to sound innocent failed.

"As opposed to what?" I was almost afraid to ask.

The nurse was exasperated and amused at the same time. "Honestly, I wish I'd had a camera. These two"—she gave them a stern glare that fooled no one—"went out to take a walk, like they're supposed to. But they went into other rooms and recruited other patients, and before we knew it, we had a conga line going down the hall, IV poles and all. I've never seen anything like it."

I had to laugh. "You've never met my grandma before, either."

This was Natalie Lindberg at her finest. She was almost killed in a wreck, and the next thing she did was befriend everyone in the hospital and get them dancing. And to think I'd soon be living with her. Never a dull moment.

"What do you have there?" Grandma Natalie pointed to the brown bag I held.

"I thought you'd need something to take your mind off being in the hospital. I should have known you'd find plenty of ways to entertain yourself." I handed her the flat brown bag. "Maybe this will keep you from causing trouble."

She gave me a sly look as if to say "Yeah, right," and tilted the bag so the contents spilled out onto her lap.

"Oh," she said in a near whisper. "Perfect." She caressed the stack for a moment. "Thank you."

"I thought you might like to go shopping now."

I'd gone to the Harley Davidson dealership and picked up flyers and catalogs for all of the available models. She was still mourning the loss of her beloved bike, but immediately declared that she'd buy another one as soon as she could take a test ride. I appointed myself her enabler and brought her a stack of eye candy to peruse.

I said, "Maybe this will keep you from causing chaos in the hospital."

"Not likely," Liz said with a laugh. "We have too much fun."

Grandma Natalie handed me a few of the flyers to pass to Liz. "I need help shopping," she said. "Liz wants to go for a ride after she's all healed up." She grabbed my hand. "Sit down for a minute and tell me what's new with you."

I pulled a chair over next to her bed. "The biggest news is that you're getting your wish." At her upraised eyebrow, I continued. "I've moved all of my stuff to your house. Shadow is shedding black fur all over your white sofa as we speak."

She gave me the sweetest, most contented expression I'd ever seen. "Good. And it's now *our* house, not mine. Heck, it's not mine at all. The deed has your name on it, and Joe's. But I'm happy to have you there. Best get well gift ever." She lifted my hand and planted a kiss on it. "Now, go away so Liz and I can shop for my new bike."

Once I knew that Grandma Natalie was recovering, I could get back to a more normal life. Other than driving out to Charbonneau twice a week to help Ada and Hal, I kept busy in Portland. I unpacked my clothes and other essentials, reminding myself that this was my home as well as hers. Shadow took over as if he'd lived there for years.

I was also able to spend more time with my friends. Rachel and Sally came to the house several times to make sure I went out and about, probably more frequently than was prudent since more often than not, their evenings out included significant quantities of alcohol. They introduced me around, so before I knew it, I was surrounded by friends and acquaintances who seemed determined that I'd never spend an evening alone. I loved it.

The nights were a different story. Insomnia set in, a new experience for me. I'd always slept like the proverbial log, out like a light at night and awake in the morning with no interruptions save the occasional bathroom break. At first, I was puzzled by it. My grandmother was healing well and would be coming home before much longer. Joe was his normal annoyingly sunny self and insisted on getting me out for long rides on my bicycle. I wasn't even angry with Patrick any longer. Ada was regaining her mobility and Hal kept us both laughing when I saw them. Sharon and Lupe kept me informed about the news in Charbonneau, and Freddy still refused to disclose the secrets to her famous pastrami.

Sure, I still had other problems. The investigation into Nicky's death was ongoing, and the shell of my dad's shop still stared me down whenever I went there.

All in all, though, wasn't my life good? And yet, most nights, I was awake for hours, my brain refusing to be quiet.

Of course, after a time I realized I knew why. Now that I was no longer consumed with worry about Grandma Natalie, my thoughts returned to the murder of Doctor Wentworth and the disappearance of my friend. I lay awake at night, staring at the darkness, wondering who would kill such a nice man and what unspeakable acts could have befallen Mo.

I tried texting Dean to see if he had any new information, but he didn't respond. I didn't *expect* a reply, but I hoped for one. I was still concerned that he thought Mo killed the doc, but my faith in her hadn't changed. On the other hand, I couldn't think why anyone would want to kill Doctor Wentworth. He'd never been anything but kind to me and the other people who worked in his home. The only show of temper he'd displayed that I knew of was his argument with Elise about Eric.

My inability to make sense of the Charbonneau events kept me awake.

One evening, when I was at a local bar with Rachel and Sally, I yawned.

"Jeez, Velasquez," Rachel said. "It's only nine-thirty. What's with you?"

I told them about my insomnia and the reasons behind it. "I can't let it go. I know the police are investigating, but I'm worried they're focused too much on Mo and may not be considering other possibilities."

By then, we'd each had a couple of drinks with dinner. I was feeling a pleasant buzz. Not drunk, but I figured I'd better wait before driving home. My friends were in a similar state. We ordered another round.

Sometimes alcohol can be inspiring.

"I know what we need to do," Sally said. "We should stake her out."

I thought for a moment. "Hey, great idea. If you guys know where there's a good anthill, I'll get the ropes. I think there's an old tent in the garage, and we can use the stakes from that. The way she treats people, she deserves it." The mental image of Elise Wentworth squirming as she tried in vain to escape crawling insects was satisfying. "Do ants bite?"

Both of them stared at me as if I'd suddenly started speaking Swahili, and then Sally laughed.

"No, you idiot. Stake her out, as in watch and see what she's doing. Like cops on TV."

"Oh." I came back to reality a little bit. "But why? I saw no indication she had anything to do with the doctor's murder. She fainted dead away when she saw his body."

"Like nobody's ever faked that before," Rachel said in a sarcastic tone. "From what you told us, she hasn't exactly been suffering. What's it been, about six weeks?"

"Mm hm."

"And what has she done? Bought herself a shiny new car to zoom around in. Does that sound like a grieving widow to you?"

She had a point that even my alcohol-impaired brain could appreciate. Still, the anthill held a certain appeal, and I gave up the idea only reluctantly.

The rest of our evening was consumed by idle chatter. I enjoyed catching up with them and wished my life was more normal. Sally told us about a woman she'd met who was interesting but a little intimidated about dating a firefighter. Rachel asked about Patrick again, so I suggested, not for the first time, that she quit waffling and ask him out.

"He's totally oblivious," I said, "so you'll have to the make the first move."

We ordered dessert and substituted coffee and soft drinks for alcohol. By the time we were ready to head home, driving was no longer a concern.

We said goodbye outside the restaurant, but before I could get to my car, Sally grabbed my arm.

"I meant what I said, Velasquez. We need to keep an eye on Number Four."

I laughed and waved her off. "I'm already in enough trouble with the cops. The last thing I need is an arrest for stalking." I gave her a hug. "Drive safe."

Two days later, the phone rang while I was making coffee. My hair was still wet from the shower, and I wore only a heavy robe and my grandma's slippers. Shadow was munching his breakfast while I watched coffee drip far too slowly into the pot. A watched pot will eventually boil, but watched coffee can drip forever.

"Annie, my dear, they're cutting me loose this afternoon." Grandma Natalie sounded as if she'd won the lottery, and perhaps she had.

I scanned the kitchen and dining room in a panic. My grandmother was a meticulous housekeeper. I had my work cut out for me.

As if reading my mind, she said, "Don't worry about the house."

Did all grandmothers have psychic powers? "It's okay, Grandma. Most of my stuff is still in boxes in the garage. All I've unpacked so far is my clothes and a few books, and some of Shadow's toys."

"Uh huh." She didn't sound convinced. "Can you pick me up around two?"

"Of course, I can. I'm so glad you're coming home. I'll call Joe and let him know."

"And Patrick? Or are you still quarrelling?"

"We didn't have an argument, Grandma. He lectured me as if I were five years old and had eaten an entire jar of peanut butter." Though I'd gotten over being angry with him, Patrick's words still stung. What could I say? He was right, and that's what irritated me.

"From what I heard, you might have deserved it." Her tone became happier again. "I'll be so glad to be home. Liz went home two days ago and I don't have a new roomie, so I've been bored. Besides, now that you're there, we'll have a great time."

After we ended our call, I called Joe and Patrick and gave them the good news. I made a mad dash through the house. Quite without trying, I'd managed to leave clothes in almost every room, like a thoughtless overgrown teenager. I threw a pile of them into the washer and turned it on. While the machine did its magic, I cleaned up two spots where Shadow had deposited hairballs. Good thing Grandma Natalie had tile and wood floors and not carpet. I swept and dusted the house and straightened photographs that adorned almost every horizontal surface in the house. I paused for a moment at a photograph that I'd seen a million times. Framed in cheap ceramic, the photo showed a blonde woman, looking like a young Natalie Lindberg. She sat in a wicker chair, a dark-haired toddler at her knee. My mother and me. For a brief moment, I wished yet again that I could remember her. The chime from the dryer reminded me that I had work to do. I replaced the photo in its usual spot and got back to work.

Joe was standing in the driveway when I pulled in with Grandma Natalie. We'd had quite a ride from the hospital since she'd insisted on bringing her entire collection of balloons home with her. They bobbed against the inside roof of the car, blocking my view. There were so many that I was constantly pushing them away from the windshield or out of from my face. She thought they were delightful, which I put down to the residual effects of narcotic pain medications. I thought it was a miracle we made it home in one piece.

We'd almost finished unloading the car when Patrick showed up. Grandma Natalie was settled into her favorite recliner with a lap blanket, happy to be home, but tired. I stacked her Harley flyers where she could reach them and made her a cup of coffee. She looked as if she might fall asleep in her chair at any moment.

"Need any help?" Patrick stood in the doorway. He had to have come from work because he was dressed in an expensive suit and shiny black shoes. His hair, about which he was almost obsessed, was perfectly combed with nary a strand out of place.

So of course I sent him out to collect the balloons from the car.

"I saw that smirk," Joe said after Patrick headed outside.

"I don't know what you're talking about," I said, feigning innocence, and then I peered through a side window and watched Patrick try to wrestle two dozen helium balloons into submission. Other than bringing my grandmother home, seeing Patrick dirty his suit and make a mess of his hair while trying not to let a single balloon escape was the highlight of my day.

The days that followed saw Grandma Natalie continue to recover from the crash. As her strength returned, so did her sassy attitude.

"Go out and see your friends. Call Joe and go for a ride. Get out of my hair for a while," she'd say. "You're turning into an old mother hen." She'd tell me that she was fine, thank you, and out I'd go.

On one of those occasions, I met Rachel and Sally at Mount Tabor park. I'd convinced them, to some small degree, that we spent too much time eating and drinking. Late February always seemed to be the coldest part of the year, so I bundled up against temperatures that refused to top the forty-degree mark. Regardless, the park was green and peaceful, and a walk to the top was definitely in order.

We caught up on each other's news on the way. Rachel was still too shy to ask Patrick out, if only for coffee. Sally and I had no difficulty teasing her about it.

"Jeez, you've had a crush on the poor man for what? Two years? Seriously, what's so hard about saying, hey, want to meet for coffee?"

"What if he says no?" Rachel sounded like a terror-stricken teenager. She confronted terrified cats, angry dogs, and demanding clients in her veterinary practice, and I thought it was funny she couldn't ask a man out for coffee.

"Then you won't have coffee with him," I answered. "You're not having coffee with him now. See, you have nothing to lose."

She squinted in my direction, as if seeking a flaw in my logic. Instead, she decided to change the subject. "Sal, what about the chick with the firefighter phobia? She still on your radar?"

"Afraid not," Sally said. "We went out to dinner last week. She's nice enough, but her range of conversation seems to entail how much she hates her boss and what new makeup tips she read in a magazine somewhere. She kept trying to convince me that my life will change if I'd only try using eye liner." She sighed. "I've never felt the need to paint my face, and I'm sure not going to start now."

"Can't you just see it?" I said. "The alarm goes off at the station, and you have to make the guys wait while you check your makeup?" I laughed at the mental image I had of Sally, six feet of muscle and courage, primping in front of a mirror.

They asked about Grandma Natalie as we walked. I told them she was doing well, and that we were still waiting to hear what charges might be filed against the man who had run the light and hit her and Ada.

At the top, we stopped to admire the Portland skyline.

"Hey," Sally said, "any progress on the case in Charbonneau? Has the chef turned up?"

"No." I gave them a quick update.

Sally said, "I still say someone needs to follow the wife. It's hard to believe she doesn't know something, given what you told us about her buying a car and all that."

"Lupe told me she goes out all the time now, and she thinks Elise comes to Portland pretty often." I looked out toward downtown Portland. Dark clouds were coming in from the west. "We should go before the rain starts."

"Maybe Lupe could tell us when Number Four heads out and we can track her." Sally wasn't letting go of her idea.

"Didn't I tell you how fast she drives? There's no way I could keep up with her. I tried one time and she left me behind in a heartbeat."

We strolled back down the hill as the breeze picked up and a few sprinkles fell.

"Yeah, but there's three of us. Four, if you count Lupe. And I'll bet your other friend, Sharon, would help, too."

"And then we'd do what? Park along where we think she's going? Synchronize our watches?" I raised an eyebrow in Sally's direction. "Did someone give you walkie-talkies for your birthday when you were a kid and then take them away?"

"Very funny, Velasquez."

"We have cell phones," Rachel said. "We could text when we see where she's going."

"Don't tell me you think this is a good idea," I said. "I think you're both nuts."

Just then, the rain came down hard. Laughing like lunatics, we ran the last hundred yards to our cars and went our separate ways.

That night, I lay awake again in my bed. Shadow was happy about that, purring and kneading the covers near my head. Nights like this were becoming too common. I hadn't had to find a job yet, so I wasn't concerned about my schedule. What annoyed me was that, in the dark, all I could think about was Doctor Wentworth and Mo. I couldn't help the doc, but I was as sure as I'd ever been that Mo was out there somewhere. I couldn't let myself believe she'd been killed any more than I could believe she'd killed the doctor. The darkness fed my imagination, convinced me that she was in peril.

I turned over and scrunched up my pillow. Shadow voiced his objections to being disturbed, but quickly resumed purring.

By morning, I'd made a decision. After breakfast, I texted Sally and Rachel: "Okay. Let's do it."

Almost immediately, I had a text back. "Park. Now."

I laughed. Not only were we acting like amateur sleuths, but we were sending cryptic messages and setting up meetings in out of the way places like spies. The whole thing was weird, but funny, too.

Twenty minutes later, I pulled into the Mount Tabor parking lot. Sally and Rachel were already there. Even though a light drizzle was falling, we decided to walk up to the top of the park while we talked.

"What changed your mind?" Sally asked.

"It's keeping me awake nights."

"Yeah, we thought you looked a bit rough," Rachel said.

"Very funny. Seriously, you know it's worried me from the start that the detective in Charbonneau thinks Mo killed the doc. He asked me if they were having an affair."

"Were they?"

"No, I don't see how. She and the doc treated each other like siblings, right down to some friendly squabbling. They got along great."

Sally said, "That doesn't mean they weren't doing the horizontal mambo on the sly."

"Mo's a lesbian, Sal," I said. "She and I dated a few times."

"She could be bi," Rachel said. "It's not outside the realm of possibility. Even if she's one hundred percent lesbian, she could have had sex with him. I've known it to happen."

I had to think about that one, but it still didn't fit. "Maybe, but somehow I doubt it. You'd have had to meet her to know what I mean."

"Okay, so what's our plan?" Rachel asked.

We reached the park's crest and sat on a bench near the statue of Harvey W. Scott. The rain had let up and a few patches of blue sky showed through the clouds, but water still dripped off Harvey, who had run *The Oregonian* newspaper sometime in the distant past. In his long waistcoat, Harvey pointed to his right as if telling his naughty children to go to their rooms. I hope that wasn't an omen.

I turned back to my friends. "Lupe's about ready to wring Number Four's neck, so I'm sure she'd let us know when she leaves in that fancy little red car, and maybe which direction she takes. A left turn out of the gate would most likely mean she's heading to Portland."

Rachel asked, "Are there roads where she could turn off?"

I got my phone out and called up the map website. "Only a couple." I expanded the picture. "The roads don't go much of anywhere, so unless she's out driving for fun, she's probably coming to town."

Sally pointed at the schematic on my phone. "One of us could park near each of those intersections and report if she turns off. Where's the next place she could turn, if she continued straight through?"

We spent the next half an hour examining the map and deciding who would be stationed at which location. Despite my initial reluctance, I was enjoying conspiring against Number Four. I'd taken enough of her mistreatment without a word of protest that I figured she owed me. With some luck—and that's what it would take—we might learn something useful.

"You look happier," Sally said, as we got up to leave.

"I am." I thought about it for a few seconds. "Ever since my dad died, I've felt stuck, as if things were happening around me and I had no choice but to bear with it. It feels better than I would have expected to actually be doing something, even if all we do is waste gas and time."

"Or get arrested for stalking," Sally said.

"Or feel stupid," Rachel said, "when we find out she's going to Nordstrom's every day."

"Or find Mo and the murderer," I said.

For the next few days, our plans were stalled by my friends' unfortunate need for employment. Rachel had patients to treat and Sally's irregular shifts made planning difficult. Their schedules made me realize I'd need to find a job soon, too.

When I broached the subject with Grandma Natalie, she said, "Nonsense! We'll get along fine. Between your savings and my retirement, we're in good shape."

"I can't do nothing, Grandma. You're much better, and as soon as you're more up and about, I'll need something to do. And I really should contribute something to the household. Grocery money?" I made myself laugh with that one. "Anyway, I'm just thinking about it. I'm not doing anything until you're well."

The truth was that she was recovering faster than any of us, doctors included, expected. Only three weeks after coming home from the hospital, she needed little assistance from me, other than taking her to her appointments because she hadn't been cleared to drive. Liz or Ada seemed to turn up on appointment days, so I was at loose ends a lot.

Since the rainy day when Joe found me at my dad's shop, I'd driven by only once and didn't stop at all. Worrying about my grandmother while she was hospitalized and taking care of her afterwards had pushed most thoughts of the charred building from my mind. Now that I had more time to myself, I was back to brooding about the shop and my dad's untimely death.

So it was that I pulled into the lot and parked, as I always did, under the trees at the far end. This time, though, I didn't sit and gaze at the ruined structure. I didn't give in to my grief at knowing how my father died there or my anger at my former partner for causing so much destruction in my life. From some hidden recess within me, the resolve to do something arose, even if I didn't yet know what.

I got out of the car and walked through the parking lot, circling the building. The shed behind the shop where the fire originated was a pile of blackened wood and ash. Shattered glass lay everywhere. Weeds grew up through the remains.

The back wall of the shop was burned away, leaving the door opening gaping. I tentatively pushed against the wall, half expecting it to collapse, but it didn't budge. Completing my circuit, I came to the front door. It, too, was burned, but not as severely as the back. The fire department had put out the worst of the flames before the front was engulfed. The bricks that my dad had so carefully laid were blackened with soot, but most of them were unbroken.

I stood before the open door for what felt like a glacial age, but was probably no more than a minute or two. Taking a deep breath, I stepped through the opening for the first time since the day I found my father's body in the smoldering ruins.

The floor was littered with burned bits of glass and the charred remains of my dad's bike shop. Almost everything was black with soot, but as I pushed the wreckage aside with my feet, I found a few pieces of metal, remains of bike parts, and one entire bicycle. Though ten months had passed, the smell of burned wood and plastic and other materials remained and my nose and throat felt raw. I didn't let it deter me.

The further into the shop I went, the more familiar it felt. The counter where Dad took payments survived, blackened and blistered by the fire, but there nonetheless. He'd built it himself. Ignoring the soot covering it, I made my dad a silent promise to try to save it. *Lo intentaré.* I'll try. Peg boards on the back wall that once held bike components and accessories appeared oddly untouched by the fire, though the pegs were gone, taken by thieves who had helped themselves to the items that had been displayed there.

I hesitated before going back to area where he'd stored his inventory, but I stood straighter, squared my shoulders, and kept going. The eight-foot-tall wood shelves he'd built were damaged, but still mostly upright. I paused at the end of the far one and closed my eyes. Could I face the sight of the old recliner where he'd been sleeping when the fire broke out?

I could.

I opened my eyes and walked slowly past the shelf unit. The chair was still there, covered in soot and surrounded by chunks of wood and other debris. The lap blanket he'd loved was piled on the floor in front of the recliner.

I stood surveying the scene, remembering there was something to be grateful for, even here in the terrible scorched wasteland of my father's dreams. The medical examiner concluded that my dad died from smoke inhalation. It appeared that he'd taken a nap in his beat-up old recliner, and startled by the explosion, tried to get out from under his lap blanket and out of the store, but succumbed to the toxic chemicals and smoke that the explosion in Nicky's meth lab had released into the air.

I could be angry with Nicky and hate what she'd done but be grateful Dad hadn't suffered for long, hadn't burned to death, had simply gone to sleep.

I turned away and finished my tour of the building. Joe and I owned this together now, but we hadn't been able to talk about what to do with it. The city inspectors gave us a deadline for getting the building removed or repaired, so we'd have to deal with it soon.

As I made my way to the front of the shop, a corner of a board caught my eye, standing out among the blackened ruins because it wasn't as damaged as the wreckage around it. One edge was burned, but two sides were intact and bore what appeared to be edging pieces. Curious, I picked it up, and at last, tears ran down my face.

It was the lower right corner of a sign. Most prominent was the right side of a large capital E, followed by an intact capital S. Part of the "BIKES" sign that had hung above the door to Dad's shop survived after all. But what took my breath away and broke through my bravado was what I saw in tiny letters at the bottom.

M. Velasquez, Proprietor

Chapter Nine

Have you taken up coal mining?" Grandma Natalie scowled at me with a raised eyebrow.

"I did tell you I was going to get a job, didn't I?" I said with a grin.

She gave me an eyeroll that would have done a teenager proud, but she had a point. My visit to the remains of Dad's shop left me covered in dirt and soot. I'd taken off my cheap canvas shoes outside and promptly discovered that no amount of clapping them together would remove the embedded blackness. I intended to drop them into the trash, but an idea was growing in my mind that made me reconsider, so I set the shoes aside and walked into the house in my socks.

"Very funny, cute girl," she said. "How'd you get so dirty? And don't even think of coming anywhere near my white sofa."

"I went into the shop."

"Did you now? Why?"

I didn't often surprise my grandmother, so I took a moment to enjoy it.

"I have to face it sometime, don't I? Today was the day. I went inside to look around. Believe it or not, I found part of the sign from above the door. I thought it was long gone."

I'd wrapped the remnant of the sign with my dad's hand lettering on it in a plastic bag and stowed it in my car. No way would I risk losing it.

She stared at me with admiration. "I've always said you're stronger than you believe, but now I think you're far stronger than I thought. I'm not sure I could have gone in there. He was a wonderful man, always kind to his mom-in-law, and you couldn't have had a better father. I'm sorry he's gone, but I'm glad to see you're coming to terms with losing him."

Until she said it, I hadn't thought of it that way. "I miss him terribly, and I'll always grieve for him. In April, he'll have been gone for a year. I don't know what we'll do with the property, but it was good for me to go there today."

"What does Joe say?"

"We haven't talked about it, probably because we haven't been able to. The building is almost a total loss, but the lot it sits on is well situated for a small business. I've wondered if we should clear it off, sell it, and move on."

She hesitated, as if considering my words. "Talk with Joe. Maybe he's ready, too." She stood up from her recliner, dislodging Shadow in the process. "Now where are you taking me for dinner? After you shower, that is."

Two days later, Sally and Rachel and I had our first opportunity to try out our tracking skills. We'd made our plans, and as I'd suspected, Lupe was delighted to help us. She told me Elise had gotten into the routine of speeding away in her hot little car at about the same time almost every other day, so we were prepared.

Sure enough, my phone beeped. Lupe's text read: *4 heading your way.*

We were ready. We'd identified two side roads Elise could take if she wasn't heading into Portland. Sally was parked near the first one and Rachel within sight of the second. I idled in a park-and-ride lot next to the nearest Portland exit. Though we were aware that what we were doing was potentially serious, we texted back and forth like schoolgirls, having more fun than expected.

Sally's message came through first. Elise hadn't turned off. Ten minutes later, Rachel reported the same thing. Depending on our quarry's speed, I had about fifteen minutes to wait. I planned to follow her, hoping city traffic would slow her down enough for me to keep her in sight.

Sure enough, she came through right on time. I pulled out as quickly as I could, but I was still a dozen car lengths behind her. Fortunately, I saw no other fire-engine-red sports cars on the road, so I was able to catch a glimpse of her every minute or two. I tried moving up, but traffic was too heavy for me to make much progress. Of course, it slowed her down, too.

I had just changed lanes to the left to pass a slow truck when I saw her take one of the exits toward downtown Portland.

She was gone. *Hell and damnation!*

I continued on until I could exit the highway and pull into a gas station parking lot. I texted my co-conspirators: *Lost her downtown.*

And try again we did. After the first few times, we found she never turned off before Portland, so we abandoned that part of the plan and tried tracking her through the city into downtown. We lost her every time, but she established a pattern, and we theorized she was either going into downtown or through downtown to the east side of the city. The latter made little sense, because she could get there faster by staying on the freeway, so we figured we'd narrow the search to the city center.

After the fourth time we'd lost track of our quarry, Sally said, "If she's going to Nordstrom's three times a week, I'll torch that damn car myself. And I know how, believe me."

I pointed a warning finger at her. "That's quite a statement coming from a firefighter."

"Damn straight." She laughed. "Okay, maybe not straight. You know what I mean. As long as we're down here, let's go get something to eat. All of this skulking around makes me hungry."

On the days Rachel and Sally were unavailable to play gumshoe with me, I parked downtown and spent a few hours on foot, keeping an eye out for a flashy little car with an allegedly grieving widow behind the wheel. Downtown Portland did me a favor by being fairly compact. I also spent time online studying the map, trying to figure out where she might go. The high-end department stores were obvious targets as were some of the more exclusive restaurants.

My chances of locating her this way were vanishingly small, but I couldn't give up. Unrelenting insomnia kept me obsessing about Doctor Wentworth and Mo. I had to do something, anything, to help me feel that I might learn something useful. The tiniest clue might lead to my friend and the doctor's killer.

One day, Joe sat across from me in Grandma Natalie's kitchen—now also my kitchen, I reminded myself. He said, "I can't believe you're downtown two or three times a week and you don't stop in at my office."

"You've been going downtown?" My grandmother looked at me suspiciously. "Why? I thought you were going back to the shop."

"You've been hanging around the shop again?" Joe said, concern all over his face. "I thought you decided to stay away from there."

"I did. But I've been back once or twice. Sometime soon, you and I need to talk about what we'll do with it. And I didn't try to see you because I figured you were busy." And I needed to keep an eye out for Elise Wentworth.

"Bullshit," he said. "You know you can stop in any time. When will you be there next?"

"Not sure, tomorrow or the next day . . . maybe."

"Let me know and I'll meet you for coffee. Now what's this about the shop?"

"She's been going inside."

I gave Grandma Natalie a glare for ratting me out.

"Inside?" Joe looked alarmed. "Why? Patrick told me the city wants to condemn it, so it can't be safe in there. Apart from that, why would you want go back in there, after—" He stopped and when he spoke again, his voice sounded constricted. "After what you saw."

"You're right, but I had to face it. I *needed* to face it. You understand, don't you?"

He had tears in his eyes, and I knew he grieved for Dad as much as I did.

I took his hand in both of mine. "Let's talk about it some other time."

The next morning, I pulled into the parking lot at the shop, but this time, instead of parking under the trees, I backed my car up to the door. After the back hatch opened, I unloaded the supplies I'd purchased. The shovel and broom went next to the checkout counter and the rest went on top. Then I moved the car to its usual spot.

I walked through the building again, formulating a plan. I was pulling on a pair of rubber gloves when I heard a truck outside, warning signals sounding as it backed up near the door. I watched a young man carefully lower a green metal dumpster to the ground. He blocked the wheels to keep it from rolling.

"This good?" he asked.

"Perfect, thanks." He'd positioned it so I could get to it easily, but where it wouldn't be in the way. I had plenty of room for the other delivery I'd arranged. I signed the form he held out and he left.

Standing in the doorway, I pivoted to examine the shop from that perspective.

"Okay," I said aloud. "Path first."

At the counter, I opened a box of large black plastic bags and pulled one free. I donned safety glasses and a face mask and, carrying the broom and shovel in gloved hands, went back to the front door.

Over the next three hours, I cleared a respectable path from the door to the counter. Each full bag of debris went into the dumpster. I kept an eye out for anything worth saving, but the fire had been intense. I found twisted metal that must have come from the bicycles Dad had hoped to sell. Tires had melted onto the floor and wouldn't budge.

I pulled my glasses and mask off, took a bottle of water from the cooler I'd brought, and opened it. Cold water had never tasted so good. I stepped back to examine the checkout counter again. Dad had built it from solid wood, and it somehow escaped the worst of the fire. I wanted to save it.

"Back again, eh?."

I yelped and spun around. Joe stood in the doorway dressed in his Team Three and a Half cycling jersey, one hand on the handlebar of his bike.

"Cripes, Joe, you scared me."

He leaned his bike against the door frame and came into the shop. "Got another one of those?"

I handed him a bottle of water.

"What are you doing?" He opened the bottle and drank half of the contents. "You keep this up, you'll be as dark as I am." He gave me a playful wink.

"I'm cleaning up."

"I can see that. But why? You know we have to tear the place down. Why waste your time?"

"It's something I have to do. I don't really know why. But look," I ran my hand along the counter top, "Dad built this, and I think we can save it. And some of the shelves in the back are salvageable, too."

He paused for a long moment without speaking. "Okay, I guess I get it. Save what we can, right? But I'm not sure what we'd do with it."

"Me, neither, but it's all that's left of his shop. He started it with nothing and made a lot of people happy."

"Including yours truly," Joe said. "Can I help?"

"Yes, but not dressed like a ninja cyclist." I thought for a moment. "Tell you what, let me work on clearing the floor. I'm having a portable storage unit delivered later on, so if you have time, maybe you can help me move this"—I put my hand on the checkout counter—"and other stuff into it."

Joe whistled. "Wow, you've thought about this, haven't you? Dumpster outside. Storage container." He scanned the room with an appraising eye. "Sure, how about this weekend?"

My shop cleaning project came along slowly. The more time I spent there, the closer I felt to my dad. People in the neighborhood stopped in to see what I was doing. The man who owned the body shop next door also came by. The fire had damaged his business as well, and he was rebuilding. With a lump in my throat, I acknowledged that though my dad was gone and his store ruined, the community was still here.

While we saved what we could and cleared almost all of the charred debris out, Joe asked a friend to examine the building. Brad was one of Joe's cycling buddies from Team Three and a Half. He was also a structural engineer with his own construction company.

"You have two options," he said after he'd inspected the charred shell. "The first one, the obvious one, is to tear it down. The worst of the damage is the back, of course, and I don't know how it's still standing. Your dad must have really beefed up the structure."

"He did," I said. "The building was old and creaky when he bought it."

"I can see that. Your second option is to save what's good and replace the rest. From what I can see, the front half is probably salvageable, but the rest is about to collapse." He looked at Joe and me. "What have you thought about doing with it?"

My brother and I exchanged glances. "We haven't talked about it yet. It's been too hard—" My throat constricted suddenly and I blinked tears away.

"I understand. Your dad was a good man. I can't imagine how hard it must be for you. As for this," he scanned the room again, "which option you choose will depend on whether you want to save it and how much money you want to spend. The least expensive option is to tear it down, but we can rebuild. If you think you'll want to try to save some of it, we should shore up the back where the structure is weakest. Don't want it falling in on anyone."

The three of us walked out to the parking lot and into the fresh air.

Brad paused by his truck. "I hope this helps. Whatever you decide, I'm happy to help."

After he drove away, Joe and I opened bottles of cold water from the cooler. We didn't speak for a few minutes and then we spoke at the same time.

"Joe—"

"Annie—"

"You go ahead."

"No," he said, "you go."

We'd done this routine many times growing up, and it usually made us laugh. Today's conversation, however, didn't allow for minor amusements.

"Okay," I said. "I'll go. What should we do with it?"

"Yeah, we can't avoid this forever, can we?" He took a drink of water. "We could tear it down and sell the lot. It's a good business location."

"That would be easiest, wouldn't it?"

"Maybe."

"Dad never did anything the easy way."

"That's where you got your bullheadedness."

"I am not bullheaded."

"Annie, you are the most stubborn person I know."

"What about Grandma Natalie?"

"Okay, you're second, but not by much." He gazed at the front of the battered little store again. "I can't think about letting this go. Dad turned my life around after my mother died, and this shop was a big part of that. Selling it would be like cutting off my other leg."

"I know, but what would we do with it?"

"I suppose we could lease it out or something. Talk with Brad about rebuilding and find a tenant?"

We discussed possibilities for another few minutes, but left without making a decision. At least we'd talked about it, and that was progress.

Over the next several days, I finished what cleaning I could at the shop and had the dumpster taken away. On the last day I made sure to lock the storage container securely. Until we decided what to do with the remnants of the shop, little was left for me to do. Brad had come back and he and Joe added two-by-fours and sheets of plywood to strengthen the walls. With the structure solidly enclosed, it looked more like my dad's old store, and I felt nostalgic and sad.

During the days I'd worked on the shop, Lupe kept me notified about Number Four's escapades. Without the cleaning project to keep me occupied, I again found myself obsessing about Doctor Wentworth's murder. After multiple failures tracking Elise, Sally and Rachel had lost interest.

Since I was fresh out of co-conspirators, I stalked Elise on my own. Every other day, Lupe texted me that the red rocket was on its way, so I'd go downtown and try to spot her. Twice I saw a red car but was disappointed each time. I never would have guessed that so many people in Portland drove bright red sports cars. Walking around downtown Portland may have been good exercise, but I was getting tired of the futility of the chase.

About a week later, I was downtown again and finally got disgusted with myself. I stopped at a hole-in-the-wall restaurant with tables on the sidewalk and called Joe.

"Can you meet me for lunch?"

He appeared within minutes and sank into the chair opposite me. "It's about time. How often have you been down here lately?"

"A couple times this week. It's a total waste of effort. I don't know what made me think I could find her, or if I did see her, how it would help. I'm so frustrated."

"You could put a GPS tracker on her car."

"What?" I stared at him. "Can I do that? Is it legal?"

"It's better than wasting your time wandering the streets. You need to find a way to stop obsessing, and if a little electronic surveillance will do the job, then go for it." He paused. "You might not want to tell Patrick, though."

"Oh, I don't know," I said with a low chuckle. "He might like it. He hasn't had a reason to yell at me for a couple of days."

We ordered lunch and talked about how Grandma Natalie was doing, where I might find a job, just brother and sister stuff. He told me his accounting firm had an opening for a receptionist. Through it all, though, part of my mind dwelled on Joe's other suggestion.

At home that afternoon, I grabbed my laptop and did some research. Sure enough, I could buy a GPS tracker online. Many websites shared instructions for installing them. I thought about it and called Lupe. She was hesitant at first, but then agreed to help, so I ordered one of the gadgets.

"I am losing my mind," I muttered, and closed the laptop.

"Done."

Lupe's text gave me the news I'd been waiting for. I had no idea how she'd managed to get the electronic tracker onto Elise's car. I'd find out later. In the meantime, I could follow Number Four—or at least her car—from the comfort of my home or my car, with a snack and a cold drink nearby. Much better.

For the first couple of days, she didn't go out, or if she did, she drove a different car. Lupe didn't work at the Wentworth home every day, so she couldn't tell me if Elise left the house with someone else.

On the third day, Lupe texted me. "Red rocket on the way." She had become an excellent informant, and I had a hunch she enjoyed it.

Monitoring my phone as best I could, I drove downtown and parked at one of the centrally located surface lots. I wanted to avoid having to exit a garage quickly if she cut through town and headed across the river. I didn't think she'd done it before; getting across Portland would be more efficient by staying on the freeway, but since I'd been unable to find her previously, I was guessing that her destination was downtown. Sure enough, the tracking unit on Elise's car showed that she got off the freeway and was driving north on Fourth Street, one of downtown Portland's one-way streets. She wasn't leaving the central city, at least not immediately.

I double-timed it toward Fourth, keeping an eye on my phone. The red dot showing the location of her car went west on Morrison Street and stopped mid-block.

The Finley Hotel. Had to be.

I arrived at the corner across from the hotel in time to see Elise hand her keys to the valet and walk into the hotel lobby.

Around the corner from the Finley, I proceeded cautiously to a good vantage point of the hotel's door. A waist-high sandwich board advertising cell phones concealed my bottom half, and I was ready to duck behind a telephone pole in case she came back out. The last thing I wanted was for her to see me.

After several minutes in the chilly breeze, I noticed a diner directly across from the hotel, its entryway and side windows affording a wide-open view of the hotel entrance. I slipped inside and got a table near the window, ordered a sandwich, and waited.

While I ate, I theorized about why Elise would visit a hotel. The Finley had a restaurant, so she could be meeting someone for lunch.

On the other hand, hotels have rooms, which have beds. I was amused at my own imagination. The Finley was a Portland landmark, in business for over a century, an elegant building, and definitely not a "by the hour" kind of place.

After almost two hours, my sandwich and patience were both long gone. The employees at the busy diner were giving me looks that said "go away, we need the table." I paid my bill, left a big tip, and went outside.

Just as I stepped through the door, Elise came out of the hotel. The valet brought her car and she left. Two hours of boredom, and what did I have for my trouble?

The next eight days provided the same result. Into the Finley in the late morning and out in the early afternoon. One of the servers at the diner commented that I needed a "reserved" sign on my little table. I didn't know if she was joking, but I supposed there were worse fates than becoming a regular at a local eatery that served up excellent sandwiches and soup. Still, watching the front of the Finley was getting boring.

Sally and Rachel suggested I was wasting my time. Even someone as disagreeable as Elise Wentworth had to have friends she might be meeting.

"Yeah," I said, "but who eats at a posh place like the Finley Hotel twice a week?"

"A woman with money and time on her hands," Sally said. "You need a new hobby."

"What I need," I said with some heat, "is to know who killed the doctor and what happened to my friend."

She and Rachel made gentle attempts to help me accept that Mo was most likely dead, but I refused to listen. She'd been missing for over three months. In truth, I'd already reached that painful conclusion, but I couldn't let it go. Natalie Lindberg's legendary stubbornness was indeed hereditary.

Everything changed on my seventh attempt to see what Number Four was up to.

I was sitting at my usual table at the diner. I'd finished a bowl of split pea soup and was trying in vain to wheedle the recipe out of the cook when Elise came out of the Finley.

She wasn't alone.

She stood on the sidewalk outside the lobby of the venerable old hotel immersed in an embrace and deep kiss with Carlton Wentworth the Third.

***

I grabbed my phone, took three photos as quickly as I could, and sent a text to Dean. He could be mad at me all he wanted, give me the silent treatment for years, but I wasn't letting that stop me. I typed: *Thought you should see this,* attached one of the photos, and pressed the send button. I left the diner and headed to my car.

I barely had time to buckle my seat belt when the phone rang.

"Where did you get this picture?" He did not sound grateful at all.

"I took it."

"You took it? You just happened to be at the Finley Hotel? And what a coincidence, look who's there." He couldn't have injected more sarcasm into his voice if he'd tried.

"Of course not. I followed her."

The silence on the phone went on long enough to let me ponder how silence could sound so pissed off.

"You *followed* her?" His voice was low and strained, and I was glad he wasn't nearby. "And you're still there?"

"Yes." It seemed prudent not to embellish.

"Why, if I may ask?"

"Well, we thought—"

"We?"

Damnation. So much for omitting details.

"*I* thought," I said, trying to emphasize the first person pronoun, "*I* thought she might know more about what happened than she let on. I don't have a job right now—"

"I could give a fuck about your work situation." He sounded as if he might be gritting his teeth. "So you've been following Elise Wentworth like a two-bit amateur detective. Do you want me to charge you with obstruction, is that it? Or stalking?"

"No, of course not. All I want to know is where Mo is and who killed the doc. The last I knew, you thought Mo did it and hopped a plane to Zanzibar. I've tried to tell you Mo isn't a killer, but you don't listen."

"I have to follow the evidence, Annie." He was sounding more normal, if still angry. "You know that. Who else is in your little gang?"

"No way," I said. I gave up pretending I'd done this alone. "If you want to charge me with something, that's up to you, but my friends are off limits." I hoped that would protect Rachel and Sally, at least a little. "What matters most right now is what's in that picture. Or should I say *who*."

He was quiet again. "You really know how to piss me off, you know that?"

"Yes, and I'm sorry."

"I doubt that." At least I heard some humor back in his voice. "Okay, yes, this is important information. I need to think about it. Are there any more photos I should know about?"

"No. This is the first time we—I've seen where she went. You know about that new sports car she got? She drives like the proverbial bat, and she kept losing us—me." I clearly had no future as a spy.

"Okay, good. Now I want you to stop interfering. Today. Right now. No more stalking Elise Wentworth. Got it?"

"Got it," I said, but mentally crossed my fingers. He had to know I wouldn't give up until I knew who'd killed the kind doctor and what had happened to my friend.

At dinner that night, Rachel and Sally couldn't get information fast enough. They passed my phone back and forth so many times I wondered if I'd get it back.

"Damn, girl, you did it." Sally shook her head in wonderment.

"Joe helped," I said. "He suggested the tracking device. Otherwise, I don't think I'd have ever figured out where she was going. Or why."

"Or who with." Rachel looked at the photo again. "He's a hunk. What I can tell from this angle, anyway."

"He's also married and has a two kids and lives in Seattle."

Rachel turned the phone toward me and said, "He doesn't seem very married to me."

"Yeah," Sally said. "If they hadn't just come out of the hotel, I'd be inclined to tell them to get a room. They're acting like over-heated teenagers."

I raised an eyebrow at her words. "Oh?"

"Not," she said unconvincingly, "that I'd ever know about stuff like that. I am impressed, though. I never had a girlfriend brave enough to do that with me in public."

"Me, neither," I said.

"Didn't you say she's been going downtown at least twice a week?"

"Yes, pretty much."

"If he lives in Seattle, what's he doing in Portland so often?" Rachel asked.

Disgusted, I put the phone away. "I sent the picture to Dean, the detective in Charbonneau. He threatened to arrest me for stalking."

"It has been a few days since you were threatened with legal action," Sally said thoughtfully. "Maybe he doesn't want you to feel neglected."

I laughed. "You're incorrigible." I paused for a moment, feeling a more somber mood coming on. "There's no way to know if there's a connection between these two and the doc's murder, so I hope Dean can figure it out. He seems like a good guy, a good cop, at least when he's not yelling at me."

Rachel said, "Maybe now you can stop obsessing about whatever she's up to. She's getting laid on a regular basis, which is more than either of you can say."

"Either of us?" I raised an eyebrow in Rachel's direction, now completely distracted from my brooding. "The last I knew, you were as single as Kraft slices."

"As single as Sister Mary Francis."

"Nuns are married to Jesus, aren't they?" Rachel said.

"Maybe so, but they're not getting laid."

We all stopped talking, processing an unlikely mental image, until I realized what Rachel had said.

"You finally did it, didn't you?" I grabbed her hand and refused to let go. "You called Patrick?"

She blushed, which is all the answer I needed.

"And how long has this been going on?"

"Long enough," Rachel said. "You've been so obsessed I thought you'd never notice."

"She didn't," Sally said with a smirk.

"You knew? And you didn't tell me?" I looked back and forth between them a few times. "How did this happen? And when?"

"It turned out he wanted to call me, but he wasn't sure he should, since you and I are friends," Rachel said. "And you thought he hadn't noticed me. Some detective you are."

Two days later, I got another text from Lupe. Elise was headed into town. Though I knew I shouldn't, I went, too, and resumed my usual spot at the diner. Sally and Rachel would have tried to talk me into giving up, but I wanted more photos, more information.

Too many questions were unanswered. Why, for instance, would Carl the Third drive to Portland, when he presumably had patients to see and a family to care for? Elise had more free time than he did. She could have easily gone to Seattle and stayed there, if they wanted to see each other so frequently. Did Carl's wife know about his absences? Surely his medical colleagues would notice.

Of course, I wouldn't get any answers sitting on my butt, but that didn't keep me from waiting and watching. The battery on the GPS tracker must have died because I no longer had the ability to know where Elise was going. It didn't matter much. The photos I got of Carl and Elise confirmed that their relationship was ongoing.

The next day, I left the diner before they came out. Sitting and watching the hotel was useless, as well as boring. I had memorized the front façade of the Finley Hotel, along with faces and little quirks of the doormen who stood there day in and day out. I'd finally had enough.

The day was one of those pristine early April days that come along unexpectedly in Oregon. The sun was shining and the breeze, while still cool, was refreshing. I stood outside the diner door for a moment and inhaled deeply, stretching my arms above my head. A walk was definitely in order.

I went toward what Portlanders call the Park blocks. Bordered by Park Avenue, the Park blocks were a series of green spaces stretching from near the Finley to the Portland State University campus. I walked on the paths that cut through the blocks, enjoying a little bit of awakening nature in middle of the city. Several blocks up, I found an unoccupied bench near a stand of trees and sat down to listen to the birds and do a little people watching.

Students from the university walked by in groups, chatting and checking their phones. A young mother pushed a stroller while holding the hand of a toddler. Men and women in business attire hurried by. A young man threw a Frisbee for his dog.

"Annie!"

I jumped when I heard my name. Before I could turn around, an arm went across my shoulders in a tight hug.

I pulled away to see who'd greeted me with such familiarity and came eye to eye with Carl the Third. Surely any passersby would believe we were friends or lovers. But despite the happy tone he'd used, I saw anger in his eyes.

"What do you think you're doing?" His tone was low and grating.

"Sitting in the park. In public. Now let go of me."

He tightened his hold on my shoulders. "Did you think you'd get away with it? Do you think I'm so stupid that I wouldn't recognize you?"

"Get away with what?" I tried bravado, but my voice quavered. "I have every right to be here."

"You've been watching Elise."

"No, I haven't." I tried to pull away again. "Let go of me or I'll scream."

He slid his hand off my shoulder, but when I started to stand, he grabbed a handful of my hair and pulled me back.

"You're not going anywhere."

I struggled again, but he tightened his hold.

"Stop! You're hurting me."

Something sharp poked against my neck and I flinched. I struggled again to free myself, but I suddenly felt weak. I couldn't focus. He was talking, making it appear as if we were having a friendly conversation, but his voice was receding, growing quieter. My vision narrowed and started to go dark. I couldn't move.

Just before I blacked out, I heard him, as if from a distance, say, "She's okay. I'm a doctor and I'll take care of her."

And then I was gone.

Chapter Ten

What seeped into my consciousness first was the stench of rotting food and human waste.

I opened my eyes, but the darkness was so deep that I had to put my hand up to my face and feel the sweep of my lashes to know that my eyes were indeed open.

My back hurt, my neck was sore, and my head felt as if I'd spent four hours on a tilt-a-whirl. I lay on a thin mattress, covered by a light blanket. I was reluctant to sit up or stand since I couldn't see anything. Trying not to move my head, I reached to my right and felt a rough wall. More exploration with my fingertips revealed what felt like horizontal seams, so perhaps the wall was built of unfinished wood planks. To my left, I encountered only empty space.

I shifted my position in an attempt to relieve the pain in my back and heard a soft clinking sound. I sat up slowly and clutched at my leg. A shackle encircled my left ankle. After a moment, my fingers touched a heavy chain attached to the shackle.

"You bastard," I whispered, my head pounding. I jerked at the chain, but it was solidly affixed. I was too fatigued, still too drugged to investigate further.

Bit by bit, I tried moving my limbs and when nothing else hurt, I turned on my side, facing away from the wall. I couldn't seem to think clearly. I pulled the blanket up around my shoulders and tried to ignore how bad it smelled. Wherever I was obviously had no heat.

I became more awake as time passed and thought through what must have happened. Obviously, Carl the Third, pretending to be my friend for the sake of passersby, had drugged me somehow.

Where was I? And why was it so dark?

I also noticed the silence. The quiet was as impenetrable as the darkness. I was either in a cellar deep underground or outside the city, but how could I tell where? I listened a while longer and thought I heard the chirping of crickets.

Unless I'd been confined to a building away from all traffic, it seemed more likely that he'd taken me out of Portland. On the other hand, the overpowering stench of the place made me wonder if he'd brought me to a building near a landfill. It was all I could do to keep from gagging.

Time and again, I peered into the darkness hoping to see something, anything, but in vain.

I must have fallen asleep, perhaps succumbed to the remaining effects of the drug he'd given me, because when I opened my eyes next, a thin gray light shone between the boards of the wall. Of course, he'd grabbed me during the day and the sedative wore off throughout the night.

I breathed a sigh of relief. At least I wasn't underground or in a cave.

After a few minutes, I realized that my head had cleared somewhat, so I carefully put my feet on the floor and sat up. There was enough light to let me see the shackle around my ankle and the attached chain. The chain led from my leg to the end of my cot.

Then I looked more closely. I wasn't attached to a cot; the surface on which I'd been deposited was a cheap metal bed frame. I pulled up the corner of the thin mattress to find metal cross bars and wires acting as support.

The dim light let me take stock of my surroundings. The space was about ten feet square. I'd been right; the walls were rough wood planks. A window opening in the first wall I'd touched had been boarded over with plywood. Opposite that wall was a half-wall topped with vertical bars made of metal. A wood sliding door, also with bars on the upper section, took up half the width of the wall. The other two walls were wood planks from top to bottom except for a couple of feet at the top, which was open. The floor was compacted dirt.

To the side of my bed stood a battered cardboard box containing half a dozen bottles of water. I grabbed one and drained it immediately. The water bottles were accompanied by a box of granola bars and three cans of soup with pop top lids. In the bottom of the box, I found a plastic spoon wrapped in paper towels.

I pushed my blanket aside and stood, careful not to trip over the chain that held me captive. As the light grew brighter, I saw something that made my stomach turn. In the far corner of my prison sat a white painters' bucket, and next to it, a grimy roll of toilet paper.

Carl clearly planned for me to be here for a while.

"Don't count on it, buddy," I muttered.

I sat on my bed and ate a granola bar. I resisted using the white bucket for as long as I could, but after a few hours, I had no choice. The raw edge of the bucket bruised my skin. After that, I had nothing to do but wait and wonder where I was and what Carl intended to do with me.

From time to time, I thought I heard rustling sounds nearby. The sound was so fleeting that after a while, I put it down to squirrels or birds. I hoped it wasn't bats.

The light seeping in from outside grew brighter and the space warmed somewhat. The building was obviously above ground and in an area open enough to let sunshine bathe the exterior.

In the following hours, I alternated sitting on my bed and lying down. The chain attached to the shackle on my leg was heavy enough to make moving difficult, and the small space in which I was confined made walking pointless.

At one point, I tried to go to the front of my cell and peer out between the bars, but I was able to go only six feet before coming to the end of the chain. Out of frustration, I grasped the chain in both hands and pulled. To my surprise, I managed to move the bed frame away from the wall and drag it far enough along the dirt floor to let me to reach my destination.

All I could see in the dim light from my new vantage point was another row of bars and more wood. The doors across from my cell had latches on the outside. They were metal, made of two pieces, a horizontal bar attached to the door and a movable piece attached to the wall that closed down over the bar. Opening it would require simply lifting the beak-shaped lever.

I reached down and felt for the latch on the outside of my door. I could barely reach it, but I managed to get the top of it between my fingers and pulled. It wouldn't budge. I stretched my arm as far as I could, almost wedging my shoulder between the metal bars on the top of the door and ran my fingers over the lock mechanism. What I found made me want to weep. The latch to my door was secured with a padlock.

Discouraged, I pushed my bed back against the wall. When I sat down, the bed wobbled so badly that I got right up again. The bed's metal leg nearest the wall was weak and had been displaced when I dragged the bed across the floor. I straightened it and sat down.

I ate another bar. I couldn't bring myself to eat cold soup, but I realized I'd have to sooner or later. I'd be in no shape to escape if I didn't eat.

Darkness fell and the few birds I'd heard earlier were silent. I still occasionally heard rustling, but since I was almost sure that I'd been taken outside the city, I attributed those sounds to the local wildlife.

Sometime during the night, I heard distinct sounds of movement nearby. I lay on my bed and held my breath, wondering what kind of creature was there. A coyote, maybe, or a family of raccoons? Whatever it was, I hoped it was friendly, because I was in no position to defend myself.

Then I heard two familiar sounds, the soft clink of chain links and the unmistakable sounds of liquid falling into a bucket.

And then a heavy sigh.

The sound of paper crinkling.

Another sigh.

Soft crying, a sound so full of despair that my heart broke.

I lowered my fetid blanket and listened for another few seconds. "Hello?" I spoke softly, unsure.

All sounds stopped.

I spoke again. "Is someone there?"

Slowly, almost glacially, I sat up.

"Please, can you talk to me?"

I waited, straining to hear.

"Who are you?" The voice from the other side of the wall was soft, scratchy, as if it hadn't been used recently.

I didn't know what to say. Should I give my name? What if it was Carl, playing some kind of cruel joke?

The voice came again, a little stronger, a woman's voice. "Are you here for me?"

"I was brought here."

"Me, too." The sobbing resumed, and then a whisper, "I want to die."

"No, don't say that." I was almost crying myself. "Who are you? How long have you been here?"

"Forever," came the whisper. "I've been here forever. You will be, too."

"No, I refuse to accept that."

She was silent again.

"Tell me your name," I said. Maybe if I could get her to talk more, I could help her feel better. What she said next knocked me flat.

"I'm Mo," she whispered. "Who are you?"

"Mo?" I jumped up from my bed so fast I got dizzy and had to put a hand on the wall to steady myself. "Did I hear you right? You're Mo? Maureen Shaughnessy?"

She was quiet for a long moment, and then, as if she couldn't quite believe her ears, she said, "Annie?"

I knew how she felt.

Knees wobbling, I fell back onto my bed and sobbed. Through it all, she tried to comfort me, which only made me cry that much harder. After a few minutes, I blew my nose on one of the paper towels from the cardboard box and wiped my face. "Honey, I *knew* you were still alive. I told the police that they had to search for you. Everyone told me you were dead or you'd run off, but I didn't believe it. I never gave up."

"You didn't?" Her voice was closer now. She was in the space next to mine, perhaps leaning against our shared wall.

"I kept telling the cops you never would have killed the doc. They wouldn't listen, but I tried, I really tried."

She was quiet for a long time, and I heard sniffling.

"Mo, you okay?"

"He's dead?"

"Yes." I already felt bad enough for her, but she'd apparently held out hope that Doctor Wentworth was alive. "I thought you'd know."

"I knew he and Carl the Third had a fight, and Carl went after the doc with my knife, but the last time I saw him, he was alive." She sighed deeply and when she spoke, her voice was constricted with tears. "Poor doc."

"And Carl brought you here?"

"Yes. I was in my room, but I went down to the kitchen when I heard noises. The doc was bleeding, and when he saw me, he yelled for me to call 9-1-1. Carl pushed him out the back door and grabbed me before I could get to the phone." She paused for a long moment. "I don't remember how it happened, but when I woke up, I was here."

"He probably drugged you, same as me."

She was quiet for a long moment. "Annie . . ."

I knew what she was about to ask.

"How long has it been? What's the date? I've completely lost track."

I didn't know what to say, so I told her the truth.

"Today is April fourth."

At that, she started crying again, this time with anger.

"Three months? That fucking bastard has kept me here for three months?"

I heard a thumping sound—Mo was pounding on the wall.

"Mo, stop, please. Together we can figure a way out of here. Please stop. You're going to hurt yourself."

The pounding stopped. "How can we get out? I've tried to escape, but I'm chained to my bed. He puts a padlock on the door. How can we get out?"

"I don't know yet, but now there's two of us, and we can find a way. We have to. We can't let him get away with killing the doc and kidnapping us."

"You know what I don't understand?" Her voice was softer again.

"What?"

"Why he's kept me alive all this time. If he killed the doc, what's he got to lose by killing me, too?" She took a deep breath. "Or you?"

I nodded, as if she could see me. "It doesn't make much sense, does it? We're definitely a risk, if we get away. Tell you what, once we have him locked up, let's ask."

Mo's voice was grim. "Yeah, I'll ask him, as long as I can do it with a sledgehammer and some wires hooked to a car battery and stabbed into his shriveled hairy balls."

"That's the spirit." After three months of captivity in the dark and who knows what other punishments, I couldn't be sure of her sanity, but an angry Mo with a purpose was better than a weeping Mo who wished to die.

"Do you know where we are?" I asked.

"No. Only that it's a horse barn somewhere remote. I don't hear traffic go by very often."

A barn. My cell was a stall. "Horse barn? How do you know?"

"For one thing, the smell. Haven't you ever spent any time around horses? And then there are the bars."

"Bars? What are they for?"

"You're such a city girl, Annie." Mo actually managed a low laugh. "Sometimes, especially in barns for show horses, the people install bars to control the horses. A pony I knew once climbed right over his stall's half-door. I've also seen horses who could open latches and get out and liberate their friends. If the wood and the floors are any indication, this is an old barn, but someone installed the bars recently."

"How terrible for the horses. They can't put their heads out and see each other."

"I know how they feel."

That explained the heavy wood planking and the bars, but without more information, our location was still a mystery.

"How often do you see him?" I had an inkling I knew his routine.

"About every other day, sometimes every third day."

"That's what I thought."

"What do you mean?"

"I've been following Elise, trying to get a clue to what happened. Turns out she's been meeting Carl the Third at the Finley Hotel on the same schedule."

"That's disgusting."

"Lupe and I agree."

We chatted until the daylight was long gone. I filled her in about the aftermath of Doctor Wentworth's death, including how I'd told Elise off when I quit my job.

"Good for you."

I told her about Grandma Natalie's accident and how I'd moved back to Portland. I remembered to tell her how much Freddy loved the carrot cake.

"Wait, you took my cake to her and didn't tell me?" She tried to sound indignant, but I could tell she was pleased.

"The surprise wasn't supposed to last this long. The bakery closed, so I thought maybe you'd want to pick up some extra work baking for the diner. She's been after me ever since to give her your name, but—" I couldn't finish.

"But you thought I might be dead," she said for me.

"Well, yeah, but not really. If that makes any sense."

"As much as anything else, sweetie."

As the darkness grew deeper, we finally felt tired enough to sleep, and I knew I needed as much rest as I could get. If Carl kept to his schedule, we'd have to face him soon.

"Rise and shine, ladies."

I couldn't believe it. The insufferable prick actually had the nerve to sound cheerful, as if we were guests at a spa instead of shackled captives held by a killer.

I remained in my bed, blanket pulled up to my shoulders. I refused to acknowledge his presence, other than watching from where I lay. Mo must have adopted the same tactic because she didn't speak, and I didn't hear the clinking of the chain that held her fast.

Carl unlocked my door and slid it open. He carried a two-by-four, held at the ready in case one of us decided to jump him. I'd considered it, but since he'd already killed once, I decided the risk was too great. Sooner or later, he'd make a mistake, and leave an opening I could use to my advantage. In the meantime, I had to be patient.

He dropped several bottles of water into the box by the bed, along with a handful of wrapped bars.

"You don't like soup?"

I glared at him without speaking.

He replaced my bucket with an empty one, slid the door closed, and locked it without looking at me again. He repeated the procedure in Mo's cell, this time without any taunts. She'd told me that she'd developed an undying hatred for canned soup, but it was better than nothing, so he had no reason to make an attempt to tease her.

Our days fell into a routine. We'd have one or two days to ourselves, and then Carl would make his visit, refill our food and water, exchange buckets, and leave. Without planning to, we'd both decided to treat him with silence during his visits. Mo told me that at first, she'd pleaded for release, promising not to tell what she'd seen, begging for freedom, but she realized fairly quickly that he enjoyed her entreaties.

"He likes feeling powerful," she said.

"Maybe that's why he became a surgeon, for the adulation."

I remembered his imperious attitude when he visited Charbonneau, the high-handed way he treated his own sons, especially Eric.

Mo said, "I still don't understand what he gains by keeping us alive."

I didn't, either, but I couldn't dwell on it. "Let's work on a way to get out of here. I'm not willing to wait and see what he has in mind."

Mo and I talked at great length, brainstorming one idea after another, but we couldn't come up with anything that seemed feasible.

Carl's choice of a barn was genius. The walls were solid without so much as a crack in the wood planks, and the plywood nailed over what had been a window to the outside was so solidly attached that I couldn't budge it.

One morning, about a week after my captivity began and the day after Carl's most recent visit, the barn seemed lighter than usual, as if the sun had somehow grown brighter. I went to the door of my cell, holding onto the chain and dragging the bed frame with me.

"Mo, can you see that?"

Carl hadn't closed the outside door as securely as in previous days, and the sun shone through the opening. Mo and I stared at it as if we'd never seen anything so beautiful.

"We have got to get out of here," I muttered to myself.

I turned to push my bed against and wall and the loose leg bent again.

"Oh, stop it," I said, irritated.

"Stop what?" Mo sounded puzzled. "What did I do?"

"It's not you. This stupid leg on my bed keeps bending. I think it's loose, so every time I move the damn thing, I have to fix the leg."

I bent over to straighten it and push the bed against the wall so it wouldn't wobble.

"How loose?" she asked.

"What?" I stood up and spoke toward Mo's wall.

"You said the leg is loose. How loose is it?"

"I don't know," I said irritably.

"So look at it."

She was speaking to me in that patiently persistent voice people use when they think they're on to something, but aren't sure enough about the idea to say what they're thinking. I complied and pushed the thin mattress aside for a clearer view.

The bed frame was a kind of metal, but it was so dirty I couldn't be sure. The horizontal pieces were bent at a ninety-degree angle. The flat part had holes drilled in it, through which wires were strung to form a base for the mattress. The side facing outward was solid. The leg was also bent in the same manner. A solid piece formed the corner, holding two sides of the bed and the leg together with a nut and bolt.

I wiggled the leg of the bed and the bolt moved.

"Mo, my lovely friend, you are a genius."

"What do you mean?"

"I think I might be able to get the leg off the bed frame. That way, I won't be chained to it any longer. And it would give me a tool to use." I didn't add "or a weapon."

"Do you think you can use it to get us out of here?"

"I don't know, but I'm sure as hell going to try."

I threw the mattress and blanket onto the floor and dragged the bed frame to the door of my cell. Carl's carelessness with the outer door and the early spring sunshine gave me plenty of light to examine the bolt and nut holding the leg to the bed.

When I moved the leg, the bolt and nut turned together. The chain holding me ended in a solid ring that Carl had threaded over the horizontal frame of the bed frame. When he'd reassembled it, he hadn't threaded the nut properly, which prevented him from tightening it enough to keep it from moving.

"If I can get this off..." I was talking to myself, trying not to hope, but unable to resist.

The head of the bolt, which faced outward, had a slot in it. The nut was in a tight corner, and I could barely fit my fingers around it, much less get a grip on it.

"I'd pay good money for a screwdriver and a pair of pliers."

"Or a shotgun," Mo said. "A bear trap. Some cyanide capsules. Wait, even better. A horse whip. Yeah, that's the ticket. We're in the right place for it."

"You do realize you can't kill him, right?" I was still unsure about her mental health.

"I know," she said with a sigh. "But a girl can dream."

I had to laugh. Mo was going to be okay.

I was able to turn the nut slightly, but the bolt moved with it. "I need something to hold this bolt still. Do you have anything that would fit in the slot, like a screwdriver would?"

"Um, soup can lid?"

I had to open a can of soup after all.

I rested the bed frame against the wall and reached into the box. The lentil soup seemed less likely to have globs of fat floating on the surface, so I popped it open. The aroma of it, muted because of the cold, made me hungry, so I rooted in the box for the spoon and took a tentative bite. I finished the soup, happy to have food in my stomach.

I didn't plan to ever eat cold soup again voluntarily, but I felt better than I had since I woke up to darkness in this place.

I wiped the lid with a paper towel and bent it in half as much as I could. Putting it under the leg of my bed and pressing down with my weight made it thin enough to fit into the slot on the head of the bolt.

"Now all I need is a pair of pliers or very strong fingers."

The can lid held the bolt fairly well, only slipping off when my concentration wavered, but I couldn't loosen the nut. When I turned it, the bolt also turned, no matter how hard I tried to hold it in place. I persisted until the light faded when the sun set, and all I got for my efforts was sore fingers and a cut on my palm from the edge of the lid.

I gave up for the night and reassembled my bed. Mo and I spent most of the night brainstorming ways to break ourselves free. Once we'd run out of ideas that we'd dismissed as doomed to fail, she added to her list of weapons to use against Carl. I had no idea a chef could be so conversant in poisons, but what I came to understand was that Mo had kept herself sane and hopeful by plotting the painful and gruesome death of our captor. If I couldn't figure out how to disassemble the bed frame, I might have to join in her plans.

Over the next several days, I kept working at the bed frame leg in between Carl's visits. The tips of my fingers were raw and bleeding from the hundreds of times I'd tried to loosen the nut from the bolt. I kept them out of sight when Carl was in the barn. For all he knew, Mo and I were beaten down, defeated, unable to fight back.

Little did he know that I'd gladly bash his brains in, if I could only get that damn bolt loose.

I was working at it again and making no progress. "What I need is some oil. Hey, Mo, think Carl'd bring me a can of 3-IN-ONE?"

She didn't answer.

"Mo? You okay?"

"What if he already did?"

"What are you talking about?"

"He's been bringing me chicken noodle soup, which by the way, is really gross when it's cold."

"I know it is. So?"

"And why is it nasty to eat cold?"

Realization dawned. "Damn, girl, you're good."

"I'm a chef. You think I don't know a thing or two about chicken fat?"

I grabbed the box and sure enough, I had two cans of chicken noodle. I popped one open and there it was, floating on the surface, several yellow-orange globs of fat.

"Do you think it'll work?" I spooned them onto a paper towel, being careful not to include too much broth.

"Can't hurt to try."

"Motto of my life," I said. "Okay, here goes."

Back at the bed, I carefully scooped a blob of fat onto my finger and rubbed it into the line where the nut and bolt met. I did my best to lubricate both sides of the nut, hoping the grease would seep in and allow me to liberate the leg of the bed frame.

"You might have to give it some time to work," Mo said.

"Okay." I was reluctant to wait too long, but after my first attempt to loosen the nut, I realized she had a point. I used all of the fat I'd harvested from the first soup can and reassembled my bed for the night.

The next day, Carl showed up again. This time, he was careful to close the outer door, but it didn't matter. I'd worked at the leg for so many hours that, like military teams who are trained to assemble a firearm blindfolded, I could have taken that bed frame apart in total darkness. I was a one-woman bed frame Seal team.

After he'd gone, I threw my thin mattress and blanket aside and leaned the bed frame against the wall. I opened another can of noodle soup and repeated the grease treatment. I secured the bolt in place with my makeshift screwdriver and applied my abraded fingers to the nut. I tried twisting the nut, but my fingers were too weak and too sore.

I looked around for something to hold the nut in place. All I could find was the plastic lid from a water bottle. The lid was only slightly bigger than the nut, but I was willing to try anything by then. I tore the hem off my shirt and wrapped it around the nut a couple of times and jammed the bottle lid onto it. When I turned the lid, the bolt turned.

On my next attempt, I gritted my teeth and held the bottle lid as tightly as I could and tried turning the bolt with my soup can screwdriver.

The bolt held fast.

I strained to turn it, my fingers throbbing.

The bolt didn't budge.

I took a deep breath and reapplied myself. Nothing.

Just when I was ready to give up, I thought I felt a slight grating sensation. I stopped, barely breathing. Had it loosened, or had my improvised pliers failed? Or was my imagination playing tricks on me? I checked the bottle lid. The fabric was where I'd put it. I applied pressure to the bottle lid and twisted the can lid in the bolt slot.

It moved.

Not much, not willingly, but it moved.

I removed the bottle lid and remnant of my shirt, and peered at the nut. Holding my breath, I put the can lid back into the bolt slot and, with my fingers, tried twisting the nut.

Slowly, with much resistance, it turned. After a revolution or two, I loosened and easily extracted the nut from the bolt.

I took another deep breath and leaned against the wall. "Mo?"

"Mm hm?" She sounded sleepy.

"Chicken fat is magic."

Chapter Eleven

Our initial elation was quickly tempered by the reality of the padlocks on our doors. I tried prying the latch loose with the leg of the bed frame, but from my position inside the door, I couldn't get enough leverage. Latches strong enough to hold horses were too strong for me, especially in my somewhat depleted condition.

I had another idea, but I didn't share it with Mo. We'd kept to our unspoken agreement to remain silent in Carl's presence, but something needed to change, and it was the only thing I could think of. I pondered it for hours before Carl's next anticipated visit, figuring the pros and cons. The former could lead to freedom. The latter didn't bear too much close analysis, or I could lose my nerve. If I could do what I had in mind, success might depend to some degree on the authenticity of Mo's reaction. I kept my idea to myself.

Two days later, Carl greeted us with his usual obscene cheeriness. I was on my carefully reassembled bed, with my blanket up to my shoulders, as usual. I was sure Mo had assumed her normal posture for his visit.

As he went about his chores, I sat up and rested my back against the wall and watched him silently. I flung the fetid blanket to the end of my bed in case Carl noticed that the chain was no longer connected to the metal frame of the bed.

He gave me a curious glance but didn't speak. He held the two-by-four in his left hand and rested it on his shoulder.

"It's about time you showed up," I said in a cold voice.

"What'd you say?" He swung around and gave me a glare of pure venom.

I pretended to be unaffected, but I kept the two-by-four in my peripheral vision, in case he swung it at me. I was playing a dangerous hunch. I had to keep my wits about me.

"I said you're late. You should have been here an hour ago."

He stared at me as if he couldn't make sense of my impertinence. After all, I'd been as quiet as a corpse for the past two weeks. I was counting on him being thrown off stride.

"Annie, no." Mo's voice was soft. "Don't argue."

Her protest did exactly what I'd hoped.

"Yeah, Annie," he said sarcastically. "Listen to your little friend. You're in no position to talk back."

"And you're a shitty housekeeper," I snapped. "You'd think that with your education, you'd know a bucket of raw sewage is unhealthy. Anyone else would be smart enough to know better, smarter than you, obviously. What kind of doctor are you, anyway?"

He raised the two-by-four, but didn't try to use it. "Are you suicidal? Do you have any idea what I could do to you?"

"You could give me food poisoning with cold soup, that's what. Is that what good doctors do?"

Carl's eyes bulged and his face grew red, but he didn't speak.

"And it's a wonder Mo didn't die from hypothermia. Seriously, you couldn't have given her a space heater? Or decent blankets? It was winter, you moron. Or here's an idea. Man up and let her go. Didn't think of that, did you?"

Mo protested again, crying harder. I hated scaring her, but I needed her honest reaction to add fuel to the fire.

His mouth worked, but no intelligible sound emerged.

I spoke as forcefully as I could. "You brought her here. You brought me here. You're keeping us in a barn, for fuck's sake. No way to stay clean, using a bucket as a toilet. It's a wonder we haven't gotten some kind of infection, living where horses used to shit. I thought you were more intelligent than that, but I guess I was wrong. I can't imagine how you ever got into medical school much less graduated. And to think that people let you treat them."

With a bellow of rage, Carl smashed the two-by-four against the bars at the front of my cell. Shards of wood flew everywhere. He dropped the remnant and turned back to me, his face purple, his eyes bulging. Blood spotted his face where splinters of wood had cut him.

My heart pounded as if it were suddenly too big for my chest, but I stayed where I was and stared back at him without saying a word. Mo's crying was verging on hysteria.

He pointed a finger at me, an inch from my face, and screamed, "You will not talk to me like that, do you understand?"

"Why," I said with as much sarcasm as I could muster. "Because you're a hoity-toity surgeon? Who cares?"

He screamed again, an incoherent howl of rage. He was so enraged he was shaking. I remained silent and didn't let my gaze waver. With too much to gain and far too much to lose, I had to hold my ground. I refused to let him see the fear I felt, the quavering in my bones, the tightness in my chest, the rapid-fire pounding of my heart. I sat still as stone and stared him down.

With another scream of rage, he kicked my makeshift toilet over, spilling the contents. He spun in a wide arc and punched me in the side of the head. I fell to the side, stunned, but still on the bed.

Mo sobbed loudly.

I sat up as quickly as I could and stared at him without moving and I hoped without expression. The side of my face felt hot and swollen. Blood trickled down my neck.

I remained silent and unblinking.

He bellowed again, his rage now sounding impotent. He left my cell and slammed the sliding door so hard it seemed to rebound. I heard the thud of angry footsteps and the outer door slid shut. His car started and wheels spun in gravel as he left.

I stayed where I was until I was sure he was gone. Only then did I relax and take a deep breath. I was relieved that Mo's crying had subsided.

"Mo, are you okay? I'm so sorry I scared you."

She didn't answer right away, but when she did, her voice trembled. "Why did you do that?" She sounded as if she might start sobbing again. "He could have killed you. He still could."

"Yes, but I was pretty sure he wouldn't."

"How could you be sure?"

"I wasn't, but his entire ego is wrapped up in being a doctor, a surgeon. When I insulted his intelligence and called his medical skills into question, he lost his temper, which is what I counted on."

"I don't understand."

"Angry people make mistakes." I went to the door, chain trailing me, to check my theory and was gratified and relieved to see that I was right.

"He's likely to be a lot angrier with us now."

"I'm sure he will be." I slid my door open wide and stepped into the passageway. I went to the front of Mo's cell. "But he can be angry in prison."

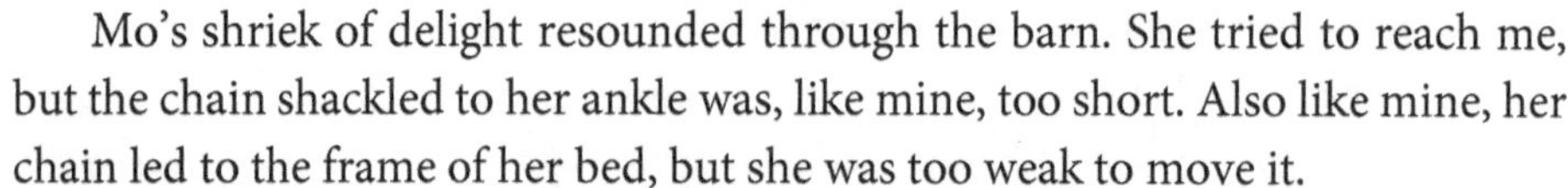

Mo's shriek of delight resounded through the barn. She tried to reach me, but the chain shackled to her ankle was, like mine, too short. Also like mine, her chain led to the frame of her bed, but she was too weak to move it.

Her appearance was shocking, and an involuntary gasp escaped before I could stop it. She was dressed in what might originally have been flannel pajamas, but were now nothing but tatters of thin, filthy cloth. Her hair was matted to her head. Her skin was grimy, and where it was visible, bones jutted out. The look on her thin face was so hopeful it almost broke my heart, but despite her excitement, she swayed where she stood. I feared she might fall.

I'd counseled Mo against killing Carl, but in that moment, if he'd reappeared, I'd have strangled him with my bare hands out of rage at what he'd done to my friend.

"Get me out of here, Annie," she said tearfully. "I can't be here when he gets back."

I went back to my bed and pulled the leg free. Back at Mo's door, I tried wedging it between the latch and the wood of the door.

"Let me see if I get this loose."

But try as I might, I couldn't get my L-shaped piece of metal behind the latch. I dug at the wood with one corner and managed to chip away some splinters, hoping to make a big enough space to let me pry the latch loose.

After what felt like four hours and was probably closer to one, all I had was a two-inch hollowed-out space by the latch, but it was too shallow. The edges of the metal leg, which had been rounded off, weren't sharp enough to cut through the wood fibers. My hands were sore and bleeding. I had a headache from Carl's blow. And my spirit was exhausted and angry.

I searched the barn for any kind of implement I could wedge behind the latch and came up empty. For a desperate moment, I wondered if Carl kept the padlock keys in the barn, but that search, too, proved fruitless. Damn him for being an intelligent kidnapper.

I went back to Mo's door and leaned my forehead against the bars. She'd resumed sitting on her bed, patiently waiting for me to liberate her. I hated to disappoint her.

"I don't know what to do, Mo," I said, almost whispering. "I can't get it loose." Exhaustion and frustration combined to wear me down, and I started crying, sobbing, wracking my chest with pain. "I can't get the lock loose."

"There's only one thing to do."

I was surprised at the strength in her voice.

"You have to run." She spoke with certainty. "Get out of here and get help for me."

"But we don't know where we are. It could be miles." I sniffled and wiped tears away. Here my friend looked like a concentration camp survivor, and she was being the strong one.

"Yes, it could, so you need to go now. If Mister Colossal Prick keeps to his schedule, we have a day, maybe a day and a half, to get out of here. It's getting dark now, so it's only early evening. You have time. Can you do it?"

"I don't know."

"You can." Her voice was insistent. "I believe you can do way more than you think you can. You're a strong person, one of the strongest I've ever met. You lost your dad—"

"You know about that?"

"Yes, I do. I've always known."

"How?"

"Tell you what, let's talk about it after we're out of here and Carl the Asshole is locked up."

Our circumstances were dire, and she was still strong enough to think up creative names for our captor. I suppose it went along with concocting ways to torture him. Sounded good to me.

"But," Mo went on, "my point is that I trust that you can do this, that you can find help and get me out of here before he comes back."

"What if I can't?" Tears ran down my face again at the thought of what Carl could do if he returned and I was gone, with Mo still chained to her bed.

"Then it wasn't meant to be" was all she said.

Back in my cell, I folded my filthy blanket in half, tied the corners together, and fashioned a sort of sling. Inside, I put two water bottles and the bars Carl had left and looped it over my shoulder and around my neck, keeping my hands free. I threaded the chain that was still connected to the shackle through part of the sling, trying to leave enough slack so I could walk somewhat freely.

I gave the rest of my water and the cans of soup to Mo. When she protested that I'd left her too much, I told her they were too cumbersome for me to carry if I wanted to move quickly, which was true enough. I also wanted her to have as much food as possible, just in case. I tossed them through the bars so she could reach them.

As reluctant as I was to leave her behind, I had to go.

"Be safe," she said softly. "Run fast. I'm counting on you."

We looked into each other's eyes for a long moment. And then I turned away before I lost my resolve.

Stepping out into the night air was a revelation. I'd never considered the pricelessness of freedom until it was taken from me. Surveying the sky, I marveled at the moonlight shining through the cloud cover and the few stars peeking through.

Fortunately, the moonlight enabled me to follow the gravel roadway leading away from the barn. I saw no homes or other buildings nearby, and no lights shone in the darkness. The barn was a hulking blackness behind me.

After a short time, I came to a paved road. I didn't have any way to gauge the time, but in what felt like ten minutes since I'd left the barn, I hadn't heard any traffic. I hoped that didn't mean we were so remote that I wouldn't be able to find help before Carl's next visit.

Taking a deep breath, I looked both ways up and down the road, hoping to find a landmark, something to help me pick a direction. The dim moonlight showed only trees and the worn white markings on the road.

I tossed a mental coin and turned left.

At first, I jogged, but the chain pulled at my left ankle and the water bottles jostled too much. After I had to stop twice to retrieve a bottle that fell out of my improvised backpack, I settled for a fast walk. The shackle scraped my skin, but I ignored it. As stressed as I was, as worried as I felt for Mo's safety, I was also able to breathe the night air and enjoy the croaking of frogs. The freshness and sounds of a normal night were marvelous.

Over the next hour, the cloud cover increased, erasing what little moonlight there had been. A breeze strengthened, which felt good at first. On top of my exhaustion and lack of decent nutrition, I was working harder than I had in a long time. The cool air bathing my skin helped rejuvenate me, but I was still bone weary.

After what I estimated to be about four miles, I saw a rectangular shape in the distance. At the thought that help might be closer than I'd dared hope, I jogged again, the chain clinking in the quiet night.

I stopped.

I was looking at one of the stone pillars flanking the gate to the Wentworth property.

"Hell and damnation!"

I stepped off the road, into the shadows of the trees, and opened a bottle of water. Obviously, I couldn't ask for help at the Wentworth house. This was a bad news-good news situation. The good news was I knew where we were. Carl had put us into the old barn I'd admired on many a bike ride. The bad news was that help was at least ten miles in the other direction, in Charbonneau. More bad news was that I had to be especially wary of cars on the road, in case someone from the Wentworth house saw me.

"I never want to see another damn Wentworth as long as I live," I muttered. I resumed my walk, this time back the way I'd come.

I kept up a decent pace and passed the barn in due time. I wanted to report in, but I knew if Mo saw me she'd think I'd given up, or worse, that I'd brought help that then didn't appear. The last thing she needed was another blow to the fragile hope she'd gained since I escaped my cell. Besides, there was always the chance that our captor might return unexpectedly, and I couldn't allow myself to be recaptured.

I kept going.

The clouds thickened overhead, and the breeze picked up. I'd lived in Oregon long enough to know what that meant. Sure enough, rain started falling. I was dressed only in the jeans and shirt I'd worn the last time I spied on Elise, and the early spring rain took no time at all to soak me to the skin. Rainwater ran off my hair and into my eyes. I'd been warm from walking and jogging, but now I felt the cold creeping toward my core.

I wanted to pick up my pace to warm up, but the heavy cloud cover and rain made the night even darker. Every so often, I inadvertently stepped off the pavement and into a puddle or mud simply because I couldn't see where I was going. Once I tripped and fell to my knees. The pain was so bad, it brought tears to my eyes. My ankle felt raw from the shackle, but as I rose and started off again, I tried not to think about the pain.

I'd gone perhaps three miles past the barn when I heard a car coming from behind. My fight or flight adrenalin told me to hide, so I bolted into a nearby stand of trees and crouched down. The car passed without slowing.

I breathed a sigh of relief and resumed walking, warmed by the fear I'd felt. If the driver had been Elise, or worse, Carl—well, I couldn't bear to think of it.

The rain fell harder, which made it more difficult for me to see where I was going. I plodded along, head down, determined to save Mo and see Carl punished. Before I'd left the barn, Mo made a joke.

"When you come back," she'd said, "bring me a car battery and some wires, would you?"

Sounded good to me. I'd happily chain Carl the Third to the nearest prison, permanently.

In the next couple of miles, two more cars passed and twice more, I hid as best I could. One time, when there were no trees to use as cover, I lay down alongside a pasture fence, but in the rain and the dark, the driver didn't see me. Mud covered my clothes.

Each time a car passed by, I wondered if I should flag it down and ask the driver for help. Each time, I worried I'd be condemning Mo to death if I did.

I kept going, munching a bar and drinking water, trying to stay strong.

When I thought I might be nearing Charbonneau, I heard another car. Yet again, I bolted toward a nearby stand of trees, but I hadn't moved fast enough.

The car slowed and then stopped. "Hey, are you okay? Do you need a ride?"

Motivated by fear, I ignored the voice and ran as fast I could toward the trees. I heard footsteps behind me and ran faster.

"Stop! Where are you going?"

The person chasing me was getting closer. Panicked, I threw off my makeshift backpack and promptly fell face first onto the ground. A sharp pain radiated from my left ankle up to my hip.

I'd tripped on the chain.

I got up on one knee and tried to stand, but the pain was too great. It didn't matter, though, because my pursuer grabbed the back of my shirt.

"Stop, goddamn it. I'm not going to hurt you."

"Let go of me," I said, panting. I struggled in vain to free myself.

"Why are you out here? I almost ran over you back there."

Dimly, through my fear and pain, I realized that the person who'd chased me sounded concerned.

"Who are you?" I asked.

"I'm Jesús Alvarado," he said, using the Spanish pronunciation of his first name. "Who are you? And why do you have a chain on your leg?"

"You're not from the Wentworths?" I had to ask, though I feared the answer.

"I don't know who that is. I live in Eugene. I'm driving to Charbonneau to visit my brother and his wife. They had a baby girl last week. But you're hurt. Let me take you to the hospital."

I couldn't help it. I started weeping, shoulder-wracking sobs that emanated from my soul. I nodded without speaking, and my rescuer helped me stand.

"Do you have a phone with you?" I winced with pain when I tried to stand on both feet. My ankle was either broken or badly sprained. Jesús let me lean on him as we made our way slowly to the road.

"In the car. Why?"

"I just escaped from a murderer. He still has my friend. We have to call the police."

He helped me into the car and handed me his cell phone. He went to the trunk and returned with a blanket. It was musty, but after my time in captivity, it smelled like freedom.

Despite the growing warmth of the blanket, my hands shook so hard I couldn't press the phone buttons. After Jesús settled into the driver's seat, I gave the phone back to him.

"Can you call, please? My hands are too cold."

I recited Dean's cell phone number. Once the call was connected, he handed the phone back to me and started driving fast toward town.

When I head Dean's voice, I started sobbing. "Dean? It's Annie."

"Annie!" His voice was sharp. "Where are you? Where have you been?"

I heard rustling and the sounds of running footsteps in the background.

"I got away, but the doc's son has Mo chained up in the old barn up the road from the doc's house." I was crying so hard I could scarcely breathe. "Hurry, please, before he comes back."

The next morning, I awoke in a hospital bed. An IV line ran from a bag of fluid down to my arm. I was dressed, if scantily so, in a hideous lavender-flowered hospital gown, but the best part was that I was cleaner than I had been in two weeks. I was sure I owed a nurse's aide or two a great deal of appreciation.

The rain from the night before had intensified and was lashing against the windows, but as far as I was concerned, it was a perfect spring day. Mo and I were safe.

I remembered everything—up to a point. Jesús had handed me his phone after helping me into his car. He sped toward town while I spoke with Dean, imploring him to send officers and an ambulance the old barn immediately. I vaguely recalled using the term "a matter of life and death." Did people say that in real life? When we arrived at the Charbonneau Hospital, Dean was already there, for once not exasperated with me. He thanked my rescuer and asked him to talk with the Charbonneau police officer who stood nearby.

The rest of the night was a blur. I must have passed out from exhaustion or been sedated.

Now I lay in my bed, watching the rain and feeling grateful. An aide took my pulse and blood pressure and brought me some tea. I asked her about Mo, but she didn't know anything. I dozed off and on, feeling groggy and not quite able to rouse myself from it.

About midway through the morning, a doctor came in. I learned I had a broken left ankle and cuts and bruises. The skin beneath the shackle was seriously abraded, but he said it would heal. They'd had to cut the shackle off, of course. I had a cast instead, and I was fine with that. I was also no longer dehydrated, thanks to the IV fluids. And despite a laceration and a massive bruise that covered the side of my head, I didn't have a concussion. My fingertips were still tender from my struggles to disassemble the bed frame and I was stiff and sore, but that was no matter.

Good news all around.

I slipped off into oblivion after he left.

"You couldn't leave well enough alone, could you?" Dean Jarrett loomed over me with a wide grin on his face.

"Of course I could," I mumbled. I cleared my throat and spoke with more authority. "But nothing about this was *well enough*."

"Okay, you win." He pulled a chair to the side of my bed and sat. "Want to tell me how you got into this mess?"

"Not really."

"Spill it."

So I did. I told him about the GPS tracker on Elise's car and ignored when he rolled his eyes.

"I should have known you'd do something stupid like that. How else would you have found her at the hotel?"

"Maybe I'm a gifted detective." And then I smiled. Even I couldn't believe that one. "Anyway, Carl must have spotted me, because he grabbed me right off a park bench. He drugged me somehow, and I ended up in the barn with Mo."

"Chained to a bed and in a padlocked stall. And you managed to escape." He looked impressed.

"How's Mo doing? They got to her in time, right?"

"Yes, they did, but she's in bad shape, Annie. They took her right to Portland, lights and siren the whole way. She's in the ICU."

My eyes filled with tears. "Oh, no. Will she be okay?"

"The docs aren't sure yet. Three months in those conditions is a long time. I'm amazed she lasted so long."

"That murdering bastard's still out there, isn't he?"

Dean grimaced. Though he didn't answer I knew what his expression indicated.

"Please tell me there's security at the hospital Mo is in," I said, trying not to let any tears fall. "He's a doctor. He'll know how to manipulate hospital personnel. He'll figure out how to get to her."

"It's okay, Annie. I asked to have a security guard at the entrance to the ICU at all times. They have his photo and all the information. She's as safe as she can be."

I lay back on my pillow, relieved that Mo was safe and in good hands.

Just then, Grandma Natalie and Joe came in, walking quietly in case I was still sleeping. Dean stood to leave, but I caught his arm.

"Get him, Dean. Take him off the streets or off the planet, I don't care which. He killed his own father. He would have eventually killed us, too."

"We will. He's probably figured out by now that you got away, especially if he was down the road with Elise and saw the activity at the barn. We didn't find him at the Wentworth house or at home in Seattle. But we'll track him down. Try not to worry about it." He stepped to the door. "Oh, when you're up and about, I have something to show you." And he was gone.

The next day, I was home with Grandma Natalie, my broken ankle resting comfortably on a pile of pillows. Joe hovered over me like a mother hen, tucking my lap blanket and bringing me cold drinks. Patrick alternated between lecturing me about following Elise and interfering in the investigation and holding my hand as if he thought he'd never see me again. Shadow all but glued himself to my lap, purring.

Grandma Natalie had tears in her eyes. "I was so worried. But I knew you'd come home."

All of my friends came to visit. Sally and Rachel wanted to hear every detail. They hadn't met Mo, but they promised to correct that mistake as soon as they could. Ada and Hal spent hours sitting with me and Grandma Natalie. Lupe brought me a fruit basket and Freddy brought me pastrami. Sharon showed up with the biggest flower arrangement I'd ever seen.

Joe said, "I never knew so many people actually liked you."

I stuck my tongue out at him, but in truth, I felt loved. These people had all worried about me for the two weeks I'd been locked away in the old barn. An argument could be made that my kidnapping was my own fault for meddling, so I felt a vague guilt at the worry I'd caused. But when I mentioned it to Grandma Natalie, she hushed me.

"You saved Mo. You risked your life for your friend. You have nothing to feel guilty about. We're all proud of you."

The next day, Grandma Natalie took me to see Mo. She was in the same intensive care unit that my grandmother had occupied.

"You go on up, honey," she said. "I've seen enough of that place to hold me for a lifetime."

I hobbled into the unit with my crutches, gratified to see a security guard at the door as Dean had promised. When I stopped at the nurse's station, I was greeted by two of the nurses who had cared for Grandma Natalie.

"I'm here to see Mo—I mean Maureen Shaughnessy. How's she doing?"

"Better." The nurse who spoke was the same one who'd stroked my grandmother's hair when we weren't sure she'd ever wake up. "She has a long recovery ahead, but she's doing okay." She directed me to Mo's room, but before I could move away from the desk, she whispered, "You got her out of there in the nick of time."

I squeezed her hand in gratitude and went to visit my friend.

In the light filtering into Mo's room, she looked worse than when I last saw her. The darkness of the barn must have masked how emaciated she'd become. Her skin appeared translucent, and patches of her hair were missing. Her breathing was harsh, and she was getting oxygen through a nasal cannula. She'd been bathed, her clean skin now revealing sores and bug bites from her time as a captive. She also had multiple bruises on her legs and arms, either from mistreatment at Carl's hands or from poor nutrition. I didn't want to think of what he might have done to her, especially if he'd discerned that she was a lesbian.

I sat near her bed, listening to the softly beeping machines. She was either unconscious or sleeping, and in either case, she didn't need to be disturbed. I was content to sit with her for a while, moving only to let the nurses change IV fluids or adjust the machines. Mo's doctors were in and out a few times and were kind enough to give me what updates they could. They felt she would recover, but it would take time. The insults to her body were extreme and healing was slow.

I visited almost every day. For the first few visits, she was either sleeping or awake just enough to know I was there. She wasn't strong enough to sit up without help or eat much, but she started to get some color back in her face. Any little step was an improvement.

In the meantime, Dean had no news about Carl's whereabouts, though I was sure he was tiring of my daily texted inquiries. My own recovery continued. The cuts and bruises I'd gotten were healing, except at a follow-up appointment, my doctor thought that the blow I'd taken to the head when Carl struck me might have lingering effects on my hearing on that side. Only time could answer that question. My fractured ankle was healing well, too. I still had the occasional bout of insomnia and suspected I'd truly believe that the last vestiges of my captivity had worn off when I lost my deep aversion to soup.

In between visits to Mo, I resumed driving by Dad's shop. Nothing had changed. The portable storage unit was there, its contents intact. The damaged building itself still stood, its fate undecided. Joe and I hadn't talked any more about what to do with it, but I had an idea to propose to him when the time was right.

Lupe kept me apprised of goings-on at the Wentworth house. She was working there only one day a week, but she said it was one day too many. Lupe told me Elise spent her days moping like a teenager with a case of the vapors because Carl had disappeared.

"She carries on like her life is over," Lupe said with disdain. "He killed her husband and she cries for him? I don't get it."

Without saying so, I wondered if Elise was crying crocodile tears. I asked Dean if he thought Carl and Elise had conspired to kill the doctor. He said it was possible, and evidence existed that their affair started before Doc Wentworth died.

One day, I went up to the ICU to see Mo. She'd been recovering slowly, eating better, and taking short walks. When I arrived at the ICU door, I found no security guard, so I hurried to the desk.

"She's been moved to a regular room," the nurse said. "She's doing well, better than expected."

I went down to Mo's new room, concerned again for her safety. Fortunately, the guard I usually saw at the ICU was sitting in a chair outside the door. I thanked him for being diligent and went inside.

Over the next several days, Mo's condition continued to improve. She was still far too thin, but her appetite had returned, which was good news. Even better, her sense of humor was back, and she regaled me with her critiques of hospital food. I'd always heard that doctors made the worst patients, but it was clear to me that chefs could give them a run for their money.

Grandma Natalie visited Mo almost every day, sometimes with me, sometimes on her own. Mo had no family in Oregon, and since she'd been living at the Wentworth home in Charbonneau, she'd never had the chance to get out enough to make many friends. She immediately adopted mine and they reciprocated with enthusiasm. There was nothing unusual in finding Rachel or Sally in Mo's hospital room during visiting hours. Grandma Natalie and I were surprised one time to find Freddy there.

After the two older women exchanged greetings, Freddy said to me, "You thought you could keep her from me, didn't you?" Her smile couldn't have gotten any wider. "Maureen indeed!"

Seeing Mo's puzzled expression, I explained. "Remember I told you I took Freddy a piece of your carrot cake? She's been wanting to find you ever since, but I hadn't told you what I'd done, so I told her your name is Maureen." I shrugged one shoulder. "Hey, I didn't lie."

"Always walking the fine line, Annie," Grandma Natalie said in a teasing tone.

"Here's the deal," Freddy said. "The Charbonneau Bakery is closed for good, and I have customers who are about to march on my place with signs and torches if I don't get some desserts back on the menu. When you're back on your feet, you think you'd be interested in helping me out?"

Mo's entire face lit up. "Would I ever! I'm going to need a job. There's no way I'm setting foot anywhere near the Wentworth house again." She and Freddy shook hands. "You have a deal."

Freddy gave me a triumphant look, Mo a salute, and Grandma Natalie a hug before heading out the door.

"This is good news for me, too," Grandma Natalie said.

"Oh? Why?"

"Yeah, now I can get a piece of this amazing cake that you've been talking about."

"You'll love it." Thinking of what Mo had said about the Wentworth house, I turned back to her. "If you're never going back to the doc's house, we'll need to get someone to pack up your stuff."

"There isn't much there. Clothes, a few books, and the usual sundries. Most of my stuff is in storage. You think Lupe could help?"

"Let's check with her. She's only working there one day a week, and as soon as she can find another gig, she's done, too."

The nurse stopped in to check Mo's IV line. "Have you been out for a walk yet?"

"No, but this is as good a time as any. I'm getting tired of lying in bed."

"Okay," the nurse said. She eyed Grandma Natalie. "But no dancing."

I broke out laughing.

After the nurse left, Mo said, "Dancing?"

Grandma Natalie laughed heartily.

I said, "Long story. I'll tell you while we walk."

Two days later, I headed to the hospital for another visit and found out that Mo was strong enough to leave the hospital soon. Without family nearby, and because she was technically homeless, Grandma Natalie and I insisted that she stay with us. Lupe enlisted the help of her nephew to pack Mo's stuff from her room above the Wentworth garage. He was kind enough to tote the boxes into the house and into the room that would be Mo's when she was discharged. She was right; she didn't have much. I'd also starting emptying her hospital room, marveling at how many gifts she'd accumulated during her stay.

"At least it's not two dozen helium balloons," I said one morning at breakfast.

"Oh, I can solve that problem for you," Grandma Natalie said. "I'll order up a bunch." She reached for her phone.

"You would, wouldn't you?"

"What do you think?"

"I think you're incorrigible. And I think she'd love it."

Later, as I hobbled on my crutches toward her hospital room, I contemplated what Mo's ten-by-ten-foot bedroom would look like with the ceiling covered in balloons. Between the stacks of boxes and the plants, fruit baskets, and other gifts I'd taken home for her, we had scarcely enough room to walk around the bed. Sure, why not add a bunch of wobbling, crinkling balloons with their trailing strings. Just what the place needed to spruce it up. Shadow would turn them into cat toys at the first opportunity.

Amused at my grandmother's antics, I headed toward Mo's room. I was surprised to see the security guard headed down the hospital corridor toward me. I waved to stop him.

"Where are you going? Is someone watching the room?"

"The doctor's in with her. I haven't had a break all day, and I gotta pee like a racehorse. Two minutes, and I'll be back."

He rushed past me and into the nearby restroom.

When I arrived at Mo's room, the door was closed, which was unusual. I pushed it open and peeked around the edge, concerned, but not wanting to intrude.

Dressed in hospital scrubs, Carl Wentworth stood beside Mo's bed, injecting something into her IV tube. Mo lay motionless, eyes closed.

"No!" I slammed the door open and crutched toward him. I screamed, "Help! Someone help me!"

He stiff-armed me away. I fell against a nearby chair and landed hard on the floor, crutches going every which way. He continued pressing the plunger of the syringe.

Still yelling for help, I grabbed one of my crutches and struck at his legs. He snatched it from me and threw it across the room where it ricocheted off the wall and clattered to the floor.

I scrambled to my feet. Only slightly encumbered by the cast on my ankle, I tackled him, driving him against the wall. He dropped the syringe.

I grabbed the IV line and jerked it out of Mo's arm, sending blood spraying onto the bed and IV fluid pouring onto the floor. She didn't move.

The security guard ran into the room, followed by four nurses and aides and two people in street clothes. A nurse avoided the tangle of Carl and me on the floor and leapt onto Mo's bed to stanch the flow of blood coming out of the torn IV site in her arm.

From my spot on the floor, it appeared that the room was filled with arms and legs and people shouting, but within moments, Carl Wentworth was immobilized.

"He was putting something into her IV," I said, pointing to the syringe. I turned to Carl. "What did you give her, you bastard?"

All he did was glare at me. I summoned all the restraint I had left to keep from smashing my remaining crutch into his face.

One of the nurses collected the syringe from the floor and put it into a plastic bag. Another nurse was taking Mo's vitals and yet a third started to set up a new IV. Within moments, a doctor from the emergency department ran into the room.

"Until we know what he was giving her, we'll assume it's some kind of drug overdose. I doubt he was giving her vitamins." The doctor injected an antidote for drug overdoses into Mo's IV line. To the nurse he said, "Let's get her up to ICU."

By then, another hospital security officer arrived. The two of them hauled a stonily silent Carl to his feet just as two Portland police officers appeared. They handcuffed their prisoner, and after I told them that he was wanted for murder and kidnapping, the cops tightened the handcuffs until he squirmed. The officers agreed to call Dean and took the killer away.

After the nurses wheeled Mo's bed out of the room, Grandma Natalie collected my crutches for me, and she and I made our way to the waiting room near the ICU. I was still quivering with rage and with fear for my friend. She'd endured so much at the hands of that monster, and just when I thought she was safe, that we were both safe, there he was, a stone-cold Grim Reaper in the shape of a human being.

I stumbled into one of the waiting room chairs as a nurse walked by. Concerned, she asked if I needed help and didn't believe me when I said I was all right. She took my pulse while I told her what happened. Grandma Natalie caught up with me and sat beside me, holding my other hand.

"You were very brave," the nurse said. "You probably saved your friend's life."

Without warning, I started crying, deep sobs that wracked my body. The nurse stopped a passing aide and sent her to get food from the cafeteria, and held my hand, trying to comfort me. When the young woman arrived with sandwiches and drinks, I started crying again.

"Thank you," I said through my blubbering. She patted my back and told me to rest. She and the aide went back to work.

Sometime later, after Mo was settled into the ICU room for observation, we were allowed in to see her. She opened her eyes and looked around, groaning.

"I hate the ICU," she mumbled. "Annie?"

"Right here, hon. With Grandma Natalie."

"Did you bring my battery?"

I peered at her. "What battery? I don't understand."

"Anyone else who wants to attach electrodes to that sick bastard's favorite body parts will have to get in line."

Grandma Natalie said, "Hmmm, I believe I wouldn't mind standing in that line."

Mo gave tried to sit up, so I found her an extra pillow, mother hen that I am, and helped prop her up.

"What the everlasting fuck did he do to me?" she said. "I feel like twelve kinds of shit."

I said, "He sent the guard away and injected something into your IV. They're testing your blood and the syringe now, but to be on the safe side, they gave you something that reverses drug overdoses. It's only been a little while and you're awake, so I think we can do the math."

"In that case, I get to kill the guard, too." Mo stretched a little and held up her left arm, which was bandaged. "My arm hurts."

I bit my lip. "That's my fault. Sorry."

She looked at me as if in disbelief. "Let me understand this. A maniac was trying to kill me, and you thought you'd twist my arm off, just to add to the fun?"

"He was poisoning you, smartass. I yanked your IV out. It was the only thing I could think to do."

"And she tackled him at the same time according to the hospital staff." Grandma Natalie beamed with pride.

Mo stared at me. "You actually saw him doing it?"

"I did. When I came into your room, he had a syringe in his hand. What else could I do?" I decided to lighten the mood before they went all hero worship on me. "Hey, I worked too damn hard to get you out of that barn to let him win. Can't let so much work go to waste, right?"

"I'm glad you have your priorities in order," Mo said.

"And don't you forget it."

Chapter Twelve

The party was in full swing when I pulled into the driveway with Mo. Joe must have taken charge of the music because we could hear the bass reverberating even though the car windows were closed. I already had a mental image of Patrick rolling his eyes and Grandma Natalie entreating Joe in vain to lower the volume.

"The neighbors are going to love this," I said. "I'll be surprised if they don't call the police."

"Maybe they did." Mo pointed out the window. "There's a Portland cop car on the street and I think this is an unmarked one right here."

Sure enough, to the right of where I'd parked sat a black car. I was sure I'd seen it before and I had a pretty good idea where.

"Oh, look at that," I said.

Stretched across the front of the house above the garage door was a massive banner reading "Welcome Home, Annie and Mo" in bright yellow on purple. I got tears in my eyes. In the darkest days in that old barn, I'd had moments when I was sure I'd never see this house again.

Mo was teary-eyed, too. "Wow," she whispered, and I agreed with her.

The decibel level in the house increased when Mo and I went inside.

"Annie! Mo!"

I doubted that Mo had ever been hugged so many times, and I know I hadn't. After the initial rush, we were shown to seats of honor and plied with cold drinks. We sat together and tried to take it all in.

Decorations covered every square inch of the house. Grandma Natalie had made good on her promise. There must have been forty helium balloons bobbing about at the ceiling. Crepe paper streamers hung everywhere. Signs saying "Welcome Home" and "We're Proud of You" were taped to every wall.

In the kitchen, I found a staggering display of food. Beef roast, fried chicken, and mashed potatoes sat alongside casserole dishes of enchiladas and macaroni and cheese. On another table sat bowls of roasted vegetables and more kinds of salad than I knew existed. To top it all off, the kitchen counter held three pies and an enormous cake.

"Grandma," I said. "there's enough food here for a small country. Are you supporting every caterer in Portland?" I was amazed by the almost unbelievable bounty awaiting us, and then I spotted something that gave it all away. "Hey, Freddy did this, didn't she?"

"How did you know?" Grandma Natalie looked puzzled.

"See this?"

In the center of the table, holding pride of place, sat a plate piled high with a food I was almost obsessed with.

"I'd recognize this pastrami anywhere. Where is she?"

"Right here."

"Freddy!" I gave her a hug. "This is amazing."

She waved a nonchalant hand. "It's nothing," she said, but then she laughed. "My kitchen staff worked their butts off to get this done. I owe them big. Including, by the way, your friend, Lupe."

"Is she here?" In the wave of celebratory greetings we'd been hit with when we first arrived, I hadn't gotten a full reckoning of who was in attendance.

"She's here somewhere," Freddy said. "You know, that girl can cook. I offered her a job waiting tables so she could quit cleaning for the dragon lady of Wentworth house, and then I found out that she makes the most amazing tamales. She's even made improvements to other parts of my menu. You've been keeping secrets from me again."

"I didn't know. But I'm glad you helped her get out of there."

"The least I could do, especially since you found me a master baker, all-around excellent chef, and my new partner."

"New partner?"

"That would be me," Mo said, appearing beside me.

I looked back and forth between them a couple of times. "I can't believe neither of you told me."

"I'm not getting any younger," Freddy said. "I started working at the diner when I was a teenager, washing dishes and cleaning tables. Since I bought it, I've worked almost every day."

"And your food is amazing," I said.

"Thanks, but I still can't bake a cake to save my soul. I'm getting tired of so much hard work, and I'd like to see a little of this world before I leave it. When you brought me that carrot cake, you thought you were finding me a source for good desserts, which was great, since the bakery went belly up."

Mo was doing her best imitation of a Cheshire cat, minus the disappearing act. I narrowed my eyes at her and prompted her. "And?"

"And without knowing it, you planted another idea. If I had a partner, someone who could cook and bake, I could cut back on work before I keel over. I had a lot of fun teasing you about who baked that fantastic cake, but I already had a pretty good idea. After all, the only people in town who had a chef were the Wentworths, and I knew you worked for them. Even I can put two and two together."

"And I'd decided long before you turned up in the barn that if I lived, I was never going back to the Wentworth house," Mo said. "I'll live in a cardboard box under the Burnside bridge before I step foot on that property again. Don't get me wrong, the doc treated me well, better sometimes than I deserved, but I've long since had my fill of that little diva he married. And we know what kind of a monster his son is." For a moment she looked sad and angry, but her face cleared. "And then Freddy showed up in my room at the hospital, so here we are."

I was speechless for a moment, and I hugged them both. "This is amazing. I'm so happy for you." I paused and turned to Freddy. "Wait a sec, does this mean she gets your pastrami recipe?" I tried to give her my best stern glare, but I must have failed, because she laughed.

"Nice try."

I spent the next hour or so making sure to visit with everyone who had come to celebrate with us. Sally and Rachel were there, of course, and there was no way to avoid seeing Patrick hovering near Rachel most of the time, while trying to seem as if he wasn't. I let him know his secret was out, and he blushed, which made me laugh. I found Ada and Hal sitting with Grandma Natalie, poring over Harley Davidson flyers while Liz looked on. My irrepressible grandmother was sharing her obsession again.

Sharon had come in from Charbonneau long enough to give me a hug and a gift. Her husband, she said, was babysitting, a turn of phrase that always made her grimace. "They're his kids, too, damn it," Sharon said. She hadn't wanted to miss the celebration, but she couldn't stay.

Lupe came to the party with Sharon, so she had to leave early, too, but not before telling me how happy she was to work at the diner.

As I'd suspected since we'd arrived, Dean was also in attendance. The car Mo pointed out was indeed his. I was a little surprised he'd come to the party, but not at all surprised to find him talking with Detective Beth O'Brien. Her presence explained the Portland police car.

"Hey, Dean," I said. "Hi, Beth. How are you doing?"

"Glad you and Mo are okay," Dean said.

Beth said, "That was quite a risk you took, Annie."

To Beth, Dean said, "I thought she'd agreed to back off. Let's you and me arrest her for obstruction."

"Oh, come on," I said, smirking. "You had to know better. You must have realized I wasn't giving up on my friend."

"Good thing you didn't," he said with good humor. "But don't tell anyone I said that, or I'll deny it."

I turned to Beth. "I want to thank you for working so hard on Nicky's case. I understand why you have to consider me a suspect, but I promise you I didn't kill her. More than anyone, I want to know who did."

She paused before speaking. "Thanks, I appreciate that. As you know, the investigation is ongoing. We're not stopping until we run out of leads to follow and evidence to examine, and probably not even then." She squeezed my hand reassuringly, but then she said "just try to stay out of the way, okay?"

We chatted for another few minutes before they, too, had to depart.

Beth slipped quickly out the door, but Dean paused and said, "When the dust settles a little, give me a call. Both Beth and I want to ask a few follow-up questions about your statement. I also have something to show you."

"You said that before. What is it?"

"You'll see. You'll like it, part of it, anyway."

After Dean and Beth left, I went back to the kitchen in search of another bite of Freddy's pastrami. Mo was there, eating macaroni and cheese from a small bowl cupped in her hands.

"Who's the babe?" She tilted her head toward the front door.

"The babe, as you so crudely put it, is Detective Beth O'Brien. She's with the Portland Police Bureau."

She gave me a sly look from the corner of her eye. "She can handcuff me any day she likes."

I laughed loud enough to draw the attention of a few party-goers. "You're incorrigible. And besides," I lowered my voice, "I'd have thought you had enough of chains to last a lifetime."

"Depends on who's on the other end," she said in a playful voice, but then she grew serious. "Wait a sec. Why do you know a Portland detective? Isn't the Charbonneau police department managing the doc's case?"

I hesitated long enough that she prompted me.

"Annie? What aren't you telling me?"

"Look," I finally said, "this isn't the time to get into details, but my partner was murdered last year. Beth is the lead investigator."

Mo was silent for a moment as she digested that information, and then her eyes widened. She whispered, "Don't tell me she thinks you did it."

"Nicky started the fire where my dad died." I felt tears start to form. "It's logical."

She set aside the bowl she held and wrapped me in a fierce hug. "Of course you didn't." She let me go and stood back a step. "Maybe it's a good sign that she came to your party."

"Our party, you dumbass," I said, laughing with relief.

Over the next couple of hours, the number of party-goers slowly dwindled. Mo had long since tired, so Grandma Natalie ushered her into her room and made her lie down under a blanket. By ones and twos, our friends left for home and other pursuits. We sent food with almost everyone, but when Freddy and I packed up the leftovers, we quickly discovered that our refrigerator was far too small.

I said, "Time to get out the big cooler. We won't have to buy groceries any time soon, that's for sure."

After everyone had gone, Grandma Natalie and I sat in the living room and contemplated the decorations.

"How long did it take to put all of that up?"

"Too long," she said. "And I don't have a scrap of energy left to take it down."

"Christmas is coming in a few months. We could leave it up and pretend. Cut down on the holiday decorating, right?"

"Sounds like a good plan."

I pulled my lap blanket up to my shoulders and sighed with contentment. "I'm never going outside ever again."

"No need to. We have enough food to sustain us for years."

With that in mind, I drifted off to sleep.

"What are you doing in here?" Dean stood in the doorway, looking puzzled. "Why didn't you go down to my office?"

I held up the book I'd brought along, in case he was busy. A murder mystery seemed appropriate for the occasion.

"This is the library, isn't it?" I asked.

He shook his head as if to say "What am I supposed to do with you?" Instead he said, "Okay, hold on. I'll be right back."

In a few moments, he returned with a laptop computer and two bottles of water. He handed one bottle to me before sitting down across the table. He opened the laptop, which started to hum.

"Okay, let's talk about what happened when you sent me the photo of Elise and Carl at the Finley Hotel."

As he took notes onto the computer, I recounted how I'd seen them together at the hotel a couple of times after I'd texted him the photo.

"I was going one last time," I said, and he rolled his eyes. "No, seriously. I figured they were having an affair, but you were right, that in itself didn't point to who killed Doctor Wentworth or where Mo could be. I was wasting my time. And I didn't want to admit it, but I thought Mo had to be dead."

He said, "I thought so, too."

"You said she'd most likely left town, especially after her car turned up at the airport. What changed your mind?"

"We'll get to that. Let's finish this first."

I quelled my curiosity while I told him about waking up in the barn, chained to the bed frame, not knowing where I was.

"Discovering Mo was a total shock. I thought for sure he was going to kill me, and when I found Mo alive, nothing made sense. She said she saw Carl arguing with the doc, that the doc was bleeding badly. Carl had a knife in his hand. We couldn't figure out why he would keep a witness alive. He had a routine of coming in every two or three days, giving us food and water. His schedule matched up with what I saw of him meeting Elise downtown."

I recounted Mo's insistence that I check the leg of my bed.

"Smart," he murmured.

I had to agree, and then I told him about freeing the leg, using it to try to loosen the door latch and failing.

"Wait a minute, so you decided to see how angry you could make him? You *are* good at making grown men furious. I'll give you that."

"Very funny. No, a couple of days earlier, he'd been agitated for some reason, and when he left, he neglected to close the outside door of the barn. I thought if he was mad enough, he might make another mistake."

"Or kill you outright."

"Or that, but we were going to die there anyway, weren't we? You saw what kind of shape Mo was in. Do you think she had much longer? I don't."

"But your plan worked."

"Yeah, well, except when he belted me on the side of the head." I rubbed my face, remembering the pain and dizziness I'd felt, but couldn't show to the enraged killer. "He screamed and yelled and smashed a two-by-four. But otherwise, he didn't hurt either of us, and when he left, he forgot to lock the stall door."

"He made the mistake you'd hoped for."

"Exactly. I couldn't get Mo's door open, so I ran for it. The rest you know." I thought for a moment. "Except that I'd love to know why Jesús Alvarado ran after me. I'd expect a driver to just keep going, but he saved me. He saved both of us."

Dean finished typing and pushed the computer away. He sat back in his chair, took a drink of water, and stared at the far wall for a long moment.

"You're a real pain in the ass, you know that?"

"My grandmother says I inherited my stubbornness from her."

"Is she the one with the Harley Davidson fixation?"

"Yep."

"That explains it." He sat forward again. "Here's the thing. If you hadn't done everything I told you not to do, we might never have caught him or found Mo." At my grin, he held up a hand. "Don't get too happy here. It's a wonder you're not dead, and by all rights, you should be. Carl Wentworth killed his own father. I still don't understand why he left you and Mo alive, but here you are."

He opened the laptop again and pressed a few keys. He turned it so I could see the screen.

"Remember I said I had something to show you?"

"Sure."

"You did something else that changed the investigation. You pointed out a security camera nobody else checked on."

I almost couldn't breathe. "The one by the back door."

"We got lucky. Since it was motion activated, it hadn't recorded much except an occasional raccoon."

"Is this what I'll like part of?" A feeling of dread was settling on me. Was I about to see the doctor's murder?

"Yes," he said in a low tone. "Are you sure you can stand to watch it?"

I couldn't answer right away, but then I said "go ahead." He pressed a button on the keyboard and a video started to play. I was immediately grateful there was no sound.

The first thing the camera recorded was the screen door being pushed open a few inches and then slamming closed. Since it recorded at night, the lights and darks were reversed, which made the scene eerie.

After a few seconds, the screen door swung open sharply, ricocheting off the wall. Doctor Wentworth stumbled out and fell down the steps, as if he'd been shoved. He stood and took a tentative step or two, holding his hands to his abdomen. Light-colored streaks showed on his hands. He was followed by a larger shape, a man whose face wasn't visible on the screen, but whose form was well known to me. Carl the Third leaped down the stairs and pushed his father to the ground. He straddled the doctor's legs, and his right arm rose and fell. He got to his feet and went back up the steps, and this time, his face was clear on the video.

Moments later, the door opened again, and Carl emerged. He wasn't alone. He pushed a struggling form in front of him, down the steps and out of the frame.

"He killed his father and took Mo," I said. "I mean, we already knew that, but wow, here's proof."

"Yes. When you accused me of thinking Mo had flown off to Zanzibar, I already knew better. I did think she was probably dead, but I knew she hadn't hurt the doctor. I couldn't tell you about this, and I'm not sure showing it to you now is the right thing to do, but I wanted you to know that, after everything, I believed you."

I took a deep breath, willing myself not to think about what the video revealed.

"You made me do something else, too."

"Oh?"

"Yeah, I had to find out where the hell Zanzibar is. You really are a pain in the ass."

Over the next several weeks, we did our best to recover from our ordeal.

My wounds healed fastest, of course, and almost before I knew it, the cast was off. I had to submit to the not-so-tender mercies of a physical therapist twice a week, but my ankle was healing quickly.

Mo's recovery was far more difficult. Even after two months, she was still thinner than I'd known her to be, but her color was back and her hair had grown in. She grew stronger by the day. Her sense of humor combined with my irrepressible grandmother meant that my life was occasionally a touch too eventful. More than once, I threatened to separate them, like mischievous children, just to get some peace and quiet.

On the other hand, she had constant nightmares, followed by panic attacks. After yet another fast trip to the emergency room in the middle of the night, she realized she needed help.

"Know a good shrink, Annie?" She said it with humor, but she sounded worried. "I can't keep doing this."

If there's any good news found in associating with police detectives, it's that they have resources. Beth O'Brien gave Mo the names of half a dozen therapists she said were worth talking with. After a few days of research, Mo chose one and scheduled regular visits. Between therapy sessions and medications, she started to improve, if more slowly than she'd have liked.

Grandma Natalie, on the other hand, developed an obsession with hovering over both of us as if we might disappear again. She waited on us and made sure we were comfortable. We tried to wave her off sometimes, but I knew I liked being cosseted, and I suspected Mo did, too.

About a week before Mo moved back to Charbonneau, we were at the kitchen table having lunch when there was a knock at the door. Grandma Natalie went to check it out and came back with Dean Jarrett.

"Coffee, Detective?" Grandma asked.

"Yes, please." He pulled out a chair and sat at the table across from Mo and me. "How are you two doing?"

"They're overgrown brats, that's how." Grandma Natalie put a full mug of coffee in front of Dean and slid the sugar bowl and creamer within his reach. She took a seat next to him. "And what can we do for you today, Detective?"

"First, please call me Dean. I think we've been through enough together that we can dispense with the formalities. As for why I'm here, I have news." He stirred his coffee and sipped, wincing at the heat. Putting the mug down, he said, "He took the deal."

I leaned back in my chair and inhaled deeply. I held it for a few seconds before letting it out. The most amazing feeling of relief swept through my body. Judging from her expression, Mo felt the same way.

"He'll do the maximum," Dean said.

"He's not likely to ever get out, is he?" I knew the answer, but I had to hear it.

"Probably not. He killed his own father for money and kidnapped the two of you. There were other charges, but any one of those would have been enough to put him away for a long time."

"No trial?" Mo's voice wavered.

"No trial," I said. I took her hand, which was trembling. "You don't have to see him ever again."

She tried a brave smile. "Good. I'm fresh out of car batteries."

Dean gave her a concerned glance, but didn't ask. I wasn't sure I'd want to explain it to him.

"It was the video, wasn't it?" Even after so many weeks, I could still see the grainy images of Doctor Wentworth stumbling down the stairs, followed by his murderous son.

"Video?" Mo sounded curious.

"From the security camera," I said in a low voice.

She took in a breath and became still. "I don't want to see it."

"No, trust me," I said, "you don't."

Dean said, "Once his defense attorney viewed it, the party was over. There's no way a jury could see that and let him go. Oregon has the death penalty, though we haven't used it for a long time—"

"Thank goodness," I said, interrupting.

"What do you mean?"

"For one thing, too many people have been sent to death row who were later exonerated, so mistakes happen. In this case, of course, there's no chance of that, but I want that evil bastard to sit in prison for the rest of his miserable life and think about how he got there."

"Fair enough," Dean said, raising an eyebrow in my direction. "Looks like you'll get your wish. Anyway, between the video and the fact that he left two witnesses, there was no way he wouldn't agree to the plea deal." He turned to Mo and repeated. "No trial. It's over."

Mo relaxed again and I released her hand. She had a great job waiting for her in Charbonneau, and Ada had found her a charming little house to rent. She was going to be okay.

"One thing I don't understand," I said.

"Why he left you alive?" Dean asked. "I know, it's a puzzler. Once the plea was signed, I asked his attorney about that. He'd talked about it with Carl, of course, and the answer makes as little sense as the rest of it. He said neither of you had done anything to hurt him except be in the wrong place at the wrong time. He hated his father, thought he'd been cut out of the will, but you two were innocent. In the end, he applied a skewed version of the Hippocratic Oath to you." He paused, thinking. "Makes as much sense as anything else, I guess."

"Do no harm, eh?" I said. Mo exchanged a glance with me, and I turned back to Dean. "I'd argue with him on that point, but we're still here, so I'll take it." Another thought came to me. "What about Elise? Was she in on it?"

"No, amazingly enough. I thought for sure she had to be, but it turned out that this big love affair they had was only Carl manipulating her. He figured if he'd been cut out of his dad's will, she'd inherit the money, and he could get it from her."

"I can't imagine how she reacted when she found out."

"From what I heard," Dean said, "she went white, clammed up, and left the room. Later she wrote checks for everyone on the staff, packed some stuff into her car, and left town."

I said, "Given what I've seen of her behavior in the time I worked there, I'd have expected her to throw a fit that could register on Richter scales in Colorado. She must have been caught totally off guard."

"She's not entirely innocent," Dean said. "Remember when her favorite jewelry was stolen? All a sham. She was sure that she was the next ex-Mrs. Wentworth, so she stashed it away. She said that she made up the whole thing so the doc wouldn't wonder why she wasn't wearing it."

Grandma Natalie said, "Can't you charge her for fraud or filing a false police report or something? I mean, what a terrible thing to do—blaming her own theft on the staff!"

Dean said, "The DA could have charged her, but she hasn't as of yet."

"She also cut Lupe's face," I said. "What about that?"

"The DA is working on it. To Elise's credit, she met with Lupe and apologized. She also paid the hospital bill. Lupe said she seemed sincere. I don't know if there will be any legal action against her at all."

"So much drama," I said. "And for what?"

"I could almost feel sorry for her," Mo said.

I gave her my best deadpan look.

"I said *almost*. She's not a nice person and the doc was too good for her, but she didn't deserve to be used by Carl like that. I do feel sorry for his wife and kids, though. They're good people."

"I agree. He killed his father and faked an affair for money, and in the end, lost it all."

Dean said, "If he hadn't let his ego as a doctor and a surgeon get the better of him, he wouldn't have left witnesses behind. And he might have gotten away with it if you hadn't pushed us to check that security camera."

"Well, then," Grandma Natalie said. "We must celebrate." She opened a seldom-used cupboard and took out a bottle of amber-colored liquid and a stack of glasses. She poured each of us a shot of Scotch.

"Here's to nosy parkers," she said, raising her glass. "May they live long and prosper."

Chapter Thirteen

On a warm mid-June day, I parked in my usual spot under the trees and gazed through the windshield of my car at the burned-out shell of my dad's shop. The counter and other things I'd rescued were safely stored, but I'd kept with me the remnant of the sign he'd so carefully created. I'd kept it securely wrapped and stowed in my car where it wouldn't be damaged any further.

Unlike past visits, though, I wasn't tearful. I'd always mourn the loss of my father, but I was learning to carry it with me, make it part of myself, rather than consider it a burden. He'd been the center of my universe, along with Grandma Natalie. Death couldn't take that away.

No, this time I felt hopeful.

I hadn't waited long when a ten-ton flatbed pulled into the parking lot. The driver maneuvered the truck into position and carefully deposited a giant dumpster close to where the other, smaller one had been. I'd used the first one for the debris I'd cleared from inside the shop.

This one was for the shop itself.

I opened the sun roof and the windows and let the early summer breeze waft through. I had enough time to once more leaf through the papers that occupied the passenger seat. I felt no pressing need to do it, because I'd created most of them myself, but I enjoyed thinking through the project again.

Patrick and Joe arrived in Patrick's Mercedes along with Grandma Natalie. Patrick was dressed, as always, in an expensive suit and Joe in jeans and a t-shirt.

"What, no Team Three and a Half?" I asked. "I almost don't recognize you in civvies."

Joe grabbed me and made to rub my head with his knuckles, but I tickled him and he let go.

"You two never will grow up, will you?" Grandma Natalie tried giving us a stern look, as she'd done many times when we were younger, but we weren't fooled this time, either.

"I won't and you can't make me," I said, sounding as much as I could like a petulant teenager. I laughed at myself for being so silly. It felt good.

"What's going on?" Patrick checked his watch. "I have a meeting in an hour."

Just then, two panel vans pulled into the lot, ladders lashed to their roofs and brightly colored logos painted on the sides.

"That's Brad's company." Joe waved to his cycling team buddy. "Why are they here?"

Both trucks rolled to a stop away from the charred building. Half a dozen well-muscled men emerged. They gathered around Brad for a few minutes. He spoke to each of them in turn while pointing to various parts of the shop, issuing instructions. The men started unloading tools and other equipment from their trucks.

"It's coming down," I said. "We knew it had to. I hired Brad and his company to help."

Patrick nodded, ever practical, but Joe looked bereft.

I put my arm around my adopted brother's waist and whispered, "Wait, there's more."

He raised an eyebrow my direction but didn't speak. Tears shone in his dark brown eyes.

I patted him on the shoulder. "Hold on, I'll be right back." I went inside and found Brad. "Ready?"

"Yep. Do you have the drawings?"

I handed him the sheaf of papers I'd taken from the car, including documents, permits, and drawings I'd made.

"I suppose we'll need real blueprints," I said. "But it's a start. You brought the mason, right?"

"Yep. He'll get to work as soon as you've made your announcement. I don't know how you've kept all of this a secret, but I love it. Joe will be over the moon."

"I'm counting on it. I'll let you know when we're ready."

I made a brief tour of the shop's interior, saying a silent farewell, more of a "see you later" than "goodbye," but no less poignant for that. I picked up the bundle that I'd deposited inside the shop and stood in the front doorway for a moment, watching as Brad's men began their demo work at the back, in the most damaged part of the shop, first dismantling the added reinforcements, and then tearing the damaged structure apart. Two men on the roof tore away what was left. The sounds of saws and hammers and protesting nails reverberated in the morning breeze as the debris pile grew.

Outside the front door, I stooped to pick up one of the light-colored bricks that had come loose from the facade. It still carried traces of soot from the fire, but rain and time had cleaned most of it away.

Grief, I thought, was much the same way. Still there, but diminished, tolerable.

I carried the brick and the bundle over to my waiting family. Joe and Patrick both looked puzzled, but Grandma Natalie nodded as if she knew what I was up to. I never had been able to keep a secret from her.

"What's going on, sis?" Joe peered at me with suspicion all over his brown face.

I handed him the brick. "Remember you and I talked about selling the property? About how we couldn't see ourselves doing it?"

"Yeah, we talked about maybe selling the vacant lot or putting up a new building and finding a business tenant."

"And you said you didn't want to let it go."

"I don't, but it makes the most sense."

"Why do we always have to make sense? If I've learned anything lately, it's that life seldom makes sense. I mean, I got kidnapped by a killer but other than making me eat cold soup and pee in a bucket, he didn't really hurt me. Does that make sense?

"You lost part of your leg in a conflict that never should have happened, so that definitely doesn't make sense. And you're happy in spite of it, riding your bike everywhere and startling people with your prosthesis. It's wonderful, but not sensible."

"Okay, but what does any of that have to do with this?"

He held the brick out on the palm of his hand, and I took it from him.

"Dad came to this country not speaking a word of English, and he built this shop. He changed peoples' lives with bicycles."

"Especially mine," Joe said.

"Especially yours *and* mine." From the corner of my eye, I saw Patrick and Grandma Natalie beaming. She had tears in her eyes.

"You don't want to let this go and neither do I. So we're taking this brick and all of the others"—I waved toward the front of the old building where the mason had begun taking the bricks down one at a time and stacking them on a pallet—"and we're going to rebuild the bike shop."

I picked up the wrapped bundle at my feet and opened it. When the corner of Dad's sign was revealed, showing his hand-lettered name, Joe took in a sharp breath.

"I thought it was gone." He sounded as if he might cry.

"I did, too, but I found it when I cleaned up inside." I put my arm around his waist and leaned against him, holding the remnant of the sign. "Let's rebuild Dad's store and put this on the wall above the checkout counter."

Joe was silent for a long moment, while Patrick and my grandmother took turns holding the burned sign and running their fingers over the lettering.

I watched the mason carefully salvaging the bricks from the front of the shop, and without thinking, I said aloud, "*Papá, Velasquez Cycles cabalga nuevamente.*"

He turned to me with a wide smile and tears running down his face and said, "Velasquez Cycles rides again."

About the Author

EJ Kindred is a recently retired Oregon attorney. Her legal career of 26 years was spent doing her best to make rich computer companies got even richer, and she's delighted to have left it all behind.

She's been a writer from an early age, penning terrible stories and wretched poems with which to torment her family, friends, and teachers. She refuses to disclose how many Star Trek scripts she wrote. Other than a first place award in a short story contest long, long ago in a state far, far away, her first published work is the story "The Other Marie," which appears in the anthology, *Time's Rainbow: Writing Ourselves Back Into American History*. The subject of the story, Marie Equi, was one of Oregon's first women doctors, a crusader for humane working conditions, an anti-war activist who spent time in San Quentin for sedition, and an unabashed lesbian—all in the early 20th century.

In addition to enjoying retirement and writing, EJ makes quilts, occasionally donating them to the fundraising efforts of various groups, primarily cat rescues. She enjoys jigsaw puzzles, old movies, spending time with friends, and, of course, reading anything and everything. She lives near Portland, Oregon, with an undisclosed number of cats. Her website is found at www.EJKindred.com.

Portland, Oregon
www.LaunchPointPress.com